It was a good world. It was a very good world—well worth a Class A bonus. Hank Shallo wiped his lips with the back of one square, hairy, big-knuckled hand, put his coffee cup down, and threw his ship into orbit around the place. The orbit had a slight drift to it because the gyros needed overhauling; but Hank was used to their anomalies.

On the ninth time around, Hank had complete surface maps of the world below. He ran them back through the ship's library and punched for that spot on one of the world's three continents where landing conditions were optimum.

Then concussion slammed the ship like a giant's hand. He tripped, caught one glimpse of the near wall of the cabin tilting at him, and consciousness dissolved . . .

GORDON R. DICKSON

MINDSPAN

Edited and with Introductions by
Sandra Miesel

MINDSPAN

A Baen Books Original

Baen Publishing Enterprises
260 Fifth Avenue
New York, N.Y. 10001

First printing, July 1986

ISBN: 0-671-65580-9

Cover art by James Warhola

Printed in the United States of America

Distributed by
SIMON & SCHUSTER
TRADE PUBLISHING GROUP
1230 Avenue of the Americas
New York, N.Y. 10020

ACKNOWLEDGMENTS

"Miss Prinks," *Magazine of Fantasy and Science Fiction*, June, 1954. © Fantasy House, Inc., 1954.

"Fleegl of Fleegl," *Venture Science Fiction*, May, 1958. © Mercury Press, Inc., 1958.

"Show Me the Way to Go Home," *Startling Stories*, December, 1952. © Better Publications, 1952.

"Rex and Mr. Rejilla," *Galaxy*, January, 1958. © Galaxy Publishing Corp., 1957.

"Who Dares a Bulbur Eat?" *Galaxy*, October, 1962. © Galaxy Publishing Corp., 1962.

"The Faithful Wilf," *Galaxy*, June, 1963. © Galaxy Publishing Corp., 1963.

"A Wobble in Wockii Futures," *Galaxy*, April, 1965. © Galaxy Publishing Corp., 1965.

"Sleight of Wit," *Analog*, December, 1961. © Street and Smith Publications, Inc., 1961.

"Operation P-Button," *Infinity One*, ed. Robert Hoskins. Lancer: New York, 1970. © Lancer Books, Inc., 1970.

"Soupstone," *Analog*, July, 1965. © Condé Nast Publications, Inc., 1965.

Ballad of the Shoshonu, Sixth Annual Edition: The Year's Best SF. ed. Judith Merril, 1961. Dell: New York, 1961. © Judith Merril, 1961.

"Catch a Tartar," *Worlds of Tomorrow*. September, 1965. © Galaxy Publishing Corporation, 1965.

"A Matter of Technique," *Magazine of Fantasy and Science Fiction*, May, 1958. © Mercury Press, Inc., 1958.

CONTENTS

MISS PRINKS   1
FLEEGL OF FLEEGL   18
SHOW ME THE WAY TO GO HOME   42
REX AND MR. REJILLA   59
WHO DARES A BULBUR EAT?   80
THE FAITHFUL WILF   101
A WOBBLE IN WOCKII FUTURES   123
SLEIGHT OF WIT   158
OPERATION P-BUTTON   180
SOUPSTONE   182
BALLAD OF THE SHOSHONU   216
CATCH A TARTAR   219
A MATTER OF TECHNIQUE   256

"As World Scouts, your keenest challenge will be to span the gap between human and alien minds. The risky and delicate business of interspecies contact must never be left to chance."

—*Orientations*, World Scout
Training Tape #011123

Miss Prinks

Miss Lydia Prinks was somebody's aunt. Not the aunt of several somebodies, but the aunt of one person only and with no other living brothers, sisters, cousins, nephews, or nieces to her name. A sort of singleton aunt. It would be possible to describe her further, but it would not be in good taste. To draw a clearer picture possibly would be to destroy the anonymity that Miss Prinks has, at the cost of a very great sacrifice indeed, maintained. Think of her then as a singleton aunt, and you have a pretty fair picture of her.

She lived on a sort of annuity in a small apartment up three flights of stairs on a certain street in a middle-sized city. The apartment had pale gold curtains of lace, a green carpet, and furniture upholstered in wine red. It had an assortment of good books in the bookcases and good pictures on the wall and a large, fat cat called Solomon on a footstool. It

1

was a very proper sort of apartment for a singleton aunt living on an annuity, and Miss Prinks lived a peaceful, contented sort of life there.

That is to say, she *did* live a peaceful, contented sort of life until one afternoon just after lunch when the grandfather clock in the corner of the living room, having gone from twelve noon through twelve forty-five, went one step farther than it had ever done before, and instead of striking one o'clock, struck thirteen.

"What on earth—" said Miss Prinks, looking up astonished from her current Book-of-the-Month Club selection and staring at the clock. Solomon, the fat cat, also raised his head inquiringly.

"*What on earth!*" repeated Miss Prinks, indignantly. She stared hard at the clock, for she was a very ladylike person herself, and the apartment was very ladylike, and there is something nearly bohemian about a clock which, after twenty-eight years of striking correctly, jumps the traces and tolls off an impossible hour like thirteen.

"Now who's responsible for this, I'd like to know?" said Miss Prinks, almost fiercely, addressing the room at large. And then it happened.

Miss Prinks had not really expected an answer to her question. But she got one. For no sooner had the words left her mouth—in fact, while the words were still vibrating in the air—a strange something like a small, busily whirling dust devil began mistily to take form in the middle of the green carpet. At first only a wisp of vapor, it grew rapidly until it was quite solidly visible and the breeze of its rapid rotation fluttered the gold lace curtains.

"I'm afraid," spoke an apologetic voice inside Miss Prinks's head, "that I am responsible, Madam."

Now this was not the sort of answer which would

be calculated to calm the fears of an ordinary person who has just discovered that it is thirteen o'clock—a time that never was, and it is profoundly hoped, will never be again. But Miss Prinks was a singleton aunt of great courage and rock-hard convictions. Her personal philosophy started with the incontrovertible fact that she was a lady and went on from there. Starting from this fact, then, and going down the line of natural reasoning, it followed that the miniature dust devil, whatever else it might be, was a *Vandal*—a clock-gimmicking *Vandal*, just as the neighborhood boys who played baseball in the adjoining vacant lot were window-smashing *Vandals*, and the drunken man who on one previous occasion had parked his car up on the apartment building's front lawn was a grass-destroying *Vandal*, and with *Vandals* Miss Prinks took a firm line.

"You're a *Vandal!*" she said angrily, to put the creature in its place and make it realize that she saw it for what it was.

This appeared to disconcert the dust devil somewhat. It paused before replying, by thought-waves, of course.

"I beg your pardon?" it thought. "I don't seem to understand that name you called me. Surely you never saw me before?"

"Perhaps not," retorted Miss Prinks, fiercely. "But I know your type!"

"You do?" The dust devil's thought was clearly astonished. Then it seemed to gather dignity. "Be that as it may," it thought. "Allow me to explain what has happened."

"Very well," said Miss Prinks in the cold, impartial tones of a judge agreeing to hear a case.

"You may know my type," said the dust devil, mentally. "But I am sure you do not know me personally. I am—" he paused, and Miss Prinks felt little light fingers searching for the proper term in her mind, "a scientist of the eighty-third Zanch dimension. I was doing some research into the compressibility of time for a commercial concern in my sector of eighty-third dimensional space. They wished to know whether it would be feasible to package and ship time in wholesale quantities——"

Miss Prinks made an impatient gesture.

"——Anyhow," thought the dust devil hurriedly, "to make a long story short, there was an explosion, and roughly an hour of the time I was experimenting with was blown into your day. Naturally, I am extremely sorry about it, and I'll be only too glad to take the hour back."

"My clock—" said Miss Prinks, coldly.

"I will take care of it," said the dust devil, or Zanch scientist, to refer to him correctly. "I will realign its temporal coordinates and make whatever spatial corrections are necessary." He waited anxiously for Miss Prinks to agree.

Now, to tell the truth, Miss Prinks was beginning to soften inside. The politeness of the Zanch scientist was making a good impression on her in spite of herself. But she did not want to give in too easily.

"Well . . ." she said, hesitantly.

"Ah, but naturally!" cried the Zanch scientist mentally. "You feel yourself entitled to some compensation for the temporal damage done to your day. Don't think another word. I understand completely."

"Well . . ." said Miss Prinks, with a hint of a deprecating smile that in a less ladylike person would have been a simper. "I know nothing at all about business arrangements of that type——"

"Of course," said the Zanch scientist. "Allow me. . . ." Light fingers seemed to touch the surface of Miss Prinks's mind. "Forgive me for saying it, but I have reviewed your condition and notice several improvements that could be made. If you have no objection . . . ?"

Miss Prinks half turned her head away.

"Of course not," she said.

It has often been recorded in history that two people have come to shipwreck upon the mutual misunderstanding of a single word. This was merely one more of those instances. Miss Prinks was a lady, and she thought in ladylike terms. To her, the word *condition* referred to a person's position in the world, and particularly to that aspect of position which is related to the financial by grosser minds. She believed, therefore, that the Zanch scientist was, with the utmost delicacy, offering her monetary damages. Such things were, out of consideration for one another's feelings, referred to in periphrasis. Her sensitivity to the social situation forbade her to do anything as gross as inquiring about the amount.

The Zanch scientist, of course, had no such intention in mind. He was telepathic, but not particularly perceptive, and he knew nothing of human mores. To him, Miss Prinks was an organism with certain mental and physical attributes. Frankly, over a cup of something Zanchly, he was later to admit to a coworker that these were pretty horrible. But such bluntness was reserved for moments of intimacy among his own people. In his way, he also had manners. Therefore he used the thought *condition*, as a manager might refer to his boxer, or, more appositely, as a doctor might refer to a patient in the last stages of a wasting disease.

"Of course not," said Miss Prinks.

"Fine," said the Zanch scientist. There was a sudden shimmer in the air of the apartment living room, and Miss Prinks felt a strange quiver run from the soles of her feet to the tips of her hair. Then the room was empty.

The grandfather clock solemnly tolled two.

"Well!" said Miss Prinks.

Now that the Zanch scientist was actually gone, she found herself of two minds about him. He had undoubtedly been polite, but then he had also as undeniably been in the wrong. However, the important thing was that he was gone. And it was two o'clock.

She had shopping to do. There was a small business center two blocks from where she lived, and when the weather was good it was her practice to visit this early in the afternoon, leaving the latter part of the day for a visit to the public library which was only a block away from the shopping center in another direction. Miss Prinks reached for her purse, which was ready on the table beside her, and arose from her chair.

Arose is indeed the best description. With the first effort she exerted to get up from her chair, Miss Prinks shot forward and upward in an arc that carried her across the room, through the good lace curtains and the window, which was fortunately open, and down three stories to the sidewalk below. She landed on her feet, and, though the sound of her landing was noisy in the drowsy summer afternoon, it did not seem as if the fall had hurt her in any way. In fact, thought Miss Prinks, standing on the sidewalk with a disturbed expression on her face, she had never really felt so well in her life.

Just at that moment, however, she became aware that somebody was calling her name. She turned and recognized her neighbor on the first floor below her apartment—a somewhat mousy little woman with the name of Annabelle LeMer.

"Oooh, Lydia!" cried Annabelle Le Mer, as she reached Miss Prinks by the expedient of running frantically out into the street. "I was watering the flowers in my window box and I saw it all. Whatever possessed you to jump out the window?"

There are some times when a lady must take refuge in a complete refusal to discuss a subject. Miss Prinks was quick to realize that this moment was one of those. She drew herself up with queenly dignity.

"I?" she repeated in tones of icy outrage. "I jump out a window? You are having one of your bilious attacks, Annabelle."

"But I saw—" babbled the little woman in desperation.

"Bilious!" snapped Miss Prinks in a tone of voice that brooked no contradiction. She glared at Annabelle with such ferocity that the smaller woman faltered and began to doubt the evidence of her own senses. "I jump out a window! The very idea!"

So convincing was her tone that Annabelle LeMer began to half feel the waves of dizziness that in actual truth preceded one of her bilious attacks. She looked at Miss Prinks and then up at the window with the gold lace curtains three stories above. She looked so long that the blood rushed out of her head and when she returned her gaze to Miss Prinks, the street wavered about her.

"P-perhaps—" stammered Miss LeMer dizzily, "perhaps you're right, Lydia." And, turning away from Miss Prinks's angry gaze, she weaved back into her own apartment, to put cold packs on her forehead and collapse on the bed.

Left alone on the sidewalk, Miss Prinks experimented. She found that by being very, very careful not to exert herself, and by attempting what she felt were tiny steps, she could walk in quite a natural manner. By the time she had this matter straightened out, she found herself at the end of the block and, so strong is habit, decided to keep on going and get her shopping done.

This decision was an excellent one, and one that might well have carried her through the rest of the day without mishap. Unfortunately fate took a hand, and the manner in which it did so was unexpected.

Now it must be confessed that, while Miss Prinks herself was every inch a lady, her neighborhood was perhaps not quite the best that a lady could live in. Perhaps it was not even the second best. One block away from the apartment building in which Miss Prinks lived, and halfway to the shopping center which she patronized and intended to visit today, there was something which for want of a better pair of words must bluntly be described as railroad tracks. Squarely athwart Miss Prinks's way they lay, and to get over them she was forced to cross a bridge beneath which the tracks lay in dark parallels and under which the trains smoked and thundered.

Usually at the time when Miss Prinks normally went marketing there were no trains, and she was able with ladylike detachment to ignore the fact that they existed. But today, owing to the particular circumstances following lunch she was later than usual and just in time for the early afternoon *Comet*, a crack passenger train possessing great speed and a mighty whistle for blowing at railway crossings and other artifacts of present-day civilization. It was a very distinctive and a very powerful whistle, and to tell the truth, the engineer who usually handled the *Comet* on its early afternoon run liked blowing it whenever the excuse offered.

Just what the excuse was this day, no one will ever know. But it is a fact that the engineer blew the

Comet's whistle as he started under the bridge Miss Prinks was on. And he blew it just as she was right in the middle of her crossing.

Miss Prinks, it has been shown, had iron courage. But she also had very ladylike and delicate nerves. So, when the *Comet* shot under her feet and the whistle blasted away practically in her ear, she could not repress a tiny start.

Unfortunately, people in Miss Prinks's made-over condition should never start. For ordinary humans it is all right, but Miss Prinks's start shot her up into the air and into a long arc that dropped her on the tracks some twenty yards in front of the charging *Comet*.

Miss Prinks took one horrified glance at the towering engine rushing down upon her, turned heel, and ran.

"Ulp!" said the engineer, and fainted dead away.

The landscape blurred by Miss Prinks and she felt her breath growing shorter. She risked a quick glance over her shoulder and nearly fainted herself. Behind her, the tracks stretched bare and empty to the horizon. The *Comet* was nowhere in sight.

Nor was the city.

Profoundly shaken, Miss Prinks leaped off the tracks, and, skidding to a stop, sat down heavily on a bank by the side of the tracks.

"Am I dead?" wondered Miss Prinks, in awe. "Did the train run me down?"

Being a practical person, she took her pulse— correctly, with the second finger of her left hand on her right wrist. Her blood pulsed strongly and steadily. That settled it, then, as far as Miss Prinks was concerned. She was alive.

Miss Prinks fanned herself with her purse and began to think. She thought back over the last few hours and she thought and she thought, and suddenly she stopped fanning herself and turned a bright pink with embarrassment.

"*Well!*" she said.

She had just realized what the Zanch scientist had meant when he used the word *condition* and what he had evidently done to her. At the thought of being altered, she blushed again.

However, one cannot go on being embarrassed forever, as Miss Prinks abruptly realized with unusual clarity of mind. She had been changed, the Zanch scientist was gone where she most probably could never reach him, and the thing to do was to investigate herself.

Her shoes caught her attention first. These were, quite literally, in ruined condition. The sole and heel of each was worn to rags. There was, in fact, little left but the tops. Torn edges stuck out over the bare arch of her foot like sad tendrils. Miss Prinks began to get some idea of how fast she had been running when she fled from the express train.

"Oh, my poor feet!" thought Miss Prinks, automatically, and then immediately had to correct herself. Her feet felt fine. In fact, they had never felt so fine, even in the dim past of her childhood when she had been allowed to run barefoot. A suspicion struck her, and she leaned over to check once more. Her bunions were gone.

Modestly, she tucked her soleless shoes under her and went back to considering the situation. She, Miss Prinks, could run faster than a train. Impossible; but here she was and—she looked back along the tracks—the *Comet* was not even in sight. If she could run that fast, how high could she jump?

She glanced quickly around the countryside. It was open and deserted with occasional clumps of trees and farmland stretching out of sight over rolling hills. There was no sign even of a building. Miss Prinks got gingerly to her feet, tucked her purse firmly under one arm, crouched slightly, and sprang.

There was a terrific rush of air, a moment's dizzy sensation and Miss Prinks found herself gasping for oxygen high in the atmosphere. Far below her, laid out in neat little checkerboard squares, the ground from horizon to horizon rocked and swayed.

"Oh my!" thought Miss Prinks in dismay as she reached the limit of her spring, turned over and started head downward toward the Earth. "Now I've done it!"

On the way to the ground, however, she thought of the proprieties and turned herself right side up again, which was, as it turned out, a very prudent move. For instead of landing on ordinary ground and sinking in about ten feet, she had the good luck to land on a large boulder which shattered into fragments beneath the impact of her falling body, but left her quite properly on the surface of the Earth.

Miss Prinks took time out to powder her nose and catch her breath.

It would be foolish to deny that at this point she was becoming somewhat excited about the possibilities inherent in her new self. When she had finished powdering her nose, she tried out a few more tests. She discovered that she was now capable of doing the following things:

(a) Felling a tree approximately two feet thick with one punch.
(b) Tying knots in sections of rail from the railway track.
(c) Lifting the largest boulder in sight (which was about ten feet high) and throwing it about eighty feet.

(d) Doing all the above without working up an unladylike perspiration.

But it was not these feats that startled her so much as a quite accidental discovery. She had untied the knots in the steel rails and was replacing them on the railway track, hammering in the spikes with dainty taps of her fist, when a tiny splinter on one of the wooden ties seemed to come to life and walk away on six legs. Earlier that morning, Miss Prinks would never have recognized it, but no sooner had its movement caught her attention than she immediately identified it as *Diapheromera femorata*, or common walking-stick insect of the eastern United States—being somewhat far west considering the present latitude.

For a moment her identification astounded her; and then she remembered reading about this particular insect some years previous, one day in one of those little squibs of general information which are used by editors to fill out columns in the daily newspaper. With letter-perfect recall, the item came back to her. For a moment she was tempted to speculate about the family of the *Phasmidae* in general, but she pushed the temptation from her, and set herself instead to considering the implications of this most recent self-discovery.

So Miss Prinks sat and thought, and, after having thought for a while, she took her way back alongside the railroad tracks at a jog trot in the neighborhood of a hundred miles an hour. On the way she passed the *Comet*.

This time the engineer did not faint. He merely shut his eyes firmly and told himself that he needed glasses.

At the outskirts of town Miss Prinks slowed down

to an ordinary human gait, so as not to attract attention, and took a streetcar back to her apartment, where she changed shoes and sallied forth once more—this time to the library three blocks away.

The library was a large, rambling building of brown brick, split up into a number of large rooms, each of which specialized in the supply of some particular class of reading material to the general public. One of these dealt with material on the more abstract branches of science, and it was this one that Miss Prinks, with some trepidation, entered.

She spoke to the woman clerk behind the desk, filled out some slips, and after a due wait was supplied with several books, in particular one rather heavy and impressive-looking volume.

It was this one she opened first. She skimmed through the first few pages, clicked her tongue disapprovingly, and went back to the desk to order several textbooks on mathematics, leading up to and including one on tensor calculus. She returned with these to her seat and flipped through them with amazing rapidity. Then she set them aside with a satisfied air, and returned to her original volume.

She sat reading this for some time, and when she had finally finished it and laid it aside she continued to sit deep in thought for some time.

A new factor had entered into her life. A social, scientific, and for all that, probably a moral and ethical problem as well. It had come as a direct result of what the Zanch scientist had done to her. And because of it she had made a serious discovery.

Mr. Einstein was wrong on several points. Ought she to tell someone?

For a long time she sat there at her library table, and her thoughts ranged far and wide over the almost limitless vista that her new abilities had opened up for her.

She was, without doubt, the strongest person in the world. The evidence she had just acquired tended to indicate that she was probably also the most intelligent person in the world. Whatever was she to do then, with all this intelligence and strength? How was she to use it? Why? Where? When? What would people think when she told them she could outrun a train?

Possibly, thought Miss Prinks, she could be useful as a sort of lady traffic policeman chasing reckless drivers. Miss Prinks shuddered a little at the thought. No, that would be too undignified, running down a street in a blue uniform at her age. Perhaps she could become some sort of government scientist. But they would probably put her to work designing some sort of super-weapon. As a member of the SPCA, she simply could not do it. Possibly——

A bell rang through the library, notifying all and sundry that the seven o'clock closing hour had arrived. Still deep in thought, Miss Prinks rose to her feet, returned her books, and made off in the direction of her apartment.

She had thought away the last hours of the afternoon, and twilight was closing down. In the soft dwindling light, she took her way down the almost deserted street, across the railroad bridge (no train this time, thank goodness), and past the closed shops on her way toward home.

She left the bridge behind her and went on in a careful imitation of her usual walk. She had half a block to go to reach the safety and peace of the green rug, the gold lace curtains, the grandfather clock, and Solomon, the cat.

And it was then that the purse-snatcher got her.

He came diving out of the shadows of the narrow alleyway between the pet shop and the hardware store, seconds after Miss Prinks had inched her way past. A few quick running strides brought him up to her—a tall, heavy youth with a scarred face and breath whistling fiercely through his straining, open mouth. With one sudden twitch, he pulled the purse from her arm, tucked it under his own and was away at a dead run down the block.

Now, of course, with her super-hearing, Miss Prinks should have heard his breathing and the pounding of his heart as he waited for her in the alley. With her super-intelligence, she should have instantly divined that he was after the contents of her purse, and with her super-reactions she should have sidestepped and tripped him up quite neatly.

Unfortunately, just like any ordinary mortal, Miss Prinks had become absorbed in her own thoughts, and the purse-snatcher took her by surprise. In fact it was a good 8.7326 seconds, as she later shame-facedly admitted to herself, before the fact registered on her that she had been robbed. When it *did* register, she reacted without thinking. With one super-leap she overtook the youth and snatched at his jacket.

It ripped away from him like so much tissue paper. Frantic with the thought that he might escape, Miss Prinks grabbed again, this time coming away with half his shirt and undershirt. Her fingers were ripping through the left leg of the purse-snatcher's heavy workpants when sanity returned to her. She gasped, stared once at the half-denuded figure fainting before her, and ran.

So, in a third-story apartment on a certain street, Miss Prinks still lives. She is still a singleton aunt on a pension, and she still has gold lace curtains on the window, the green carpet on the floor, and wine-colored upholstery on her furniture. The grandfather clock and Solomon are intact and present. She does her housecleaning in the morning, her shopping in the afternoon, and still visits the library late in the day, on nice days.

But she never goes in the science room, and she never requests Mr. Einstein's book again. Sometimes, in the evening when she has finished supper at home, she will sit down in her favorite chair to see what the news is. Then, with hands that are capable of crumpling three-inch steel plate, she picks up the evening paper. From the table beside her chair she picks up glasses and fixes them firmly in front of eyes that can see a fly crawling up a window pane two miles away. And, with a perception that is capable of scanning and memorizing a page at a glance, she plods through the news stories, word by word.

And sometimes she comes across an item on the front page reporting the construction of an atomic airplane, or a new discovery of medical science, or a release on the latest Air Force rocket—or on flying saucers. When this happens she reads it through, then shakes her head a little, then smiles. But that is all. She puts the paper down again and goes to bed.

For Miss Prinks made up her mind in that split second of realization that came to her in the heat of her flurry with the purse-snatcher. For the first time she had put her newly acquired powers to use, and in that moment she realized that it never could be.

For perhaps it would benefit the world to have a Miss Prinks who can outrun an express train, jump over the Empire State Building, or correct the Theory of Relativity. These things might be good and they might not. Miss Prinks does not know.

But there is one thing she does know. And it is the reason the world will never see Miss Prinks doing any of these things.

For Miss Prinks is a lady, and such goings-on are far too dangerous. There is no doubt about it, and you are just wasting your breath if you try to argue with her. For there is too great a risk—far too great a risk (and Miss Prinks blushes at the memory) that such exercise of her powers might lead to another such occasion as that in which she—a lady—suddenly found herself *tearing a man's clothes off on the public street*! Further such doings are not for her.

No indeed! Not for Miss Prinks!

"Despite the most careful scientific planning, you must still expect complications when alien minds meet."

—*Orientations*

Fleegl of Fleegl

James Godow woke up just in time to see it happen. His alarm clock had just gone off in the bedroom of the small house he had inherited from his aunt Martha. The four blue-and-green flowered wallpapered walls were all about him—and then suddenly they weren't. That is to say, two of them still were, but the other two had been cut off by what appeared to be a wall of thick, misty glass extending through both floor and ceiling.

Jim did not react immediately. Instead, he lay cautiously still, gazing at the misty wall and turning over in his mind all the things that could cause him to experience such an hallucination. Nerves? Incipient insanity? Degeneration of the optic nerve? After several minutes had passed and the wall was still there, he stretched out a slow hand and touched it where it passed close to his bed. It was quite solid. Solid as steel.

After thinking this over, he got out of bed and looked out the one window that had been left to him. What he saw was a continuation of the white wall, reaching up into a dome to enclose the unfenced back yards of three other houses at his end of the block and portions of the houses themselves.

As he watched, a bedroom window of the amputated house-portion directly opposite was pushed up, and the oval-shaped face of a girl with somewhat rumpled blond hair emerged to stare right, left and center, finally focusing on something which in the general excitement had escaped Jim's attention. It was a large, metallic-looking cube, some eight feet on a side, sitting in the center of the four yards. It gave no sign of life. From this, she looked around the enclosed area again, and spotted Jim, hanging out *his* window. Jim felt that it was time to enter into communication.

"What is it?" he yelled across at her.

"I don't know!" she called back. "Don't you?"

"No!"

"It must be something!"

There was a slight pause.

"Tell you what!" shouted Jim. "I'll get dressed and meet you in the back yard in a few minutes. I'll have to come out the window. I'm walled off in my bedroom here!"

"Me, too!" she answered. "It's right across my bedroom door. I'll get dressed, too, and—oh!" Apparently just realizing the implications of her last statement, her head popped back out of sight through her window. Jim pulled his own head in and went in search of clothes.

Half the dresser and all of his closet was available to him. He was equipped with everything but shirts, which he kept in the closet of the spare bedroom. He compromised on slacks and a clean t-shirt, and crawled out the window.

The girl was already out in the back yard by the metallic cube. She was dressed in slacks and a light summer blouse. With her was a neighbor boy of about twelve in a boy scout uniform; and a heavy man in his sixties, wearing pajamas and a purple-wool dressing gown, whom Jim recognized as Mr. Harvey Bolster of the segment of the large house the back of which was diagonally opposite his own.

". . . get a pry-bar," Bolster was saying excitedly, waving his arms in outrage. "Break it open. Smash the machine inside!"

"Maybe there isn't any machine," said the boy scout, happily. "Maybe the box just resonates a signal beamed in from somewhere else, and makes the force-field that way."

"Resonates!" exploded Bolster, glaring at the boy. "Force-field!"

"Sure. Just like—"

"Be quiet, boy!"

"You'll see," said the boy scout. He went over to examine the surface of the cube closely.

"Uh-hello," said Jim. The girl and Bolster looked over at him. "I'm Jim Godow. I just moved into Mrs. Lee's house last month. She was my aunt. . . . You're Mr. Bolster, aren't you?"

"How d'y'do. Harvey Bolster, yes." The two men shook hands. "You know Jennie Coram, here? Miss Coram, Mr.—uh."

"Jim Godow."

"Hi," she said. "The neighborhood's been talking about you. You write Christmas cards, don't you?"

"All sorts of greeting card verse," said Jim.

"That must be fascinating."

"The point is," broke in Harvey, "what're we going

to do? Here we are, cut off, in my case without even a pair of slippers—"

"It's opening," said the boy scout.

They all went over to the cube, which was beginning to crack down on one side.

"Hi," said Jim to the boy scout. "I'm Jim Godow. Who're you?"

"Rodney Wasla," said the boy scout. "We better stand back. The extra-terrestrial atmosphere from the interior of the ship may be poisonous to humans."

"Oh, nonsense!" snapped Harvey. "What I think is—"

The cube opened up suddenly, revealing what appeared to be a small, square room crammed with instruments. A large, rabbit-like creature with long drooping ears and four arms came out, waving its hands at them.

"All right, all right now," it said pettishly in a rather Vermont-like accent, "get back, don't be in the way."

They retreated slightly.

"Welcome to Earth," said Rodney Wasla.

"What's that?" said the creature, focusing on Rodney. "Oh, *Welcome*. Thank you." It patted Rodney on the head. "That's a good boy." It produced something like a large turnip from what appeared to be a natural pouch in the front of its body, and rammed the vegetable into the turf of a back yard—Jim's, as luck would have it.

"I declare this planet planted in the name of Fleegl," the creature said. "I, Nugwik, being a duly accredited planter of Fleegl on Fleegl. Good sproutings!" It went back into the ship.

"Well, of all the blasted nerve!" exploded Harvey. "Hey, you—Nugwik, or whatever your name is—come out here."

"Now, now," said Nugwik, emerging from the

cube's interior with his four arms full of miscella-
neous gadgets of a metallic nature. "No time to gab.
Particularly with criminal psychopaths. Stand back
there while I get my spacetube started."

"Gab!" roared Harvey. "Psychopaths! What're you
talking about?"

"Come, come," said Nugwik, beginning to put his
gadgets together. "Nothing to be ashamed of. You're
all paranoiacs here on Earth. But we'll cure you, just
as soon as I can get the necessary equipment here
from Fleegl on Fleegl. Insanity's completely unknown
at Fleegl on Fleegl."

"What—" Harvey was beginning to pop and froth
again. Jim took him by the arm and led him away,
beckoning to Jennie Coram to follow. When they
were out of earshot of Rodney and Nugwik, Jim
spoke again.

"Let's not go off half-cocked," he said. "This thing
looks like it's too big to be fiddled with. Let's see if
we can't get together and decide what's best to do."

"Oh, yes," said Jennie.

"Well," said Harvey, calming down with an effort,
"you may be right. It's just the infernal nerve of
that— What do you suggest?"

"Is there someplace we can talk?" asked Jim.

"Not in my bedroom," said Harvey. "There's less
than a bed and an armchair left."

"I'm in about the same condition," said Jim.
"Er—Jennie?"

"Oh, no!" she said quickly. "I haven't much more
than the rest of you and it's all in a mess. But
Rodney's got all his bedroom, and a bathroom, too,
he says. Why don't we . . . ?"

They adjourned to the segment of the Wasla house
and compared notes.

There was little they could tell each other—they'd
all been asleep when the wall came.

"We need help," said Jim.

"Yes, but how do we get it?" demanded Harvey. "No blasted telephone. You can't see through that wall, let alone hear through it. I tell you something's got to be done! What's wrong with the police—and the fire department? They should have been here an hour ago, cutting their way in."

"They can't," said Rodney, appearing at the window. He proceeded to climb into the room. "No power on Earth can break that barrier."

"Who says so?" demanded Harvey. "That rabbit?"

"The Fleeglian," explained Rodney.

"I don't care whether he fleegls or floozles!" snapped Harvey. "He can't do this to us. Who does he think he is, anyway?"

"He's a survey Fleegl," said Rodney. "He happened to be passing by this solar system, and, luckily for us—"

"You've been talking to him," said Jim.

"I just asked him where he came from."

"Where?" asked Jim.

"Oh, he can't make us understand, we're too dumb," said Rodney. "Besides, we're all psychofats."

"Psychopaths, Roddy," corrected Jennie.

"Yes, and this place he comes from, it's an island called Fleegl. It's the only land on the planet Fleegl. He just happened to be passing by after many years on space duty and he saw at a glance that we were dangerous."

"Why?" asked Jim.

"On account of we're going to conquer Fleegl if he doesn't cure us. We hate Fleegl and all it stands for."

"Never heard such nonsense in my life!" barked Harvey. "Is that all it is?" He got to his feet. "Let's go straighten him out."

"Well, maybe . . ." said Jim, doubtfully. They all followed Harvey back out the window. He strode up to Nugwik. The Fleeglian had got his bits and pieces of equipment put together. From somewhere inside them a shimmering cylinder rose up as they watched and passed through the top of the dome. Every so often Nugwik would do something to a control panel and the cylinder would appear to flow upward at an incredible rate. Then it would stop, and Nugwik would make another adjustment on his panel.

"Hey!" said Harvey, tapping Nugwik between the shoulder blades. "Hey, you! None of us here're mad at Fleegl. Nobody ever heard of the place."

"Yes, yes," murmured Nugwik absently, his gaze on the panel. "Run along, now."

"Run along! Why, blast you—*you* run along!" Harvey purpled. "Pack up and get out. You've made a mistake."

Nugwik stiffened and turned.

"A mistake?" he said icily.

"You heard me!" cried Harvey.

"Barash!" exploded Nugwik, stabbing a finger suddenly at Harvey. He turned back to his panel, in an outraged tone muttering to himself something that, whatever it was, certainly was not English.

Harvey continued to stand there. After a second, Jim nudged him.

"Let's go back and talk this over some more," he whispered. "Back at Rodney's."

Harvey turned about like a clockwork soldier and marched off toward the boy's house. He continued marching until he came to the wall of the house. There he stopped. The other humans hurried after him.

"Mr. Bolster!" said Jennie. "Are you all right?"

Harvey jerked his head around and looked at her glassily.

"All right?" he said. "Of course not. I'm wrong, all wrong."

Jim and Jennie looked at each other. After a second, Jim turned to Harvey again.

"Let's all get back inside," he said. Harvey obediently scrambled over the sill into Rodney's room, and the rest followed. Jim heard a continuous beeping sound coming from somewhere.

"Sit down on the bed, Harvey," he told the older man, and turned about. "What's that noise?"

"Oh, boy!" yelped Rodney, diving for a card table cluttered with junk. He scratched most of this aside and revealed a telegraph key, a sounder, and a couple of dry-cell batteries, all hooked together.

Eagerly, Rodney began to manipulate the key. "It's my line to Jerry Burr, down the block," he said. "We're going to be ham operators—" he broke off suddenly, listening to a series of answering beeps. "Hey, that's somebody else talking! That can't be right."

"Wrong. Dead wrong," said Harvey to himself, on the bed. "How could I be so wrong?"

"He's a general, a real general!" cried Rodney, jittering in excitement. Busily, he began to send himself. The small telegraph buzzed back and forth and the minutes stretched on.

"What's going on?" Jim asked finally.

"He's asking all about Nugwik," said Rodney, blissfully. "I'm telling him. He's listening, too. He's an Air Force general from the air base at Leesville."

"Perhaps I was born to err," Harvey told himself. "When I think how wrong I've been, day after day, year after year. . . ."

"Let me talk to him," said Jim.

"Always wrong," muttered Harvey.

"Just a minute—he wants to talk to you, or somebody grownup—" Rodney turned for the first time from the key to look at Jim. "Do you know code?"

"Code? Oh—no, you'll have to send for me," said

Jim. "Is the general listening? Ask him what we ought to do?"

Rodney tapped his key, paused and listened.

"He says," said Rodney, "observe the alien carefully. Take notes on everything he does."

"But what about us?" said Jim. "We want to get out. Tell him to break through this wall here and let us out."

"He says they're working on it now. Meanwhile, he wants full data on the alien, and in particular on the space tube the alien is projecting. It's already a number of miles high. This alien may be a threat to the very existence of the United States. It is imp— imperative to discover his intentions and that of the government he represents. Repeat, it is imperative to discover his intentions."

"How does he expect us to do that?" demanded Jim. "Am I supposed to just go ask him?" The set beeped.

"Affirmative," said Rodney.

"What?" said Jim. "Affirmative? Affirmative what?"

The set ceased sounding. Rodney looked sadly up at Jim.

"Don't you know that?" he said. "That's the way they say *yes* in the Air Force."

"Oh," Jim looked at Harvey—he was shaking his head despairingly at his own reflection in a dresser mirror—and over at Jennie. "Well," he said. "I suppose . . ."

Leaving the rest of them there, he climbed out over the window sill and went back out to Nugwik, who was still busily jacking up his space tube.

The alien did not seem to be aware of Jim's approach, so Jim coughed a couple of times. "Say," he said, when this produced no response, "can I ask you a question?"

"Yes, yes," said Nugwik, "just a minute." He twiddled a couple of dials and straightened up. "Tiring," he said. "Very tiring." He turned around toward Jim and produced what looked like a small bunch of flowers from his body pouch. He sniffed them. "Ah, that's better." He put the flowers away, "And now for your question."

"Why don't you just leave us alone?" said Jim.

"And give you the chance to conquer and enslave Fleegl on Fleegl? Hah!"

"But nobody here is mad at Fleegl on Fleegl. We never even knew there was such a place."

"You would, shortly. What do you mean, not mad? You're all mad, here. If I ever saw a species so unethical, carnivorous, given to delusions of persecution, bloodthirsty, hysteric—"

"But—"

"No interruptions, please," said Nugwik, sternly. "You are monsters—fortunately, rather stupid monsters . . . but monsters. Now, have you any other questions to ask, before I knock off for a sniff of nourishment?"

"Yes," said Jim. "How come you speak English so well?"

"Come now!" said Nugwik, stiffly. "As if there were any trick to learning your simple dialect."

"Well, look," said Jim. "If you'd just tell me something about this Fleegl of yours—"

"Words," said Nugwik, "cannot possibly convey to you the essence, the grandeur of the island-wide Fleegl City on Fleegl Island on Fleegl. Why, if I were to attempt to describe to you just Fleegl Hall on Fleegl Boulevard—I doubt very much you'd be able to take it. It would be too much. You would collapse."

"Try me," offered Jim.

"No," said Nugwik, shaking his head. "It would be too cruel." He turned away and reentered his cube.

Jim went back to Rodney's room. Harvey was still

on the bed and weeping softly as he explained to Jennie how he had been wrong-natured from the start. Rodney looked up from his telegraph set, as Jim climbed in over the window sill.

"General Farber has a message for you," he said. "You're to tell Nugwik if he does not emerge from this protection of his and enter personally into negotiation with United States authorities, serious steps will be taken. You are to tell him—" Rodney consulted a piece of paper—"that if he wishes to consider this as an ultimatum, he may do so. The deadline is two hours from now at 1300 hours. . . . And," wound up Rodney, "I'm hungry and my mother says you have to make Nugwik see that I have something to eat."

"Thanks," said Jim, dropping wearily down on a corner of the bed.

"Oh, that's all right," said Rodney, generously.

"However," said Jim, seeing Jennie's eyes, too, upon him, "Nugwik's gone inside his box to have his own lunch; and I can't get at him. As soon as he comes out I'll talk to him again. How's Harvey?"

"He's not very happy," said Jennie. She patted the older man consolingly on the shoulder. "There, there, Mr. Bolster. You never were *that* bad."

"Oh, yes I was," said Harvey. "I was worse, much worse. You don't know me like I do." He snuffled quietly into the pillow of Rodney's bed.

"Can't you get Nugwik to change him back?" asked Jennie, turning to Jim. "He's such a problem this way."

"Well," said Jim, doubtfully. "I hate to ask him for too many things at once. Let's just try out the food question first."

"How long do you suppose before he comes out again?"

"No way of telling," said Jim. He glanced again

out the window. The cube was still closed up, looking as if it were cast out of one piece of solid metal,
and Rodney had left them again for another examina-
tion of it. From the bed a gentle snore apprised
them that Harvey, worn out by his self-recriminations,
had dropped off to sleep. "We'll just have to wait,"
said Jim. He looked at Jennie and cleared his throat.
"Funny situation, isn't it? I mean, meeting this way."

"I've seen you lots of times," said Jennie. "Around
your aunt's house. But you didn't seem to have too
much to do with the neighbors."

"Well, you see," said Jim, "when you work at
home the way I do, it's awfully easy to get distracted
from work you ought to get done. . . ."

They chatted in low voices while Harvey slum-
bered. Jennie, it turned out, was in her senior year at
Dumbarton U. Her major was Education. She wanted
to teach history. Jim had always liked history . . .
some day he intended to write an historical novel.
Their first names both began with J. . . .

"Nugwik's back out at work now," said Rodney,
after an indeterminate time, appearing at the window. "And I'm hungry as heck."

"Oh," said Jim, coming back to the realities of
their present situation. "All right, I'll go ask him."

"Be careful he doesn't get mad," said Jennie.

"Yes," said Jim. He went out the window and
approached Nugwik. The Fleeglian was happily at
work, jacking up his space tube.

"—er," said Jim.

"Now what?" snapped Nugwik, his good nature
vanishing in a flash. He turned about, his ears literally
dragging on his shoulders.

"Well, you've got us cut off here without any
food—" began Jim.

Nugwik winced, but turned back to his panel and
made some adjustments on it.

"All right," he said. "Go get your—" he winced again, "sustenance."

"Thanks," said Jim. Nugwik turned back to the panel. Jim hesitated.

"Uh—" he said, after a second. "Just where do I go to get it?"

Nugwik threw up all four hands and turned on him.

"Where do you usually go?" he snapped. "To a refrigerator."

"Refrigerator?"

"*His* refrigerator!" Nugwik jabbed a finger at Rodney, and turned back to work, muttering. Rodney turned and raced off toward his bedroom window.

Jim continued to stand around, peering at the panel at which the Fleeglian was working. There did not seem much to what Nugwik was doing. A twist of a rheostat, a glance at a dial, and the white column seemed to flow upward for a short period of time.

"Well, what are you staring at now?" demanded Nugwik, without turning.

"The—uh, space tube," said Jim.

"Eighteen thousand miles out already," said Nugwik with satisfaction. "Propagation increases in ratio to the square of the established length. Won't take long now."

"Fleegl isn't Mars, is it?" asked Jim.

"Mars!" Nugwik snorted. "Are there any oceans on Mars?"

"Venus?"

"Certainly not. None of your scrubby little planets. For your information—much good it'll do you— Fleegl is light-years from here. Hundreds of light-years." He waved a hand absently at Jim. "Now, go seek your sustenance and leave me to my work here."

Jim went back into Rodney's bedroom. There was nobody there. Going down the hall toward the bedroom, he discovered the wall had been extended in the form of a tunnel which led him to the kitchen of the Wasla house. Rodney, Jennie, and even Harvey were seated at the kitchen table, eating chicken sandwiches.

"Coffee?" asked Jennie, getting up as Jim came in.

"Thanks," said Jim. He looked around him. "Are we still walled in?"

"You can't open the kitchen door," said Rodney, with his mouth full. "It's all white outside it, and the windows, too."

Jim sat down at the table somewhat dispiritedly. Jennie brought him some coffee and a chicken sandwich.

"What did he say?" asked Jennie.

"He just said to go to the refrigerator here."

"I mean," said Jennie, "to the general's ultimatum."

"Oh, Lord," Jim said, getting to his feet. "I forgot to tell him." He went back out in the direction of the back yard; and returned in a few minutes, looking rather pale.

"What did he say?" Jennie asked again. Jim sat down heavily at the kitchen table.

"He said," reported Jim, "to let them drop their silly little fission bombs."

He looked at them. Jennie and Rodney stared back at him. Harvey remarked that that was all right, he, Harvey, deserved it.

"That does mean—atom bombs or H-bombs, doesn't it?" faltered Jennie.

"I don't know what else it could mean." Jim perspired slightly. He cleared his throat and took a gulp of coffee. "Maybe I could find something to hit him over the head with. I thought of that. But how would I find out how to turn off the wall?"

"Couldn't you just experiment with the controls—"

"If I could just get him out of the way for a while,

I could try it." Jim bit thoughtfully into his sandwich. "Wait a minute—Harvey!"

"I'm sorry," whimpered Harvey. "I didn't mean to do it—whatever it was."

"No, no," said Jim. "I was talking to Jennie. Jennie, you go tell Nugwik that Harvey's in some kind of coma. Say it's his fault. He won't believe you, but he ought to come just to make sure you're wrong. I'll hide in the bathroom, and after he goes by, I'll run out and see what I can manage to figure out with his controls."

"But Harvey isn't in a coma," protested Jennie.

"He will be," Jim said. He stood up, winced, murmured "Excuse me," and hit Harvey squarely on the jaw. Harvey collapsed.

"Man!" said Rodney. "With one punch!"

"It's not my muscles," explained Jim, modestly, "it's Harvey. He's agreeable to anything now, even to being knocked out. I figured on that." He turned to Jennie. "Hurry."

Jennie went out hurriedly. Jim followed her and hid in the bathroom. After a minute or two he heard the sound of double footsteps pass his closed door, and the voice of Nugwik snorting—"Ridiculous!"

He opened the door and peered out into the kitchen. He saw Harvey still obligingly being unconscious and everybody else bending over him.

Jim hurried out through the bedroom into the backyard. The cube stood open before him. He entered it.

There were only two panels of controls visible. On top of one of them was a small something like a tv screen, in which a miniature cube stood open in the middle of some back yards.

"That's for driving it, I suppose," muttered Jim. He turned to the other panel. This was surmounted by a like screen, which was blank. Below it were a couple of knobs like rheostats and a small keyboard, of which some of the keys were depressed. Jim hastily punched other keys at random and twiddled the knobs. A face like Nugwik's appeared in the screen.

"Koji?" it said, staring at Jim. "Wun vark?"

Jim hastily stabbed other buttons. The face disappeared, but blinked back on again a second later.

"Woji!" barked the face.

"Sorry, I didn't mean to get you. Wrong number!" stammered Jim, frantically poking buttons. The face in the screen flickered, but stayed put.

"Lari, orri, Shkarri, sawri—sorry. Enjefli nu. Paji? Poji. Sawri, I didn't min tawgt oo. Ah, *chifleni!* Who you? What you are doing, calling from Fleegl number? Explain this, please."

"Just a mistake," said Jim, trying wildly with the controls to erase it.

"Kindly cease attempting to alter your wavelength," said the face sharply. "You are connected with Survey Headquarters, Aberrations Tracer Unit One. How does it come you are operating a Fleeglian communication device?"

"Sorry, got to go now," said Jim. He slammed down both hands on all the keys at once, succeeding in blanking the screen, and sprinted for Rodney's house. He was just in time to duck into the bathroom before Nugwik passed, muttering angrily to himself.

After Nugwik had gone, Jim came out and went back to the kitchen. The other three were still there, Harvey sitting up and looking something like his natural self.

" 'Lo," he grunted as Jim came in. "I'm fixed up now. How'd you do?"

"No good," said Jim. "All I could make work was his radio, or his telephone, or whatever it was." He told them what had happened. "How'd Nugwik fix you up?" he wound up, looking at Harvey.

"Must be hypnotism," said Harvey. "It's those eyes of his. He looked at me and said something."

"Did he find out why you were unconscious? Uh—sorry about that punch, by the way."

"No," said Harvey. "That's all right. Fortunes of war. Look, what'll we do now? If the Air Force's actually going to bomb us—"

"I think we better talk to that general again," said Jim.

They went back to the bedroom and Rodney unlimbered the telegraph. As soon as he had the general on the wire, Jim dictated an account of the present situation and recent happenings.

". . . what do you advise us to do?" he wound up. There was a short period of silence from the far end of the wire.

"Sit tight for the moment," came back the answer. "You may hear from us in about fifteen minutes."

They sat tight. About a dozen minutes later there was a small jar, like a minor earthquake, that rattled the hunting prints on Rodney's walls.

"What happened?" asked Jennie, turning startled eyes on Jim.

"I don't know," said Jim. "Call them back, Rodney, and ask what's going on."

Rodney did. "They say, wait a minute," he reported.

They waited. About ten minutes later, the telegraph began a plaintive beeping. Rodney hurried to it.

"It's the general again," he said. "He says—we are finally in a position where our only hope is to appeal to you. Our most powerful weapon has been tried against the defense of the alien, with no effect. The alien's space tube now reaches hundreds of thousands of miles into space and continues to grow unchecked. Clearly the safety not only of the United States but the whole world is threatened. In this sad and fateful hour our only hope rests upon you four. We must appeal to you to make whatever effort lies within your power to put this creature or his apparatus out of commission. Whatever the cost or whatever the results may be, you must make this effort for the sake of every living creature upon the face of the globe. We can offer you no hope and no help, but our hearts are with you. Goodby."

The telegraph fell silent. They continued to sit in that same silence, for a long minute.

"Well," muttered Harvey, at last. "That's all very touching. But what can we do?"

"Take a chance at putting Nugwik out of action," said Jim. "That's all we can do."

"Easy enough to say it," said Harvey.

"Well, there's just a chance," said Jim. "If the Fleeglians are as advanced, as it seems, Nugwik may not be used to physical violence. We could sneak up on him—"

"All he has to do is look us in the eye. And then what?" Harvey said.

"I thought of that," answered Jim. "We put something over his head, see, and—"

Shortly thereafter, armed with a couple of baseball bats, Rodney's lasso and a large brown paper shopping bag—all held out of sight behind their backs— the four of them emerged from the bedroom window and advanced on Nugwik, busy at his outside panel.

"Go away! Go away!" snapped Nugwik as they came up behind him. He continued to work without turning his head. "I can't get anything done when you're constantly interrupting me—"

"Now!" yelled Jim. They all jumped him. Jennie jammed the shopping bag down over his head. Rodney hit the bag-enclosed head with a baseball bat.

Jim and Harvey threw the lasso around him and began to wrap him up tight. Jennie, with the other baseball bat, dodged around making small attemptive swings that had to be checked at the final second for fear of disabling one of the men.

Jim, Harvey and Nugwik rolled around on the grass in a tangle of arms and legs that eventually resolved itself into three parts. Jim and Harvey got puffily to their feet. Nugwik, trussed and paper-sacked, lay still on the ground, emitting muffled noises that were not, whatever else they were, words in English.

"Whoopee!" yelped Rodney, dancing on the grass.

"Are you all right?" said Jennie.

"Fine," said Jim. "Harvey?"

"Little short—breath—that's all," wheezed Harvey. "Now what?"

"Well," said Jim, drawing a deep breath, "now we try to figure the wall."

"Oh, do you think we can?" said Jennie, gazing up into his eyes.

"Er—no," said Jim, running an index finger around the inside collar of his t-shirt, which seemed to have shrunk somewhat. Jennie was a particularly pretty girl, he was realizing. "But we can try."

"What if we don't?" said Harvey.

"Then," said Jim, "we can always starve quietly, all of us, including Nugwik. That way nobody outside, at least, is any worse off."

"Ought to give him a hit on the head right now," growled Harvey. "Settle his hash once and for—"

"Certainly not! That would be barbarous!" snapped a new voice over their heads. Looking up, they discovered a new visitor floating down through the beam of the space tube. This was a tall thin man dressed in a cutaway coat and striped trousers. His face was thin and sensitive, his ears were large and he wore an enormous top hat. He was carrying a pencil and a notepad, and was making notes of some sort as he gently floated down to stand on the grass, facing them.

"Shocking situation!" said the newcomer. "Shocking. You shouldn't try to concentrate so hard."

He gestured at Nugwik. "*Ajash!*" The rope and paper sack disappeared. Nugwik climbed to his feet somewhat glassy-eyed, and marched to the space tube. He rose it up out of sight.

"Professor Johnson-Fleegl, at your service," said the top-hatted man, bowing to them all. He turned to Jim and took him confidentially by the elbow. "Come with me, my boy."

He led Jim off into the shadow cast by the eaves of Jennie's house.

"Listen—" began Jim. Professor Johnson-Fleegl held up a hand.

"Not a word," he said. "I insist. Let me be the first to congratulate you. I will be your best man—in fact, that's why I'm here."

"Best man?" Jim stared at him. "Best man for what?"

"Best man in your upcoming marriage to Jennie, of course," said Professor Johnson-Fleegl. "You young rascal, I know you've been secretly in love with her for some time. All those sonnets you wrote about her."

"But I didn't write any sonnets about her!"

"Come, come," said Professor Johnson-Fleegl. "Jennie knows nothing about it, of course, but you can't hide such things from a psychologist like myself. You were smitten with her the first time you saw her, but you didn't dare hope until last Monday when you happened to see her turning into the Alhambra theater, downtown. You sat in a seat two rows behind her all through the *Alice in Wonderland* feature. *I* saw you. I was seated two rows behind you."

"I don't know what you're talking about!" cried Jim.

"Tut-tut," said Professor Johnson-Fleegl. "Let me remind you again that you're talking to a psychologist. It was in that show that you finally decided to let her know of your love, come what might. But you had no chance until all this happened. And now—" he clapped Jim on the back— "the prize is yours. And what a prize she is! Surely, the most wonderful, beautiful girl in the universe."

"Well, I wouldn't say that," said Jim. "After all, there's Mar—"

"Of course she is. A gem without a flaw—except perhaps the fact that during experiments she *will* try to concentrate too hard."

"Experiments? You know, Professor, this is all becoming more and more like a dream. What experiments?"

"Nothing that need concern you, my boy. Although she has a great talent, a very great talent."

"Uh—I see," said Jim. A very strange idea was burgeoning in his mind. He peered curiously at Professor Johnson-Fleegl. "Look," he said. "You're right. I admit it, being secretly in love with her. Now, I wonder if you'd do something for me."

"Anything," beamed the Professor. "Anything."

"I haven't bought her a ring yet, of course. I wonder if you'd go over and—kind of subtly, you know—try to find out just what she'd like in the way of an engagement ring. Would you?"

"Of course!" said Johnson-Fleegl, patting him on the back again. "Just leave it all to me." He went off.

Jim threw a quick glance at the others. They were all—Harvey Rodney, and Jennie—clustered around the open cube, peering inside it. Everyone's back was turned.

He turned about quickly, went down along the side of Jennie's house to her open window and hoisted himself inside, wriggling through and falling to the inner floor with something of a thump.

He sat up and looked about him. He was in the midst of the perfumey clutter of a young girl's room. The footboard of the bed was just beside his head. He stood up and looked over it.

Jennie, hair spread out on the pillow, was peacefully slumbering there, a happy smile on her lips.

Jim glanced out the window. Jennie was also out there, engaged in earnest private conversation with the Professor.

Jim swallowed. He went up to the head of the bed and stood over the sleeping Jennie.

"Uh—" he said. "Jennie—er—wake up."

She did not stir. Uncertainly, he reached out and nudged her shoulder, gently. She slept on. He thought for a moment, and nodded wisely. He cleared his throat rather desperately, leaned over, and kissed Jennie on the lips.

She sighed ecstatically, stretched out slowly and happily under the blankets, and lazily opened her eyes. Slowly they focused on Jim, standing over her; and she smiled.

Then suddenly her eyes flew wide open. She shot upright in the bed, clutching the covers protectively to her. And screamed.

And that was the last Jim remembered for a while.

He opened his eyes rather woozily. Professor Johnson-Fleegl, minus the top hat, was bending over him where he lay in some sort of bed.

"How're you feeling?" asked the Professor.

"Fine," said Jim. "Or am I?" He moved cautiously

on the bed. Everything seemed to be working all right.

"That's right," said the Professor. "There shouldn't be any ill effects. By the way, I'm Professor Alan Johnson—"

"Johnson-Fleegl, isn't it?" said Jim then checked himself. "What am I talking about? Of course Fleegl was all in her dream."

"So you understand about that," said Johnson.

"Some of it, I guess," said Jim. "Was it really real—or did we all just imagine it?"

"It was real all right—the dome, the space tube and all," Johnson smiled down at him. "I'm a psychology research fellow at the University Foundation across the river. Jennie was one of my subjects in psi research. We knew she was a strong talent—but never how strong until today. When she was awake, she had a slight block . . ."

"I know," said Jim, "she used to concentrate too hard."

Johnson looked slightly surprised.

"You and I are going to have to get together for some more talks," he said. "I'd like to hear more of what my dream counterpart told you about Jennie. Naturally, most of the dream was made up out of whole cloth."

"Where did she get the name Fleegl?"

"Fleegl Dry Cleaners," said Johnson. "It's the out-fit her family sends laundry to. I don't know where she got the majority of her details about the place, but the effect of *Alice in Wonderland* was very apparent all the way through."

"You were a sort of mad hatter," said Jim.

"So I gathered. And a lot of the rest of it will undoubtedly turn out to be highly symbolic on a subconscious level." He paused and shook his head a little ruefully. "What a girl!"

"You can say that several dozen times," said Jim. "By the way, where's Jennie now?"

"Jennie?" Johnson shook his head again. "I don't think you'll be seeing her again. I may not even see her again, myself. The army's got her under lock and key, now. You can imagine what an impenetrable dome like she threw up would be worth to them—as well as the other possible uses of her talent, after they get that symbolism under control." He looked down at Jim. "Why? You weren't actually in love with her, were you?"

"Heaven forbid," said Jim.

"Then it's just as well you won't be seeing her any more."

"I'd say so," agreed Jim. He thought of the space tube probing thousands of miles into space, and he shivered again. "Somehow," he said reflectively, "I've got the feeling I never would have been able to live up to her dreams."

"Nevertheless, even an ineptly managed operation can yield valuable insights to the alert student."
·—Orientations

Show Me the Way to Go Home

"Come, come," said Kris Ilis, "Cheer up, Meki."

"I can't," groaned Meki Ton.

"Have some of this pressed duck and Napoleon brandy; there's a good fella. It'll make you feel better."

"No thanks, Kris," said Meki, hollowly. "It would choke me."

The two Cuperians were seated in the palatial living room of the Princess suite at Chateau Hotel in Miami. Luxury surrounded them. A feast fit for a king was laid out on the table in front of them; but they were doing it poor justice. This, however, was not surprising. They had been on Earth for two weeks now and the strain was telling on them.

"Buried," groaned Meki. "Buried alive. Oh, these stupid humans."

Kris Ilis looked anxiously at his friend, knitting his black brows worriedly. They looked remarkably alike, these two—but then Cuperians always do, conform-

ing to a general type which is tall, brunette and
Mongoloid in appearance—but to anyone experienced
in Cuperian physiognomy it would have been apparent immediately that Kris was the older and more
responsible of the two.

"Look," he said soothingly, "why don't you go tell
it to the cat."

"That stupid animal!" said Meki bitterly. "It'll *never*
understand. I've been trying to get the situation
through its thick skull for five days now."

"Try again," urged Kris. "It may be stupid, but it's
our strongest hope right now."

"The trouble with it," said Meki, "is that it hasn't
any sense of social responsibility." He sighed. "Oh,
well. Come here, cat."

A fine blue Persian, which had been napping on
the cloth of gold bedspread in the master bedroom
came strolling in through the door in response to
Meki's telepathic command. It sauntered to a position on the carpet facing the two men and sat down.

"I'm here," said the cat. Kris looked over at Meki
with a slight expression of surprise.

"Oh, you've taught it to talk?" he said.

"Yes," sighed Meki. "I had a wild hope that it
might get to gossiping with the bellboy or something
like that. But it can't seem to grasp the concept of
talking for the pleasure of it."

"Oh," said Kris, "well, go ahead." Meki nodded
and turned to the cat.

"Now, pay attention," he commanded sternly. "Who
are you?"

"I'm here," said the cat.

"I know you're here, you pea-brained idiot!" yelled
Meki. "I asked who you were."

"Gently, gently," remonstrated Kris.

"Well, who are you?"

"Cat," said the cat.

"And who am I?"

"Nice," said the cat.

"I am not nice," roared Meki. "I'm Meki. I'm one of the evil Cuperians that's going to blow the world up and destroy all the fish and pour all the cream down the sewers. Now, who am I?"

"Meki," said the cat. Meki mopped his brow with relief.

"And who is he?"

"Kris."

"Good, good," said Meki. "Is he an evil Cuperian, too?"

"Yes," said the cat. Broad smiles broke out on the faces of the two Cuperians. They leaned forward hopefully.

"Now," said Meki, "think carefully. How did we get here?"

"Your ship crashlanded," said the cat. "And both of you had been conditioned never to let inferior creatures like humans know of the presence of superior creatures like evil yous. So you automatically buried the ship and hid all traces, and have been waiting here for someone to rescue you. There are more yous out on the moon, but they don't know you're in trouble because you have no way to signal them. But if people knew you were evil Cuperians—Cuperians—Cuperians—"

"—then the scanning station—" prompted Meki.

"—then the scanning station with their psych scanners would notice it and investigate, and find you and take you away. The scanning station can't find you now because it is set for human minds. So all you can do is let the humans find out, but you can't let humans find out because you are conditioned not to let humans find out. But—" finished up the cat, "I'm not an intelligent creature, so you can tell me."

"Fine, fine," said Meki. "Now, don't you think you should do something about it?"

The cat looked at him blankly.

"Idiot!" exploded Meki, suddenly. "I'm telling you to—to—" He choked off suddenly, vocal cords straining, face turning a bright crimson in his unsuccessful attempt to force the forbidden order to betray their presence past his conditioned block.

"Relax," said Kris, patting his friend on the shoulder. "If the creature can't understand, it can't understand."

"I'm hungry," said the cat.

With a furious gesture, Meki swept his plate of pressed duck onto the floor in front of it.

"Here!" he bellowed. "Eat; stuff yourself! Choke! Ungrateful beast!"

"Not ungrateful beast," said the cat gravely. "Hungry beast."

"Oh, go away," said Meki, despairingly, and the cat, much to its own disgust, turned obediently away from the pressed duck and trotted into the bedroom. There it meowed piteously until Meki wearily remembered himself and carried the pressed duck in to it.

I really don't know," said Meki, sadly, coming back from the bedroom. "We've tried just about every way conceivable to attract attention."

"Did the hotel manager get in touch with you about the bill we've been running up here?"

"Oh, yes," sighed Meki, "my reflexes took over and I talked him out of it. He ended by suggesting we stay here permanently. I can't take it, I tell you!" he added, wildly. "I'll develop paranoic tendencies, see if I don't!"

"Come now!" said Kris, shocked. "We've been in

some tough spots before this. Remember the ice
fields of Urana, or the lava prospecting on Drusus."

"But that," said Meki, his voice cracking, "that
was plain ordinary hardship. It's this insane barbaric
opulence. I ask for a glass of cold water and they give
me a glass of warm water with chunks of frozen water
in it—" his voice rose to a scream. "Isn't that funny?
Isn't that ridiculous? Ha-ha-ha—" and he went off
into a shriek of hysterical laughter.

"*Meki!*" roared Kris.

"Not cold water," screamed Meki, "half-cold, half-
warm. Tricky, eh? Clever, eh? Ha-ha-ha-ha—"

Kris slapped him, sobering him up.

"Now, that's better," said Kris, as Meki buried his
nose in the Napoleon brandy. "Keep your chin up.
I've got the feeling that cat will be the saving of us
yet. Meanwhile, we'll do what we can."

"If I ever get out of this," said Meki fervently, "I
swear I'll never go prospecting again."

"And I, too," said Kris. "However, let's get down
to ways and means. What all have we tried so far?
We started a fire—"

"And they arrested that little old lady on our rec-
ommendation," said Meki.

"We robbed a bank—"

"The morning paper says the police are baffled."

"And we called on that scientist—what's-his-name?"

"Luodomann," said Meki. "The one who was preparing a report on ten years of work to prove the
existence of extra-terrestrial life."

"Oh, yes," sighed Kris glumly. "He shot himself
when we proved logically that he was wrong. But—"
he said, brightening—"there's something you don't
know about. I sent in a fake income tax return under
your name."

"I know," said Meki. "I spied on you, stole the
return back from the mailman and burned it."

"Oh," said Kris. There was a moment of bitter silence. Suddenly however, he sprang from his chair, jubilantly.

"I've got it," he cried. "Let's take the cat and go get drunk and get picked up by the police. One of us is bound to babble."

Meki's face lit up.

"The very thing!" he echoed. "Here, cat!"

The cat came running eagerly into the room. Meki picked him up.

"Come on, boy," said Meki, jubilantly. "We're going to paint the town red."

Arming themselves with a good supply of the money stolen from the bank, they hurried out of the hotel and hunted up the worst section of town. It was a dirty, dingy saloon below street level where a slovenly bartender lazily flicked flies from the glasses with his bar-towel. The three comrades lined up at the bar, the cat on top of it.

"Gimme a shot," said Meki.

"Gimme a shot," said Kris.

"Gimme a shot," said the cat.

The bartender stared at the cat.

"A talking cat?" he said incredulously.

Meki's face lit up. But Kris's reflexes had already taken over and the words flowed in a smooth stream from his mouth.

"Of course, naturally," he said cheerfully to the bartender. "You've heard of this play, Harvey, where the hero has an invisible rabbit, or Pooka. Well, Pookas may be invisible, but cats are not. You've certainly seen cats before. And this is a Persian cat. If a Pooka can talk, so can a Persian. Of course—" he leaned across the bar and shook the bartender warmly by the hand. "Of course, I knew you'd understand. As I said to my friend, bartenders aren't surprised by anything. And you aren't. Hah! Hah!" and he laughed heartily.

"Hah, hah," echoed the bartender weakly, not sure whether this was a joke or not. And then Meki, much to his own disgust, found words forcing themselves past his lips.

"My friend," he said confidentially, leaning over the bar, "is a ventriloquist."

"Oh," said the bartender, relieved.

"Gimme another," said the cat.

"Heh, heh," said the bartender, pouring another shot glass full for the cat. "Cute little devil, isn't he?"

"Er-yes," said the two Cuperians, watching in some surprise as the cat tossed off his second shot glass with flying tongue and shoved it forward for a refill. For the first time a sinking sensation made itself felt in the breasts of Meki and Kris.

"You know," said the former, voicing this in a whisper in the latter's ear. "Maybe it would have been just as smart to leave him at home."

Meki's fears were only too well-founded, the next couple of hours disclosed. At the end of that time the two Cuperians, drink as they might, were only slightly high; but the cat, owing to its smaller blood content, was roaring drunk. It staggered down the bar, cater-wauling happily.

"Shh," said Meki, nervously, grabbing it by the shoulder.

"Lemme go," said the cat, making an ineffectual swipe at him with one paw, "I can lick any tom in the room."

"But," pointed out Kris, "there aren't any toms in the room here."

"Then lesh go find some," said the cat, embracing him. "I don't want to fight you. You're my buddies. You're the nicest, most evil Cup-Cuperians in the world."

The faces of Kris and Meki lit up, but a split second later their reflexes had taken over and they were holding the cat's jaws firmly closed.

"What did he call you guys?" asked the bartender, suspiciously.

"Canarians," said Kris, glibly. "From the Canary Islands, you know."

"Oh," said the bartender, and they carried the struggling feline outside.

"Damn it!" said Meki. "If we'd only been able to stay there, maybe the cat would have talked some more."

"Well, there's other bars," Kris pointed out reasonably. "Suppose we try one down the line here a way."

The other bars, however, proved to be pretty much of a repetition of the first. That is to say, they would have a few drinks, the cat would start talking, and at the first suspicious word, they would find themselves, hustling it outside. To top all this off, the cat passed out in the fifteenth bar and could not be persuaded to say another word. The two Cuperians sat in dispirited silence in the last bar, a small cosy place by the name of Louie's Nite Club and gloomed at their drinks. That is to say, they gloomed until Meki was suddenly struck with the bright side of the matter.

"Say," he said, happily, making a grab for his glass and missing. "Kris. I do believe I'm getting a little drunk."

"Well, I'll be flipped," said Kris, trying to focus on his glass which seemed to be doing a sort of geometric dance with four or five hazy duplicates of itself. "I think I am a little that way myself."

"Of course," said Meki, closing one eye slyly, "we aren't really drunk. Not us Cuperians on this weak human liquor. But maybe we're just a little bit high enough to get by. Do you suppose we're drunk enough to be picked up by the police?"

"Could be," agreed Kris. "Let's go find out."

"Let's," said Meki. "But first, let's take a little nap."

"Good idea," said Kris. "Just the thing. Good night."

But Meki, his head down on his arms, was already snoring; and Kris, with a tolerant smile at the younger Cuperian's ability to hold his alcohol, lost no time in following his example.

He woke up later—but after that things got hazy.

Kris returned to consciousness because Meki was shaking him. Through bleared and aching eyes, he looked around him. Five inches in front of his nose was a cement wall on which somebody had scrawled in pencil:

> *"Stone walls do not a prison make,*
> *"Nor iron bars a cage."*

He pondered this for a few seconds, becoming conscious of an aching head and the fact that he appeared to be lying on some rather hard surface. Finally, deciding the matter was worth investigating, he rolled over to discover the fact that he was in a cell and that Meki was standing over him, excitedly waving a newspaper.

"Wake up!" Meki was shouting. "That cat has got us in a fine mess." He shoved the newspaper into Kris's hands and indicated an article on the front page. "I hypnotised the jailer into getting me a copy of the morning paper. Read what it says about us."

Kris groaned, sat up, and focused with difficulty on the item indicated:

MANIACS PLEAD CAT AS ONLY
DEFENSE

Kris's eyebrows shot up in surprise. He read on:

"Two maniacs were taken into custody this morning after a drunken debauch with a cat leading through a number of bars. Bartender Otto Bikonsky at the Blue Point Bar called police when the maniacs ran out of money and insisted that the cat write a check for further funds. When the cat made no move to do so, a loud argument ensued, climaxed by the arrival of the police. Upon being taken to Headquarters, the maniacs refused to furnish any information about themselves, referring all questions to the cat and stating loudly that since it (the cat) had gotten them into this, it was up to the cat to get them out. To date the cat has refused to utter a word and a sanity hearing is scheduled before Judge Custer P. Polk, affectionately known in courthouse circles as 'Committin' Custer.' A careful check of city banks today revealed that the cat possesses no checking account."

"Well?" said Kris, looking painfully up at Meki.

"Kris," said Meki, shaking him. "For Snark's sake, Kris, I'm frightened. You see what it says—*maniacs*. Kris, maybe they're right. Maybe we are going insane. Remember those two just like us that got marooned on Kathol? When the survey station found them they were already in an insane asylum and so badly infected they had to be left there. Remember?"

Kris shuddered.

"I hadn't thought of that," he said.

"Kris, we've got to get out of here."

"All right, all right," said Kris, supporting his aching head. He took a minute to sort out his thoughts and then sent out a mental call.

Some seconds elapsed, and then a portly individual in an olive-drab uniform came waddling down the corridor between the cells. He stopped before their door and stared at them glassily.

"Well, open it up!" snapped Meki, impatiently. The portly individual stared, shook himself, produced a key and unlocked the door.

"Now, show us the way out," said Kris. Automaton-like, the jailer preceded them up the corridor, ran headlong into a steel door and knocked himself out.

"Now isn't that just like a human?" said Meki in deep disgust. "Can't think for themselves at all under hypnosis. Now, how are we going to get through the door?"

"It doesn't seem to be locked," said Kris, pushing at it cautiously. It yawned open and they stepped through into a room containing a high desk and several uniformed individuals in various poses of relaxation.

"Jailbreak!" yelped one, whipping out his gun. He stared at it in surprise and then began to suck child-ishly on the barrel. The others smiled and nodded and indicated a door in the far wall.

They went through the door into another corridor, down an elevator and out of the building. They went back to the Princess suite at their hotel, and opened the door.

The cat, uttering glad cries, flung itself into their arms. . . .

"Now what?" asked Kris morosely, when they had finished a light but nourishing snack of crepes suzette and opened a jereboam of champagne.

"I ran away," said the cat, proudly.

"We know!" snapped Meki. "You've told us fifteen times already."

"I didn't say a word," added the cat, preening itself.

"Thanks," said Kris, sourly. He poured some cham-pagne into a coffee cup. "Drink that and keep quiet."

The cat lapped happily. Kris turned back to Meki.

"Now what?" he repeated.

"Kris," said Meki, desperately. "We can't waste any more time. I can feel paranoic tendencies nibbling at my sanity right now. Varve yourself and see if you don't notice the same thing."

Kris did, and shuddered.

"You're right," he said. "That foolish business of getting drunk speeded up the process."

"Listen, Kris," said Meki. "We've got to signal the moon direct."

"But how?" protested Kris. "All they've got on this godforsaken planet is radar, and I don't know a thing about that. And an operation as delicate as that can't be handled by direct hypnosis."

Meki groaned.

"Oh, why didn't I study my ancient sciences like Professor Smrgi wanted me to. If he said it once, he said it a hundred times, 'Meki, you never know when it may come in handy to be able to make a catapult or to levitate yourself.' And I just laughed. If I can just get out of this, I'll make it a point to go back and apologize."

"I've got it," said Kris, snapping his fingers. "How about a large mirror? We could flash them a message in interstellar code."

Meki grimaced sourly.

"It's a penal offense to make backward natives work for you," he said.

"I know," said Kris, solemnly. "But think which you prefer. Fifty years at hard labor or an indefinite stay—maybe a permanent stay, if we become mentally infected—on Earth."

The alternatives were only too clear. Meki faced up to them like the Cuperian he was. He shook hands solemnly with Kris.

"We'll do it," he said.

"I'll help," said the cat.

"Oh, no you don't," said Meki, swiftly. "We don't

want you balling up the works again. Kris, what can we do with him?"

Kris thought.

"I've got an idea," he said. He turned to the cat. "How would you like to learn to read?"

"Read?" repeated the cat.

"You'd love it," said Meki, heartily. "Everybody does when they first learn how. Kris, you teach him while I order up some material." He picked up the phone and put in a call to the cigar counter in the lobby for all the blood-and-thunder they had in the way of pocket books and magazines. By the time a bellboy came staggering up with an armload of these articles, Kris, with the aid of the morning newspaper had rendered the cat semi-literate.

"You'll pick up more words as you go along," Kris informed the cat, as he and Meki left the feline surrounded by garish covers. "Oh, one other thing— you've seen Meki and I answer the phone?"

The cat nodded.

"Well, you know how it's done. If anybody should call while we're gone, you tell them we've left town and take a message. Got it?"

"Yes," answered the cat.

"Good," said Kris, and they went out.

After driving around in a taxi for some time, they decided that the best thing would not be one big mirror, but innumerable smaller mirrors, mounted on all the rooftops in town and operated in unison. Accordingly, they got out of their taxi in a central portion of town and sent out a mental call.

Immediately, all through the business section, normal activity ceased. The butcher, the baker, the candlestick maker (the president of Waxies, Inc., that is, who happened to be vacationing in town at the time) to say nothing of innumerable other people in all sorts of trades and professions, immediately felt a sudden distaste for their usual functions and a corresponding overwhelming urge to rush up on the rooftop of whatever building they happened to be in and construct mirrors. Cheering and laughing happily, they threw away their typewriters, adding machines, stethoscopes, and monkey wrenches, tore down all sorts of reflecting surfaces and went scurrying up stairs and out onto shingles, eaves, or tiles. Within a certain rough circle of area, the town took on an air of carefree holiday and festival, while outside that area people pointedly ignored what was going on within—unless, that is, they happened by accident to cross the boundary line, in which case they were struck by the industrious madness that went on around them.

"Very good," said Meki, to Kris, watching a bank executive smash a store window and take out a large dressing room mirror, while the proprietor of the store cheered happily. "But I wish they'd hurry. I'm beginning to get a funny feeling."

Kris mopped the perspiration from his brow.

"I must be out of shape," he said. "I'm having a rough time handling these people. Are you sure you're doing your share?" He looked suspiciously at Meki.

"My share?" muttered Meki, avoiding his eye. "Me? Certainly? Why not? But why? Why—"

"Meki!" cried Kris, staring at his friend. "Snap out of it. What's wrong with you?"

"Me?" answered Meki, in an odd tone. "Nothing. Nothing could be wrong with me. But—" he suddenly clutched at Kris's sleeve.

"Look!" he hissed. "That little man, over there. He's staring at me."

"Nonsense," said Kris, trying to disengage himself. "He isn't even looking at you."

"He is. He was," said Meki wildly. "But you won't admit it. You're all against me. All of you. But I'll beat you yet. You want to take me back to Cuper for psycho-conditioning. But I won't let you." And, under the sudden surge of Meki's mind, little bodies of men around the town began pulling down their mirrors and getting into fights with others who were still putting theirs up.

Kris fell back, the horror of realization printed on his face. They had delayed too long. Meki was already mentally infected. That meant that he with his only slightly higher stability rating had only a matter of minutes left. The scanning station personnel would have to reach them in less than six hours in order to save them. After that the damage of infection would be beyond repair. There must be some way to get through to the station in time. In a last surge of desperate effort, his mind sought for an answer—and found it. . . .

Leaving Meki madly engaged in tearing down what they had built, he groped his way to the nearest telephone. And as his mind sunk into insanity, the last thing he remembered was his voice babbling desperately into the mouthpiece.

He awoke to the blissful peace of the infirmary in the scanning station. An orderly was bending over him.

"Am I—" he croaked.

"You'll be all right," said the orderly, his kindly Cuperian face beaming down on him. "How do you feel? Want another shot of nerve-titillator?"

"No thanks," sighed Kris, relaxing. "Meki?"

"He's all right, too," said the orderly. "And the cat sends you his love. We offered to take him off Earth with you two, but he preferred to stay with the humans he was used to. Affecting scene at the end, there, though. He took my hand in both paws and shook it with tears in his eyes."

"Did he?" said Kris, feeling, despite himself, a little touched. "Tell me, what happened?"

"Well, according to what he told me, you didn't make too much sense over the phone. But as you surmised, there had been all sorts of noble heroes in those books and magazines he had been reading, so that when you told him that the city was doomed to be destroyed by invading Cuperians, but that he could save himself, he bravely decided to stick by his guns and warn Washington.

"He immediately made a long distance call to the FBI and informed them of the situation, insisting that he be put through to the President. I gather they gave him a rough time, but knuckled under when they found where the call was coming from. I guess they figured anyone with enough money to rent the Princess suite deserved to be listened to for a minute or two. The upshot of it was that the cat spoke to the President and told him off rather sharply about the inadequacy of the space-warning set-up in that area of the country. At any rate it was enough to make the FBI start a routine investigation, and of course our scanners picked it up at once and deducted your presence."

"And—" ventured Kris, hesitantly, "—the mirrors?"

"What mirrors?" asked the orderly. "You were both babbling about them, but we didn't see anything out of the ordinary about the mirrors where you were."

"Never mind," said Kris, happily, relaxing. "Just a hallucination I guess. Ah, it'll be good to get back to Cuper."

"To Cuper?" said the orderly, surprised. "Oh, I forgot you didn't know. It's been decided to raise Earth to interstellar apprenticeship level, and all citizens having any knowledge of the planet have been requisitioned for work in the human cities—with adequate mental shields, of course. For you and Meki it'll be quite familiar territory, won't it?"

There was a long moment of silence.

"I think I'll take that shot of nerve-titillator after all," said Kris, in a dull voice. "Better make it a double."

"The achievements of certain untrained persons suggest that the gift for penetrating other minds may be an inborn talent."

—*Orientations*

Rex and Mr. Rejilla

At that moment, Lucy came into the kitchen. Tom Parent ducked the bottle behind him, but it was too late.

"Oh, no, you don't!" She came across the new Luster-Glo floor and took it away from him. "You heard what the ambassador said. No smoking or drinking while Mr. Rejilla's here. Oprinkians don't like it."

"Well, for cripe's sake!" protested Tom. "He isn't going to get down on his hands and knees and smell poor old Rex's breath. And it's not going to ruin my Foreign Office career if he does."

"How do you know?" said Lucy. She put the rum bottle back on the shelf above the Freezador. "Maybe Mr. Rejilla has a very acute sense of smell. Besides, it won't hurt that booze-hound to lay off for one night in over six years."

She poured out the rum and milk and refilled

Rex's pan with plain milk, setting it down on the floor before him. That booze-hound—he was an enormous Great Dane—sniffed at it, whined and looked up at her mournfully.

"No!" said Lucy. "No, Rex. Not tonight. Drink your nice milk."

Rex moaned softly and despairingly under his breath and lay down with his paws covering his eyes.

"There!" said Tom. "See what you've done? Now he thinks we're mad at him. He's always had his nightcap, Lucy—ever since he was a puppy."

"Well, he can just do without it this once. I'm not going to have the representative of the most intelligent alien race we've bumped into yet going home and telling the other Oprinkians how immoral we are. Besides, it's time Rex learned that life isn't all rum and milk. Ordinary dogs don't get grog rations."

"But he isn't any ordinary dog, honey. Remember who his father was. Rex Regis took Hollywood by storm. A genius among dogs, they called him. He could do everything but talk—"

"What can Rex do?"

"Well, the point is—"

"I said," repeated Lucy, "what can Rex do? I'll tell you what Rex can do—our Rex—this hooch-swilling, vase-smashing, overgrown lump off the old block. Nothing! That's what our Rex can do."

"Owooo," said Rex mournfully to the floor between his paws.

"No, you don't!" snapped Lucy at the huge canine. "You aren't going to get anywhere trying to play on my sympathies this time. And you, Tom Parent!" she continued, rounding on her husband, who took a step backward and almost tripped over the collapsed Rex. "Here we are chosen—chosen over *everybody else* in the Foreign Office—to give the Oprinkian Representative a real glimpse of human home life, and after I've spent two days trying to get the house just perfect, what do you do? You try to botch it all up before he even arrives."

"I—"

"And you'd better get your jacket on, because Mr. Rejilla's coming in on the midnight copter and we're late leaving for the community port now. This is a great start!"

She went out. Tom paused long enough to give Rex a consoling pat between the dejectedly drooping ears.

"Sorry, old son," he said softly. "C'est la guerre."

He hurried out.

Daneraux, the Washington Chargè d'Affaires to the visiting Oprinkian representative, and a hard-faced man named White, from the Internal Security Branch, were waiting at the copter port to give Tom and Lucy last-minute instructions.

"All right now," said Daneraux. He was a small man who had a habit of going up on his toes when he got excited. He was very much up on his toes now. "Now listen, both of you. You'll be completely covered at all times—"

"Right," said White.

"Right. And what we want is that you two just act normal. Just normal, you understand?"

"Sure," Tom replied.

"Remember, Rejilla's the representative of a greater race than any we've encountered to date. They may have all sorts of abilities. We absolutely can't afford to take a definite line with them until we find out just what their potentialities are."

"Right," said White.

"Right. We have a feeling, now—in fact, it's practically a certainty—"

"Check," said White.

"—that they're as much in the dark about us as we are about them. That's why Rejilla's asked for this chance to spend twenty-four hours with a typical human couple in a typical human household. Theoretically, it's just academic interest. Actually, he probably wants as much data as he can get. Now you remember the taboos?"

"No smoking while he's visiting," said Tom. "No drinking. No fresh plants in the house. He's not to be disturbed once he's shut himself in our spare bedroom, until he comes out again. Keep the dog out of his room—" Tom sighed. "We should have sent Rex away for the weekend. It'd be easier."

"No, no!" cried Daneraux. "That's one reason you were picked. Because of the dog. The Oprinkians don't have pets. He specifically asked for a family that had a pet. He wants you to act with perfect normalcy."

"Perfect," said White.

"All we ask is that you spend an ordinary twenty-four hours—only just remember that the Oprinkians outnumber us and that—this is restricted information now: they seem to be somewhat more advanced than we are technically—and furthermore—"

The announcer's voice broke out overhead from the metallic throat of the loudspeaker.

"Please clear the stage. Please clear the stage. Eastbound copter landing now. Eastbound copter now descending for a landing."

"How come they didn't send him out in a private ship?" Tom just had time to ask as they all moved off to the stage entrance.

"He didn't want to," replied Daneraux.

"He wanted to ride out to your community here just like any ordinary citizen. Ha! Every seat on the copter except his is taken by Security agents."

* * *

They brought up short against the chest-high wire fence that enclosed the stage. A gate had swung open and a flood of passengers from the copter were streaming out. Rather curiously, in their exact midst, emerged the tall, thin, black, furry-looking form of the Oprinkian alien.

He was swept forward like a chip in the midst of a mass of river foam and deposited before the four of them.

"Ah, Daneraux," he said. "It is very good of you to meet me."

He had a slight, lisping accent. Aside from this, he spoke English very well.

"Mr. Rejilla!" exclaimed Daneraux exuberantly. "How nice to see you again! This young couple are your host and hostess for the next twenty-four hours." He stood aside and Tom and Lucy got their first good look at the alien.

He was tall—in the neighborhood of six-feet-five— but very thin, almost emaciated. Tom guessed him at less than a hundred and thirty pounds. He wore no real clothing in the human sense, only an odd arrangement of leather-looking straps and bands that covered him in what appeared to be an arbitrary rather than a practical fashion. Evidently his curly black body fur, or hair, gave him some protection from changing temperatures, since the late April night was in the low fifties and the chilly air seemed to leave him unaffected.

"May I present," Daneraux was saying, "Tom and Lucy Parent. Tom is an ambassador's staff member, here in Washington. One of our crew. Lucy was on our clerical staff before she married Tom."

"Hay-lo," said Rejilla. "To you both, haylo. Do we shake right hands now?"

They shook right hands. Rejilla's furry grip was fragile but firm.

"I am so most indubitably honored to be a guest within your walls," commented Rejilla. "The weather, it is fine?"

"Very fine," Daneraux agreed.

"Good. Though perhaps it will rain. That would be good for the crops. Shall we go?"

"Right this way," said White.

The Security man led them out and to the Parents' car. White slid behind the wheel in the front seat, Daneraux behind him. Rejilla insisted on sitting between Tom and Lucy in the back.

"I understand," he said to Lucy, as the car pulled away from the parking area, "that you have two lovely grandparents."

"Well—" fumbled Lucy. "As a matter of fact, I have three still living."

"Three!" cried Mr. Rejilla joyfully. "How wonderful! I dote myself on grandparents very much. I write them poems. Yes." He turned to Tom. "And you, sir?"

"Uh—one grandfather," said Tom, "only."

"The ways of Providence are mysterious," replied Mr. Rejilla, putting a comforting hand on Tom's knee.

"Uh—thanks."

"How black the night," said Mr. Rejilla, gazing out the window of the speeding car.

"We're almost there," White said.

After White and Daneraux had dropped them off back at the house, Mr. Rejilla insisted on retiring to his room immediately, which gave Tom and Lucy a chance to escape to theirs.

"My!" gasped Lucy, when the bedroom door was

safely closed upon them. "He isn't anything like I imagined." She set about getting ready for bed. "I expected someone who would be more—"

"More what?" asked Tom, hanging up his jacket.

"Oh, I don't know. More positive. More dangerous, sort of."

"You can't tell dangerousness from outside appearances."

"Well, you know what I mean."

"An alien culture must present some dangerous points, just as it must present some advantageous and congenial ones—" He continued explaining the subject as he undressed.

"How well you explain it!" said Lucy, in admiration, as they climbed into bed.

"Part of the briefing they gave us in the Foreign Office training school," said Tom. "Oh!"

He climbed out of bed again and went over to the closet.

"What is it?" asked Lucy, sitting up in bed. She caught sight of her reflection in the mirror and adjusted one of the shoulder straps of her nightgown. It was a new nightgown.

"Sealed orders, I guess," said Tom, rummaging in an inside pocket of his dress jacket. "Daneraux slipped it to me as we were getting out of the car."

He produced an envelope and brought it back into bed with him. He ripped it open and unfolded a single sheet of paper.

"'Information received by special courier on same copter as Rejilla'," he read. "'Advices from Oprinkia Major Three indicate Rejilla actively engaged in studying *homo sapiens* for weak points which may be exploited in interracial diplomatic field. Be on lookout for any unusual activities on part of Rejilla and offer no information that you believe might be harmful in Oprinkian hands'."

Tom sat for a moment, staring at the letter.

"Well," he said, "there's a nice general warning."

"We'll just have to do the best we can," said Lucy. "Keep our eyes open and our mouths shut."

"*What* weak points? That's the problem."

"We'll just have to be careful, Tom."

"Easier said than done."

"Well, anyway," answered Lucy, "there's nothing you can do about it tonight. Put that letter away in the nightstand drawer. Here. Now that's that for tonight. Sufficient unto the day are the cares thereof. What do you think of my new nightgown?"

"Wha-huh?" said Tom, waking up. Sunlight was filtering through the closed slats of the venetian blinds. "Whazist?"

"Tom! Wake up!" whispered Lucy urgently, shaking him.

"Whazamatter?"

"It's Rex. Rex!" she cried, clutching his arm.

"It's what Rex? Rex what?" demanded Tom crossly. "Rex?"

The Great Dane was standing by the side of the bed with his tongue hanging out in a friendly manner. The bedroom door was ajar. The doors in this new house of theirs, unfortunately, had a push button type of latch and one of the few things Rex had learned was to push the button on the doorknob with his nose until the door opened. Tom had cited it to Lucy as an instance that Rex had, after all, inherited his great father's brain. Lucy had remained unconvinced.

"I love you," said an unmistakably masculine voice.

Tom blinked and struggled up into a sitting position. He glanced around the room. He peered under the bed.

"Huh?" he said.

"I love you. Get up," said the voice.

"Lucy!" croaked Tom. "Who is it? Where is he?"

"That's what I'm trying to tell you!" said Lucy frantically. "It's him—Rex. It's Rex!"

"I love you. Play ball? Fun? Go walk."

"Rex!" Tom stared at the dog. "Lucy! He's—I mean he isn't, is he?" With a sudden explosion of energy, Tom jumped out of bed, lunged across the room, closed and locked the door. Turning about with his back against its panels, he regarded the canine interlocutor before him.

"How can he talk?" he said thickly. "With *his* mouth? Say something, Rex."

"Play ball? Nice Tom."

"See—" yammered Tom. "His mouth doesn't move—"

"Nice Lucy. I love you, Lucy."

"I don't care what you say!" snapped Lucy. "That's Rex and he's talking."

"Nice Lucy and Tom. I'm hungry."

The two humans stared at each other.

"I'm nice, too," said Rex.

"Well, there you are," Tom said insanely. "I always said he had his father's brain—and Rex Regis could do everything but talk. Rex just decided to learn to talk. That's all."

"Don't be funny!" said Lucy sharply.

"Who's being funny? You hear him, too, don't you?"

"Of course I hear him. But he can't talk. That's impossible."

"How can it be impossible when he's doing it?"

"I don't care. How can he talk with *his* mouth? You said that yourself."

"Well, he is, Rex, say something again."

*   *   *

Rex was nosing after what might be a flea or just a stray itch.

"Rex!" Tom ordered in a sharp, no-nonsense voice.

"I'm Rex! I'm Rex! I'm here, too!" said Rex, looking up cheerfully. "See me? Play ball? Nice Tom. I love Lucy, too."

"Wait a minute!" Tom snapped his fingers. "I've got it!"

"Got what?" asked Lucy.

"Ball?" asked Rex. "Ouch! Got flea? Flea! There flea. Take that! Bite, bite, bite, bite! Crunched flea."

"We really ought to get some more of that flea powder and dust him good," said Lucy thoughtfully. "I could run down to the drugstore after breakfast—"

"Will you listen?" Tom demanded. "Listen, Lucy!"

"Another flea?" queried Rex, checking a hind leg. "Where flea?"

"Lucy, it's telepathy."

"Telepathy?"

"That's right. Look, his mouth doesn't move. And he speaks English, doesn't he? All right, he couldn't just do that overnight. But if he was just *thinking* these things he says—and our own minds were putting them automatically into words—"

"Oh, Tom! That's just downright silly!"

"Why?"

"Well, it just is," said Lucy. "How could he go telepathic all of a sudden?"

"You think I don't have the answer to that, too?"

"You do?"

"I certainly do. Remember how smart his father was? Well, Rex is even smarter."

"But—"

"Let me finish. The point is we never realized how

much smarter he is because Rex here was drunk all the time."

"Drunk!"

"I don't mean staggering drunk," said Tom excitedly. "I just mean he had his rum and milk every night and probably the alcohol was just enough to inhibit his telepathic powers. You made him lay off last night—and this morning, here he is, beaming thought waves at us."

"Pet me," said Rex, nuzzling up against Tom's knee.

"Down, Rex! Not now!" Tom said, pushing him away.

Ears drooping, tail sagging, Rex hung his head and burst into heart-breaking sobs.

"Tom! How could you?" cried Lucy. "He was just trying to attract your attention." She was out of bed in a flash and threw her arms around the dog's neck. "Poor Rex! There, there, that's all right. Tom didn't mean it. No, he didn't."

"Love Tom. Love Lucy," gulped Rex. "Good Rex?" He looked up hopefully and flicked out a long wet tongue, which Lucy dodged.

"Boy, what a cry-baby!" said Tom. "I certainly never suspected—"

"Well, he's just a dog!" said Lucy indignantly. "Good Rex. Good boy. That's better now. You're too hard on him, Tom."

"*Me?*" yelped Tom in outrage. "Me? How about you—like last night when you wouldn't give him his drink? Just because you can hear him now—"

"Well, I had to." Lucy straightened up and sat back on the edge of the bed. "Tom, what're we going to do with him?"

"That's the thing," said Tom, lowering his voice.

"Rex here is probably the most valuable piece of property on Earth at this moment, from every standpoint, including the military. And you realize who we've got under the same roof at this same moment?"

"Who . . . *Oh!*" gasped Lucy. "Mr. Rejilla."

"Right!" said Tom grimly.

"Well, we've got to get Rex out of here. Right away!"

"And tip Rejilla off that there's something special about him?"

"Oh!" said Lucy. There was a moment's taut shuddering silence. "What'll we do?"

"Let me think."

Tom walked across the room to the dressing table, turned and walked back again.

"Look," he said. "You go out and try to keep Rejilla occupied. We'll shut Rex up in here. I'll try to get in touch with Daneraux."

"Are you going to phone him?"

"No, no," said Tom. "Too much of a chance. Who knows what Rejilla might be able to do with an ordinary telephone? Maybe he carries a little portable wiretap or something. I'll run out and phone from the drugstore."

"Go walk?" asked Rex.

"Sorry," said Tom, dressing hurriedly. "Later—if we're lucky," he added nervously.

The drugstore was empty, as it should have been at a little before nine o'clock in the morning. Daneraux's office informed Tom that Daneraux had not yet come in.

"Hell!" said Tom.

He went back home.

Lucy was drinking coffee in the living room. Mr. Rejilla was seated opposite her in the big armchair, playing a flute.

"Good morning," said the Oprinkian as Tom came in, and lowered his instrument. "Take a condolence, please."

"Uh—I beg your pardon?" asked Tom, dropping down on the living room sofa.

Lucy hastily handed him a full cup of coffee.

"I was just telling Mr. Rejilla how sick Rex is," she said, with a meaningful glance. "How you had to go for the veterinarian. Did you get him?"

"He wasn't in his office yet. *Ow!*" said Tom. He breathed violently through his open mouth.

"Well, you might have known it was hot," said Lucy.

"You find yourself internally dismayed by hot liquids?" inquired Mr. Rejilla. He produced what looked like a small slate and a crayon from under one of the straps of his harness. "May I make a note?"

"Oh—sure," said Tom.

"I am endeavoring to understand humanity as a means to establishing the bonds between," explained Mr. Rejilla. "That is my twenty-four-hour mission here. Do you like music?"

"Well, yes," Tom said warily.

"I will play you a small composition," said Mr. Rejilla. He did so. The tune that came out sounded like anything but a tune. "Does it provoke you?" he inquired politely.

"It's very original," volunteered Lucy.

"Indeed. Eighty per cent original," said Mr. Rejilla proudly. "It is a theme upon one of your human melodies."

"Oh?" questioned Tom, searching his memory for a single similarity.

"A Chinese melody, I am so told," said Mr. Rejilla, driving his point home.

"Have some coffee," offered Tom. "What would you like to do today, Mr. Rejilla?"

"I would like to peep," said Rejilla.

"Peep?"

"In on your lives. How fascinating, the living process, don't you agree? You are embound with so many things that on Oprinkia are unthought of. This pet of yours, now in malady. Has he existed for a number of years?"

"Five," said Tom.

"No, dear—six," corrected Lucy. "Don't you remember—"

"Five," repeated Tom firmly.

"Has he offspring?" Mr. Rejilla wanted to know.

Tom sipped cautiously at his coffee, which was starting to get down to a tolerable temperature finally. "Not only that, but his offspring has offspring."

"A grandfather!" breathed Mr. Rejilla.

"Well, yes."

"How noble!" said Mr. Rejilla enthusiastically. "I will make a special effort to remember him in my thoughts. Now I must not detain you both. There will be housing affairs to demand your attention, no doubt. I would wish that you concern yourselves as customarily. Pay no attention to me. I shall merely peep." He stopped and looked at them expectantly.

"Well—" said Tom. "Uh—maybe I better—uh—mow the lawn. Don't you have to bake a cake or something, Lucy?"

"A cake?" asked Lucy, staring.

"A cake."

"Oh, a *cake!* Why, of course! Why don't you two just putter around? I'll get my cake started—and when I get a chance, I'll try and give the veterinarian another ring."

"Superb!" said Mr. Rejilla. "So this is how the human day inaugurates. I am complete attention."

The meeting broke up. Tom went out and fired up the power mower. Mr. Rejilla accompanied him. Lucy went off to the kitchen and hunted around for a cookbook. An hour and a half later, as Tom was pruning some rose bushes and Mr. Rejilla was watching, she appeared, crossing the lawn in the direction of the next-door neighbor's and returning a few minutes later with a cup of flour.

"I'm going to try again!" she called gaily, waving to them, and disappeared in the direction of the kitchen.

Tom talked Mr. Rejilla into trying his hand with the pruning shears and hurried off to the kitchen himself. Lucy was standing before a cluttered kitchen table with flour up to her elbows and even a dab of it on her nose.

"Tom, this is absolutely fascinating!" she bubbled as Tom came in. "Whoever thought it would be so much fun to cook! Phooey on that old roboserver. I can do better any day."

"What are you doing?" asked Tom distractedly.

"Well, the first two went wrong, somehow," said Lucy. "But I'll get it this time. Honey, will you run down to the market and get me some vegetable coloring for the icing? Pink."

"And how about Mr. Rejilla?"

"Oh, he can come watch me cook. Please, Tom."

"I'll do that," said Tom between his teeth. "I'll do just that. And while I'm at it, I can manage to make another call to the veterinarian."

"The vet—whatever for—*oh!*" said Lucy. "Oh, dear, I forgot. But then you can do it, as you say. Pink coloring."

"Pink coloring!" barked Tom, and slammed out of the house.

"Daneraux!" bleated Tom, when he finally got the

Foreign Office man on a private phone down at the supermarket. "Listen—"

He outlined the situation.

"Now, Tom," said Daneraux soothingly.

"I tell you, it's the truth! Come out here and see for yourself, if you don't believe me."

"Security said to keep hands off so Rejilla wouldn't know they were keeping the situation covered. I can pass the word on to them, if it'll make you feel better."

"Pass, nothing! Lucy's up to her ears in baking a cake, which nobody in their right mind's tried for fifty years, Rejilla's taking notes, and Rex is locked in the bedroom, ready to blab his head off. I tell you, we've got to get that dog away where he's safe. Do you know what it'd mean to have even a *dog* that could telepath? Rex ought to be covered with Security men ten feet deep. He shouldn't be able to breathe without a man on each side of him. Now you listen to me—"

"All right, all right," said Daneraux. "I'll be right out. I think you're suffering from hallucinations, but just on the wild chance there's some truth to this— wait where you are. I'll be right over and pick you up. We'll go back to your house together, and if you're right, we'll figure some way of slipping Rex out so Rejilla won't suspect."

"Well, hurry!"

"Keep your shirt on," said Daneraux, and hung up.

Tom paced back and forth sweatily for an inconsolably long fifteen minutes. At the end of that time, Daneraux pulled up at the front entrance of the supermarket in an official runabout.

"Hop in," he said.

White, the Security man, rose up in the back seat like a business-suited demon from the nether regions.

"Hop!" he said.

"You again!" Tom said to White. "It's about time." He walked around and got in the front seat.

"Tell it again," ordered White.

Daneraux pulled out into the street.

By the time Tom had run through his story for a second time, they were back at the house.

"It checks," said White.

"Checks with what?" asked Daneraux.

"Our suspicions of Rejilla," replied White, with gloomy satisfaction. "Where is he?"

"In the kitchen with Lucy—I'll say you just happened to run into me at the market—they're right in here—"

They went through the door. Lucy was still at her kitchen table, which was more cluttered than ever. Rejilla was conspicuously absent.

"You got the pink coloring?" Lucy asked. "Oh, hello," she said to Daneraux and White.

"Here," said Tom, hastily handing it over. "Where's Rejilla?"

"Oh, thanks!" sang Lucy. "Tom, I've really got it at last! A cake, baked all by myself—just like Grandma used to tell me about. I'll tell you what I did. I took a full cup of butter for shortening—"

"Where's Rejilla?"

"I don't know. Anyway, it's all done—"

"Where's Rex?"

"Why, he's back in the bedroom, isn't he—oh!" Lucy's hand flew up to cover her mouth.

"What is it?" snapped White.

"Mr. Rejilla said he was just going to look in on him—"

The three men made a dash for the bedroom in the forepart of the house: Tom leading, Daneraux right behind him and White bringing up the rear. Lucy followed.

When they burst open the door to the bedroom, they discovered Rex lying on the floor and Mr. Rejilla tightening a leather strap around the dog's neck.

"Stop!" yelled Tom, and made a dive for the Oprinkian, only to be brought up short by some complicated sort of wrestling hold which White had clamped onto him.

Mr. Rejilla rose with a surprised expression. Rex got to his feet with the strap dangling and wagged his tail.

"He's the accredited Representative of an Alien Power!" hissed White in Tom's ear, and let him go.

"I beg your pardon?" Mr. Rejilla was saying. "Am I in violation of some custom? Observing that this grandfather appeared to enjoy the wearing of collars, I was impelled to decorate him with another as a token of affection and get-well-quick."

"Like furry man!" said Rex, happily and audibly, flicking a tongue in Mr. Rejilla's direction. "Play wrestle?"

"All right!" cried Tom, before White could stop him. "Go ahead—deny it now! You found out Rex could project his thoughts—telepathy. So you came in here to shut him up permanently!"

"Fight?" queried Rex doubtfully.

"No, no. Shut up, Rex," said Tom. "Now—"

He was interrupted by Daneraux tapping him on the arm.

"Tom," said Daneraux. "Did I understand you to say that this dog of yours was telepathizing right now?"

"Of course," said Tom. "Didn't you hear him? Now, Mr. Rejilla—"

"No," said Daneraux.

"No?" demanded Tom, wheeling on the Foreign Office man.

"No, I did not hear Rex say or broadcast anything," said Daneraux.

"Rex? I'm Rex," announced that individual.

"Well, *there* you did," said Tom. "What're you talking about, Dan? You heard him that time all right and—you *didn't?*"

"No," said Daneraux.

"No," said White.

"But—but—" sputtered Tom.

"Pardon me," interrupted Mr. Rejilla, "but do I understand your implication, Tom, to the effect that this grandfather is broadcasting his intentional statements by non-auditory way?"

"Of course he is!"

"And you, too, are receiving the grandfather clear and strong?" Rejilla asked Lucy.

"Why, yes—" said Lucy. "Don't you?"

"Woe," said Mr. Rejilla. He turned about and walked into the living room, where he collapsed on a couch and fanned himself with a magazine from the coffee table alongside.

The humans followed him in bewilderedly.

"I don't understand," said Daneraux.

"It is over," said Mr. Rejilla. "I resign myself. I am surrendered. I admit all, while requesting an asylum from politics to remain on this world. How mysterious the ways of grandfathers! Ah, well. I am not unhappy at this termination, being by nature dutifully non-combative."

"Sir," said Daneraux, "could you perhaps explain it all a little more clearly?"

"Indubitably," Rejilla said. "I shall confess. What is of all universal relationships most important? Responsibility of teacher to teach, pupil to learn. Consequently grandfathers, percolating wisdom down to younger generations, are venerated. Oprinkian nature and sociological development cast us in roles of teacher. But what if pupil prove refractory? By stern duty, I compelled myself to investigative procedure. Spy. You understand."

"I'm afraid not yet," said Daneraux.

"During unconsciousing hours of nighttime for fine young couple here, I investigated exploratoratively. This is result."

"Tom!" gasped Lucy. "He means he read our minds last night while we were asleep!"

"You Oprinkians have that ability?" snapped White.

Mr. Rejilla nodded. "Matter of training only. Astonishing as results were, yet I defer action until, first, amazing chemical investigation of Lucy leading to discovery of almost extinct art of cake-baking and now this. Overwhelming average citizens in pupil-ability."

"Well—" began Daneraux.

Mr. Rejilla held up his hand and continued. "Affection basis for instruction. Consequently, I am informing Oprinkia no need to fear humans unteachable and set in motion defensive-offensive mechanisms of science to determine survival of Oprinkia over Earth. Myself, I intend to follow duty here with continuing instruction chosen pupils Tom and Lucy Parent."

"But what's all this got to do with Rex broadcasting his thoughts?" exploded Tom. "*He's* the important one around here."

"No," said Mr. Rejilla.

"No?" demanded Tom.

"No," stated Mr. Rejilla. "This grandfather, though venerable and praiseworthy, has discovered no unknown talent. His simple emanations always in existence. Only now, new sensitivity triggered by my mental investigations of your and Lucy's minds last night render you capable of reception and interpretation of simple animal thoughts."

Everybody stared. There was a moment of peculiar silence.

"You mean—" croaked Tom finally—"it's *us*?"

"Yours. You. Yourself and Lucy."

"But—"

"With training I shall supply you with ability to eventually receivi-transalatable more complex intelligent human and Oprinkian thoughts."

"Wait a minute!" commanded White suddenly. "Do I understand you to say that these two people here are now telepathic?"

"You understand," said Mr. Rejilla courteously.

"Don't move," White said. "Not any of you. Not even the dog." He went out the front door.

"What's got into him?" Tom blurted, staring after the Security agent.

"I think," said Daneraux nastily, "he's gone out to get some more people from Security. I think we're going to be covered with agents ten feet deep. I don't expect we'll be able to breathe without a man on each side of us. Just like you said for Rex—only it'll be you now."

"Rex? I'm Rex," telepathed the Great Dane, wandering into the living room with tail awag. "Love everybody. Pat me."

"A most magnificent grandfather," said Mr. Rejilla admiringly.

Tom and Lucy stared at each other. They looked at Mr. Rejilla, at Rex, at Daneraux. Lucy essayed a tremulous smile.

"Would—would anybody care for a slice of cake?" she inquired with a fine, false brightness.

"The utmost tact is imperative when intervening in alien affairs."

—Orientations

Who Dares A Bulbur Eat?

I

"Me!" said Lucy. "At an Ambassadorial Banquet!"

"Don't be like that now," said Tom, pausing in the night shadow of a ten-foot-high alien plant, something in the shape of a bear-trap. He took a last couple of drags from his cigaret and ground it out underfoot, on the footpath of terrazzo tile.

"How should I be?"

"Nonchalant," said Tom. "You do this sort of thing every day. Ho-hum."

"But certainly the Jaktal ambassador knows you're only a third assistant secretary in the Foreign Office's Department of New Governments—"

"We hope they won't know me at all. Heh-heh."

"You sound nervous, honey."

"I am not nervous."

"Then why are you biting your nails?"

"I am not biting my nails. I never bite my nails. I just thought I had something stuck between my front teeth, that's all. I don't know why you always keep talking about me biting my nails, when you know as well as I do . . . Ah, good evening, Spandul. My card. I am Thomas Whitworth Parent, and this is my mate, Lucy Sue Parent. Beware the zzatz."

"You are welcome, sorr!" hissed the Spandul, which was about three feet high, black, lean as a toothpick, and had a mouth full of vicious looking needle-sharp teeth. It stood just within the golden glow of the light from the high arched doorway to the Jaktal Embassy in Washington. Its large eyes glittered at Lucy. "Welcome alssso, Lady. Enter please. Here you will be safe from zzatz."

It took their cloaks and they proceeded on through the entrance into a long, high-ceilinged hall, already well-filled with humans and aliens of all varieties, all in evening dress.

"What's 'zzatz'?" muttered Lucy in Tom's ear.

"Means 'a most unfortunate fate'," muttered Tom back. "Ah, good evening, Monsieur Pourtoit," he said in French, "I don't believe you've met my wife." And he introduced Lucy to a tall thin gentleman with a sad face and a broad red ribbon crossing his white dress shirt under a dinner jacket. The gentleman acknowledged the introduction gracefully.

"*Elle est charmante*," he said, bowing to Lucy.

"Why, *thank* you, Mr. Ambassador!" said Lucy. "I can see—"

"However if you'll excuse us," said Tom, catching Lucy by the hand, "we must be going."

"Of course," said M. Pourtoit. Tom towed Lucy off.

"Well, all I was going to say was—" whispered Lucy.

"Ah, Brakt Kul Djok! May I present my wife, Lucy Sue Parent?"

"Well, well, honored I am positive!" boomed a large alien, looking something like a walrus with a stocking cap on. "A fine young lady, I can see at a glance, hey, boy?" The walrus-sized elbow joggled Tom almost off his feet. "See you coming up in the world, hey? Hey? Wonder what type entertainment and food this Jaktal puts out, hah? Never tell about these new alien types, hey, ho?"

Tom laughed heartily and they moved on, Tom introducing Lucy every few feet to some new human or alien of the diplomatic circle in Washington. Finally they found themselves at the punch bowl, and were able to fill a couple of glasses and find a small alcove out of the crowd.

"What I don't understand," said Lucy, "is how they can have a banquet for so many different kinds of people and aliens. I should think—"

"Well, they do have a number of different foods for those who can't eat anything but their own special diet. And of course it's necessary to stay clear of what might offend anyone," said Tom, after a large swallow of the punch. "But you'd be surprised how much in common tastes are among different intelligent, animal life forms. It's all flesh and plant food, in every case."

"But don't some of them taste . . . ?" said Lucy.

"Some, of course," said Tom. "But a lot of alien foods are quite tasty. I've liked all sorts of diverse items I've run into."

"Oh!" said Lucy.

"What's wrong?"

"What do you think's in this punch?" said Lucy, examining her glass with suspicion.

"Fruit juice and alcohol. Now," said Tom, "let's just run over the schedule for the evening. First, we'll be having entertainment."

"Oh, Tom, wait a minute," said Lucy, interrupting. "Listen. How sad!"

"What?" he said—and then he heard it. A voice, around the corner from their alcove and through an archway leading back, was pouring out a thin, sad thread of song. He stiffened suddenly. "Wait a minute. I'll see."

He got up and went around the corner. Through the archway he could see a farther doorway from which light was showing. He went forward and looked into the lighted room beyond. At this moment Lucy bumped into him from behind.

"I told you to wait for me!" he whispered angrily at her.

"You did not. You said, 'wait a minute.' Anyway," said Lucy, "there's nothing here but that great big jelly mold on the table." And she pointed to an enormous three-tiered mass of what seemed to be pink, green and yellow gelatine on a silver box set on a white tablecloth. The tablecloth was on a table which was the only furniture in the room.

"You know what I meant!" said Tom. "And somebody was singing here."

"It was I," said the jelly mold in sweet and flawless tones of English.

Lucy stared at it. Tom was the first to recover.

"May I present my wife?" he said. "Lucy Sue Parent. I am Thomas Whitworth Parent, Third Assistant Secretary in the Foreign Office Earth Department of New Governments."

"I'm awfully pleased to meet you," said the jelly mold. "I am Kotnick, a Bulbur."

"Was it a Bulbur song you were singing?" asked Lucy.

"Alas," said Kotnick, "it is a Jaktal song. A little thing I composed myself but sung, of course, in Jaktal—though unfortunately with a heavy Bulbur accent."

"But you sing so beautifully!" said Lucy. "What would it sound like if you sang it in Bulbur?"

"Alas," said Kotnick, "there is no Bulbur to sing it in. There is only Jaktal."

Lucy looked bewildered.

"You don't understand," Tom said to her. "There are a number of intelligent races on the Jaktal planets. But the Jaktal are the ruling ones. The language and everything takes its name from the rulers."

"Indeed, yes," said the Bulbur. "And properly so."

"I knew about Spanduls, and Gloks, and Naffings," said Tom, looking at it. "But we haven't heard much about you Bulburs compared to the rest of the inferior races of the Jaktal."

The Bulbur turned pink all over.

"Pardon my immodesty," it said, "but I have come especially for the occasion."

"Ah?" said Tom. He stepped closer to the Bulbur and lowered his voice. "Perhaps, then, you can tell me—"

"Did the sorr and lady wisssh somesing?" interrupted a sharp, hissing voice. The two humans turned abruptly to see a Spandul like the one that had admitted them to the embassy. It was standing in the doorway. Beside it was a sort of four-foot worm with fang like teeth curving down from its upper lip.

"Oh!" said Tom. "No. Nothing. Nothing at all. We heard this Bulbur singing and wandered in to meet it."

"It ssshould not sssing!" hissed the Spandul, looking at the Bulbur, which quivered and went almost colorless.

*　　　*　　　*

"Well, it wasn't really singing. Sort of just humming. Well, we'll have to be getting back to the punch bowl. Glad to have met you, Kotnick." Still talking, Tom herded Lucy before him past the Spandul and the wormlike being and out into the shadowy area giving on the hall. The wormlike being slithered past them into the room and the Spandul fell in beside the humans, its needly teeth glittering at them.

"Guestsss," it hissed, "will find it mossst comfortable in main hall area."

"I imagine you're right," said Tom. "We'll trot on back. Nice of you to show us the way. See you later, then. May there be no zzatz beneath this roof tonight."

"There will *be* no zzatz beneasss ssis roof tonight," replied the Spandul, fixing them with its glittering eyes as they moved out into the hall.

"Well," said Tom. "How about another glass of punch, Lucy?"

"I should say not," said Lucy. She took hold of his sleeve and led him back around to the privacy of their alcove. "Now, suppose you tell me what's going on."

"Going on?" said Tom.

"Yes, going on," said Lucy. "And you might as well tell me now because I'm going to keep after you until you do tell me. I thought we were just going to a banquet. You didn't give me any notion that it was something undercover or something like that. Now I want you to tell me right now—" she broke off. "What are you making faces like that for?"

Tom, besides making faces, was scribbling on a piece of paper torn from his checkpocket. He passed it to her.

Will you keep quiet? the paper read. *The walls have ears. I can't tell you. It's top secret.*

"Oh!" gasped Lucy. Tom took the paper from her hands and held it up to her lips.

"Eat it!" he whispered.

"I certainly will not!" whispered back Lucy, revolted.

"Then I'll have to." said Tom. He took it, and he did.

"Oh!" said Lucy, impressed. Tom was looking at her in an unusual way. She shrank back a little.

"Shall we dance?" said Tom.

"D-dance?"

His eyebrows wigwagged angrily at her.

"Oh, *dance!*" she said. "Of course!"

II

Tom led her out across the hall and into a sort of garden area where a band was playing. When they were well out into the middle of the dance floor, he put his lips close to her ear and murmured into it.

"You might be able to help after all."

"Yes?" whispered Lucy.

"The Office Upstairs," whispered Tom, "is very concerned about this Jaktal race. Six months ago, we didn't even know they existed. Now we suddenly discover they have a spatial empire at least as large as ours. Not only that, but the Jaktal themselves—I mean the dominant race—seem to have a conqueror psychology, judging by their expansion and the intelligent races like the Spanduls, Naffings, and Gloks."

"Was that one of them—that wormlike thing with the fangs?" Lucy asked.

"A Naffing," said Tom. "They are not much more intelligent than an adult chimp. But dangerous. But to get back to the important part of the business, recent information seems to indicate that even with our alien allies, we'd be at the mercy of the Jaktal Empire, if they decided to move against us right now."

"Would they?" Lucy shivered.

"We don't know. That's it. Their ambassador talks peaceful relations; but we can't make this match up with the character he and his subservient races show. You'll see what I mean when you get a look at Bu Hjark, the Ambassador."

"But what's it all got to do with us—with you?"

"Well, you remember how they thought we did a good job with that Oprinkian? Well, there's a new addition to the embassy here. That Bulbur we just saw. He—or it, we don't even know that much yet—seems entirely different from the rest of the crew here. So what does it mean? What's his place in the organization? What does his showing up here mean in terms of the Jaktal attitude toward us and our alien allies?"

"I see what you mean," whispered Lucy. *"Ouch!"*

"What happened?"

"You just stepped on my toe."

"Oh. Sorry."

"It's all right. Go on."

"It's hard to concentrate on two things at once. As I was saying, the Office Upstairs thought I might be able to get the information where somebody better known in our diplomatic corps might fail. Easier for me to be inconspicuous. Of course, that's why I brought you along, too."

"Well, I like that!"

"I'm sorry. But that's the way diplomacy is. Now, we've had one stroke of luck already. We've found out where the Bulbur is, and we know he's off without a crowd around him. The next step is up to me. I have to have a chance to talk to him alone."

"Oh, I see."

"Yes," said Tom, "and I think that's where you can help."

"Oh, good."

"Do you think you can get that Spandul out of the way while I have a talk with the Bulbur? I can gas the Naffing. It can't talk and report what's been done to it. But the Spandul could, if I gassed him."

"Well," said Lucy, biting her lower lip, "I don't know. It isn't as if he was a man, or something. What'll I do?"

"He has to be polite to you—especially if you can get him out where people can see him. You'll think of something."

"I hope," said Lucy.

"Sure you will. Let's go," Tom started to lead the way off the dance floor and suddenly noticed that she was limping. "Ohmigosh, I didn't realize I'd stepped on you that hard!"

"It's all right," said Lucy, bravely. "Maybe I can use it as an excuse to make him stay with me."

"That's an idea," said Tom. They were off the dance floor now and he lowered his voice. "I'll tell him I want him to take care of you while I go for a doctor to make your foot more comfortable. Then, when I leave you with him, you get him away from the entrance there any way you can."

He broke off suddenly. A fanfare of something like trumpets had just silenced all the talk in the room. The crowd was splitting apart down the middle, leaving the center of the floor clear. Luckily, Tom and Lucy were already on the side of the room they wished to reach.

"I wonder what's happening?" said Lucy. "Oh, dear. I wish we had Rex with us."

"Rex!" said Tom. "What good would it do to have that moose of a dog along?"

"He could keep us in touch with each other."

"How? Just because we picked up enough tele-pathic sense from that Oprinkian to understand Rex doesn't mean he'd be any use to us now. What I wish is that we'd been able to go one step further and understand people's thoughts. Even each other's thoughts. That's what we need now."

"If Rex was with you and trouble came, he'd start broadcasting excited thoughts, and then I'd know you were in trouble."

"What good would that do? You couldn't do anything about it. No, believe me, Rex would be just what we needed to bollix things up," said Tom. "Besides I'm happy to have a rest from those inane canine thoughts of his. *'Good Tom,' 'Good Lucy,' 'play ball?'*—all day long."

Tom broke off suddenly. The trumpets had sounded again, a wild, violent shout of metal throats. Now, bounding down through the open lane in the middle they could see an alien fully eight feet tall, approaching and bellowing greetings to people in the crowd.

"It's him," said Tom. "Him, the Jaktal Ambassador, Bu Hjark. Just look at him!"

Bu Hjark was a huge lizardlike alien, with a heavy, powerful tail. Elbows out, huge hands half-clenched, he danced down the open space like a boxer warming up in the ring. Brilliant ribbons and medals covered his silver tunic and shorts. Into a gem-studded belt was fastened a heavy, curve-bladed sword.

"Ho! Ho! Welcome! Welcome!" he roared. "Great pleasure to have you all here! Great pleasure. Greetings, Brakt Dul Jokt. Evening, Mr. Vice-President! Great evening, isn't it? Find yourself seats, respected entities, and let me show you how the Jaktal entertain."

"What does he need a sword for?" whispered Lucy, staring. "With those teeth and nails?"

"And that tail," said Tom. "Just part of his costume, no doubt. Wait until the entertainment starts. Then we can slip off while everybody's watching."

"Positions, everybody!" shouted Bu Hjark, and added something in Jaktal. A crowd of apelike beings in full metal armor trotted in and formed a protective wall in front of the audience. Laughing hugely, Bu Hjark took off his sword-belt and tossed it to one of these.

"Gloks," explained Tom in answer to Lucy's inquiring gaze, nodding at the beings in armor. "A little brighter than the Naffings, not so bright as the Spanduls. Sort of high-grade morons. But extremely strong for their size."

"First," Bu Hjark was crying, "let in the Bashtash!"

There was a moment's pause, then a gasp from the far end of the room, drowned out by a sudden bestial bellow. Something the general shape of a rhinoceros but not so large, charged down the aisle full tilt at Bu Hjark, who met it with flailing hands and tail, and a deep-chested shout. Amid roarings and snarlings, they rolled on the floor together.

"I can't look," said Lucy, hiding her eyes.

"It's all right, it's all over," said Tom, a few moments later. "He wrung its neck. See, some Gloks are carrying it off."

"Now, for the armed Wlackins!" shouted Bu Hjark. And a moment later, a herd of five small, centaurlike creatures, clutching sharpened stakes, galloped down upon Bu Hjark, who joined battle with them gleefully.

"Let's get going," whispered Tom.

"Yes, let's," said Lucy with a shudder. They threaded their way through the staring crowd to the

shadowy corner which led back to the room where
they had discovered the Bulbur.

"Limp more!" said Tom. He guided her toward
the lighted doorway. "Hey! Spandul?"

The Spandul they had seen earlier emerged from
the room. Its eyes glittered suspiciously upon them.

"What iss the masser?" it hissed. "Guests will be
more comfortable in main hall."

"My mate has hurt herself. I insist you give me a
hand here," said Tom. "I need help."

"Help?"

"I must get a doctor. Right now!" said Tom. "You
understand? Find her a chair. Look after her while I
find a doctor!"

"Doctor?" hissed the Spandul. It glanced back into
the room behind it, and then out again at Tom and
Lucy.

"A chair," moaned Lucy, clinging to Tom.

"What're you waiting for?" snapped Tom. "Is this
the way you do things here at the embassy? I'll speak
to the ambassador himself about this!"

"Yesss, yesss. I help," said the Spandul, gliding
forward. It took hold of the arm of Lucy which Tom
was not holding. "Chair. Thisss way."

"Good. Stay with her," said Tom. "I'll go after a
doctor."

He turned and plunged back into the crowd. As
soon as he was out of sight, however, he stopped,
waited for a moment and then slowly began to work
his way back.

III

When he arrived once more at the shadowy entrance, it was empty. He slipped quickly back to the
doorway, taking what appeared to be a lifetime
fountain pen from his pocket as he approached the

doorway. Holding it, he peered inside. The Naffing, curled up in a corner, reared up at the sight of him.

He pointed the pen at it and pressed the clip. There was an almost inaudible pop. The Naffing wavered a minute and then sank down to lie still on the floor.

"What is it?" fluted the jelly on the table, paling to near transparency. "Have you come to kill me?"

"No," said Tom. He glanced behind him and saw the entrance still deserted, the crowd still occupied with the combat going on. He slipped into the room. "I want to talk to you."

"Take my worthless life, then," keened the jelly. "I have nothing worth talking about."

"Yes, you have," said Tom. "You can tell me about yourself."

"Myself?" A little color began to flow back into the Bulbur. "Ah, I see. It is not me. It is the high role I have been chosen to play that makes me an object of interest to you."

"Oh? Oh yes, that of course," said Tom. "Let me hear you describe it in your own words."

The Bulbur turned pink.

"I am not worthy," it murmured.

"Tell me," said Tom. The Bulbur turned flame-colored.

"I am . . ." it began and then its voice almost failed it, "the . . . most important item . . ." At that its voice did fail it.

"Go on," said Tom, drawing close to it.

"I cannot. The emotion involved is too strong."

The Bulbur had deepened its red color until it was almost black. Its voice seemed strangled and unnatural. Tom cast another glance at the doorway.

"All right," he said. "Let's talk about things you can talk about for a moment. Tell me about yourself—aside from what you're supposed to do here."

"But I am nothing," said the Bulbur, paling relievedly. "I am a mere blob. A shameful blob."

"Shameful?" said Tom.

"Oh, yes," said the Bulbur, earnestly. "A shameful quiver of emotions. A useless creature, possessing only a voice and the power of putting forth weak pseudopods to get about. A pusillanimous peace-worshipper in a universe at war."

"Peace?" Tom stiffened. "Did you say *peace*-worshipper?"

"Oh, yes. Yes," fluted the Bulbur. "It is the main cause of my shame. Ah, if only the worlds of the universe were oriented to my desires!" Its voice sank, and took on a note of sad reasonableness, not untouched with humor. "But obviously, if it had been meant to be that way, all life forms would be cast in the shape of Bulburs—and this, manifestly, is not the case."

"Look," said Tom with another glance out the doorway, to see that the way was still clear, "I'm afraid I don't understand you. What do you mean, *peace*-worshipper?"

"If you will permit me," said the Bulbur humbly. "I might sing you a little melody?"

"Well, if it'll help," said Tom. "Go ahead."

The Bulbur turned a pale, happy pink. A thread of melody began to pour forth from it. Up until now, Tom had been too concerned to figure out how a three-layer aspic, even one of large size, could manage to talk and sing. But now, looking closer, he perceived, palely moving and pulsating within the body of the Bulbur, almost transparent organs and parts—heart, lungs, and throat among others, with a clear channel leading to a small mouth in the very top of the being. He was also suddenly aware of pale, almost transparent eyes ringing the upper tier like decorations on a wedding cake in jelly form.

But almost as soon as he had seen this, he began to forget all about it. The melody he was listening to began to pass beyond mere sound, began to pass beyond mere music. It moved completely inside him and became a heart-twisting voice speaking of peace, beyond any other voice that could possibly speak in opposition. He felt himself swept away. It was only with a sudden, convulsive effort that he broke loose from the hold of that voice upon him.

"Wait! Hold it!" he gasped. "I get it. I understand."

The Bulbur broke off suddenly, with a sound very much like a sob.

"Excuse me," it whispered. "It's shameful, I know, but I was carried away."

"Well, it's not shameful, exactly," said Tom, clearing his throat. "I mean—there's more to life than that, of course. But I don't see why you think you have to be ashamed of it."

"Because," said the Bulbur, going a sad, translucent blue, "it is my mark—the mark of my difference from all the rest of you. I cannot stand to force my opinion on anyone else. I have no virtues. It is quite right that I should suffer."

"Suffer?"

"Ah, indeed—suffer. Oh," said the Bulbur, pinkening again, "it's a great honor, I know. I should be rejoicing. But I'm a failure at rejoicing, too." And now it did sob, quite distinctly.

"Wait a minute, now," said Tom. "You seem to have things all twisted up. What gives you the idea nobody but you prefers peace to fighting?"

The Bulbur turned completely transparent. "You mean you also find peace to be a pleasant and desirable thing?"

"Of course," said Tom.

"Oh—you poor creature," breathed the Bulbur. "How you must suffer."

"Suffer? Certainly not!" said Tom. "We like it peaceful. We keep it peaceful."

"You *keep* it peaceful?"

"Well—most of the time," said Tom, a little guiltily.

"But what do you do with such as the Jaktals, the Spanduls, the Gloks and the Naffings?"

"We—well, we stop them," said Tom. "By force, if necessary."

"But force? Isn't that coercion?" said the Bulbur, turning pink, chartreuse and mauve in that order. "Isn't that fighting fire with fire?"

"Why not?" said Tom.

The Bulbur went slowly, completely transparent again.

"Oh, I couldn't!" it said at last.

"Certainly. That singing of yours is a strong argument. I'd think you'd use it."

"Oh, no," said the Bulbur. "What if I was successful? That would make me a dominator of the Jaktals—and the Spanduls."

"To say nothing," said Tom, "of the Gloks, Naffings and so forth." He stopped suddenly, wondering what had just alarmed him. Then he noticed that the sound of battle from the main hall had suddenly ceased. "Why shouldn't you have things peaceful if you want them?"

"Why, it's not natural," said the Bulbur. "Look at the matter logically. If beings had been intended to live in peace—"

"Good-by!" interrupted Tom, sprinting out the door. He had just noticed the crowd stirring and opening in the direction of the shadowy entrance and this room. He made it to the fringes of the crowd in the main hall just as a lane parted through them and a platoon of Gloks appeared, marching toward the room. Tom slipped down the open space behind them to the edge of the open area in the center of the floor. A table had just been set up in the middle of the floor. A Naffing, operating a sort of vacuum cleaner, was busy cleaning up a few last spots of pale blood. Bu Hjark, wearing a few neat bandages, his sword replaced, was standing by the table directing the Naffing. Tom gained a ringside position, and all but bumped into Lucy, limping around the ring in the opposite direction.

"That Spandul finally insisted on going to get a doctor, himself. I came to warn you to get out," she said. "What happened?"

Before Tom could answer, there was a fanfare of trumpets. The crowd opened up again alongside them and the platoon of Gloks, now bearing the Bulbur on its silver stand, marched out to the table and set stand and Bulbur up in the middle of it. Bu Hjark raised his hand for silence and barked at the Naffing with the vacuum cleaner, which scurried off.

"Respected Entities!" boomed Bu Hjark. "I now bring you the climax to the evening's entertainment and the commencement of the banquet itself. I have no doubt, respected Entities, that you have on occasion tasted rare and fine dishes. However, tonight I mean to provide you not merely with the finest-tasting food you have ever encountered—a food which all beings who have yet tried it rate better than any other thing they have tasted—but with certain preliminaries and appetizers. After which I shall, with my own hand, prepare and serve the dish to you."

He drew his sword and stepped a little aside from the table.

"And now," he said to the Bulbur. "Commence!"

"R-respected Entities," the Bulbur began with a slight quaver. It turned remarkably transparent, then washed back to blue again. "It is a great honor, I assure you, to be the appetizer to your banquet tonight. We Bulburs are a worthless lot, fit only for pleasing the worthwhile palates of our betters. It is our one pride and pleasure, to know that you find us good to—" the Bulbur swallowed audibly and then took up its speech a little more rapidly as Bu Hjark scowled at it—"eat. I cannot express the intense enjoyment—" it said rapidly "—that it gives me to be here tonight, awaiting my supreme fulfillment as appetizer to the banquet you will shortly be having. To ensure your unalloyed enjoyment of me, I will now," it said, speeding up even more under Bu Hjark's steely, lizardlike eye, "sing you a mouth-watering song to increase your appreciation of my truly unique flavor." It broke off and visibly took a deep breath, turned pale, but came steadily back to a solid blue color.

"Tom!" Lucy clutched Tom's elbow with fingers that dug in. "It can't mean we're going to *eat* it? Tom, do something!"

"What?" said Tom as a small beginning thread of golden melody began to emerge, growing in volume as it continued, from the mouth of the Bulbur.

"I don't know. But stop it!"

Desperately, Tom looked around him for inspiration. He thought of how he had almost begun to convince the Bulbur that its attitudes were not unique in the universe. He thought of how effective the Bulbur's gift of song had proved in the room when the Bulbur sang to him. *What we need is another Bulbur to sing it into resisting the Jaktal*, he thought—

and, with that, inspiration came to him. He opened
his mouth and, in his best bathroom baritone, burst
into song:

"*Allons, enfants de la patrie—*" he sang.

Almost with the first word, Lucy chimed in with
him. Her untrained but clear soprano picked up the
second line.

"*—Le jour de gloire—*Sing!" she cried to Monsieur
Pourtoit, who was standing across the open space
from them. He bowed to her gravely. He looked a
little puzzled, but after all he was a Frenchman. He
opened his mouth and joined a resonant, trained
voice to her tones and Tom's.

"What is this?" roared Bu Hjark, spinning around
to face Tom. His lizard face was agape, showing great
dog teeth. He lifted the sword ominously in his
hand. Tom swallowed, but continued to sing.

The *Marseillaise*, the anthem of France, was beginning to sound its battle cry against tyranny from
other confused but cooperative lips. The sword swung
up. The Gloks turned as one man toward Tom. Suddenly a clear, pure note, two octaves above high F,
trilled through all the sound of the room, striking
them motionless. The whole room turned toward the
table.

The fine, thrilling note was proceeding from the
Bulbur. It had stretched upward until it was almost
twice its original height. From what well of knowledge it had picked up the necessary information Tom
was never to discover, but it had changed color. Its
lowest tier was now red, its second tier blue, its top
tier white. As they all stood, as if at attention, it broke
magnificently into the French anthem to liberty:

"*Against us long, a tyranny,*" it sang in wild, mas-
terful accents. "*A bloody sword has waved on high!*"

It was pitching its notes directly at Bu Hjark. Those assembled saw the full power of the Bulbur's melody-born emotional might driving through the savage ego of the Jaktal like a metal blade through the tender body of a Bulbur. Now it caught the whole assemblage up in its song. Spellbound, a chorus of diplomatic and government personnel harking from old Sol to the furthest of the Pleiades, roared to the tune of the *Marseillaise:*

> *Too long have you kept us subject,*
> *With your Spanduls, your Naffings and your Gloks!*
> *Why shouldn't peace be sweet?*
> *Who dares a Bulbur eat?*
> *Have done! Have done!*
> *Let there be an end!*
> *It's be-autiful PEACE—*
> *From this hour on, my friend!*

And, as the last great chord of voices crashed into silence, the huge figure of the Jaktal ambassador could be seen to shiver through all its length and, leaning more and more at an angle with eyes glazed, topple at last to thunder upon the floor like some mighty ruined tower. And the voices of the Spanduls and Gloks present rose in one great wail, crying, "Zzatz! Zzatz! Zzatz . . ."

When their cries at last died away into silence, the Bulbur on the table could be seen to have taken on an all-over shade of perky pink.

"Jaktals," it mentioned, in mild but audible tones as it leaned above the fallen Bu Hjark, "are also supposed to be very good eating."

"And that remark," said Tom the evening of the next day, after he had finished work, waded through the softball game in the street before their house, patted Rex, the Great Dane, and kissed Lucy, "will undoubtedly go down in the history books as the harshest statement ever made by an adult Bulbur."

"But what's going to happen to the Bulburs now?" asked Lucy, as she gave Tom a Martini and Rex a bowl of Scotch and milk.

"Well, this one told us his race doesn't want anything to do with running the Jaktal Empire. He turned the authority over to us humans. All other Bulburs, he said, would ratify that move, if they were contacted by us—if for no other reason than that they wouldn't want to hurt his feelings by disagreeing with him."

"They must be so sensitive!" said Lucy.

"Sensitive," said Tom, taking a glum sip from his Martini, "but shrewd. The Bulbur knew very well he was turning the authority over to people who'd regard it as a scared trust. 'Greater love hath no being than to take on authority as a duty rather than a privilege,' he said."

"You must admit that was quite a compliment," said Lucy.

"Yeah," said Tom, gloomily. "We're in for one hell of an expansion. They're going to make me a first assistant secretary with a full department under me. Twice the work—and a ten per cent raise in pay."

"But imagine," said Lucy radiantly. "Me! The wife of a first assistant foreign secretary!"

Tom sighed heavily. Rex licked his hand. In the pause in the conversation the yells from the softball game outside penetrated through the livingroom walls, in spite of their being set on full sound-block. It sounded to Tom a little like Glok and Spandul voices in the distance, faintly and forebodingly crying "Zzatz! Zzatz!"

"If interspecies misunderstandings are unavoidable, exploit them."

—*Orientations*

The Faithful Wilf

I

"I suppose you think of it sometimes," sighed Lucy Parent, as their Mordaunti spaceship descended on the world that was its midway stop to the Mordaunti capital world of Cayahno. Cayahno was something like six hundred light years in toward the center of the galaxy from Earth. The Mordaunti Ambassador, Arknok, had explained it would be necessary to let down here at Bug'raf to replate the drive chamber.

"Think of what?" said Tom Parent. He was pacing up and down by their stateroom viewer. He alternated between casting glances at the glittering cityport toward which they were descending and glancing at the top-secret subspace communication that had just reached them from his superiors back on Earth. The communication was, of course, in code. But Tom had had keys to all recent codes hypnoed into him before they left Earth.

101

Lucy sighed again. "About what it'd be like not being married again."

"Not married? What?" said Tom, stopping his pacing suddenly. "Why, of course not. Certainly not. What made you think of that?"

"Oh, nothing," sighed Lucy.

"If you don't mind," said Tom, "I have something urgent on my mind at the moment."

"All men do," said Lucy, studying her fingernails. "I suppose it's only natural. Women aren't like that. Marriage means a lot to a woman."

"Lucy, if you don't mind—" Tom was suddenly interrupted by the gentle chiming of their stateroom door. "Come in."

The door opened. A seven-foot humanoid looking like a satanic Tarzan in purple robes stepped into the room. A weapons harness covered the robes, various types of weapons depending from it. The humanoid touched pale green fingers to his winged skullcap.

"Good morning, Mr. Ambassador," said Tom, touching his own brown crew-cut in similar fashion. "May the Mordaunti live forever."

"And yourrr own rrrace also," replied the ambassador, rolling his r's like a Scotsman. His black eyes glittered as he added affably, "I thocht I'd tell you therrres time for you to stroll about the Bug'raf capital below, if you wish. We'll be here at least half a day."

"Stroll? Well! Well, that's just fine!" cried Tom, happily. "Yes. We will. Thank you so much, Mr. Ambassador."

"Think nothing of it," replied the other. Touching his head again, he went out.

"You go by yourself," said Lucy sadly. "I think I'll just stay here."

"You will not!" Tom snapped. Lucy sat up and stared at him.

*   *   *

Half an hour later the ship was down, and Tom and Lucy strolled off the landing area into the winding, colorful streets that looked as if they had been lifted out of the illustrations of some old fairy-tale book. The streets were aswarm with a hundred alien races. Once out of sight of the ship, Tom started walking at a pace that had Lucy almost trotting to keep up.

"Tom!" She grabbed hold of his arm. "Slow down! I can't—"

"Just around this corner," said Tom, dragging her around it and down at seats of something like a sidewalk cafe. A robot rolled up. "Alcohol and cold distilled water, two," he said in the local lingua franca. The robot rolled away. "I couldn't talk on the ship. Something's come up."

"But you're on vacation!" cried Lucy. "This is supposed to be our second honeymoon!" She broke off suddenly and eyed him sharply. The robot rolled up and deposited two squeeze-bulbs before them. Tom produced his identity papers with the Mordaunti seal. The robot punched a hole in them and went away.

"Well—" said Tom.

"Or is it?"

"Well," said Tom, avoiding her eye.

"You told me—you *told* me this was a vacation! I might have known there was something wrong the way you've been acting. So. . . . So *absentminded* about things. Well," said Lucy, "it doesn't matter, of course. I don't mind. Go right ahead." She fumbled angrily in her wrist purse and produced a small lace handkerchief.

"Good!" whispered Tom. Lucy checked herself, surprised, with the handkerchief half-raised.

"Good?"

"We're away from the ship but there still may be spies. That'll confuse them. Look, Lucy, I didn't know about this myself until I got the sub-space message just now. The Office Upstairs back on Earth just said they might have a little job for me on Cayahno. They didn't even let me in on it—after all, I'm still only a first assistant secretary in the Foreign Office's Department of New Governments."

"You let me think it was going to be a real vacation!"

"Now, honey, be reasonable."

"I won't!"

"Our lives are in danger."

"Oh!" Lucy closed the mouth she had just opened preparatory to saying some more, looked around and put the handkerchief away. She leaned toward Tom. "In danger?" she whispered.

"That's what I've been trying to tell you," said Tom in a low voice, "and it's not my fault. The Office Upstairs just gave me the idea they wanted me to do some little red-tape thing, like make a duty call on one of the Mordaunti authorities. Now, this message lets me in on it. And it's so secret they couldn't even trust me with the knowledge before we left."

"Tell me," said Lucy.

"I'm not supposed to—"

"Oh!" gasped Lucy. "It's all right if my life is in danger; but I'm not supposed to know why!"

"—But," said Tom, "as I was going to say if you'd ever let me finish saying something, I'm going to. You may have to carry on if anything happens to me."

"Tom!" Lucy's eyes grew suddenly large.

"No use not facing things," said Tom bravely. "Well, here it is. On Cayahno—the capital world of the Mordaunti to which we're headed—there's going to be a gathering of representatives from the forty-three great interstellar powers in this section of the galaxy."

"Forty-three?" squeaked Lucy. "The Oprinkians, the Mordaunti, us—and who else?"

Tom, said sadly, "We are not listed among the forty-three. The Jaktals were, of course. And everyone knows we've taken over their empire* by now. But no invitation has been sent to us."

"Why, that's terrible!"

"More than terrible. Dangerous. It means the other forty-two great interstellar empires are thinking of dividing our own and the Jaktal territory between them. The Oprinkians** are still our friends, of course. They suggested we secretly send a man and have him just walk in and take over the Jaktal chair at the meeting."

"You?" said Lucy.

"Me," said Tom. "The Office Upstairs thought a minor official like myself would never be suspected of being sent to speak for the whole human empire. Of course, I won't actually speak for us. I'll simply grab the Jaktal seat and hold it. Once I'm there, I'm safe. No one will act against me for fear of endangering his own immunity as ambassador. But I've got to get there first."

"Let's go back to the ship and lock ourselves in and throw away the key."

"That might not be a bad idea. However—" Tom broke off suddenly and looked up. A sudden hush had fallen over the street. Everyone seemed to have disappeared. Then, suddenly, around the corner floated a metal platform with two odd-looking aliens of different species on it.

*WHO DARES A BULBUR EAT?
**REX AND MR. REJILLA

II

The first was a stubby individual wearing a harness draped with guns, knives and other fierce gadgets. He wore nothing else. He appeared completely hairless, his skin a leathery brown. His face looked something like a bulldog's. The other alien beside him was about three feet tall, wearing a robe, a sort of magician's cone-shaped hat and a long white beard, above which showed a bulbous nose and two large, purple trusting eyes.

"Greetings!" boomed the harnessed individual, in the local lingua franca, bringing the platform to a halt at their table. As it settled to the ground he took a device from his harness and looked through it at Tom. "Magnificent! Just as advertised! .72 on the ferocity scale. Congratulations, my boy. I am Drakvil, Master Assassin—and you are my apprentice."

"Apprentice?" said Tom.

"Hard to believe, I know. But you are. I just picked you."

"Pardon me," said Tom. "But overwhelming as the honor is . . ."

"Tut-tut," said Drakvil. "Say no more."

"—I must decline—"

"WHAT?"

Drakvil suddenly paled all over his body until he was almost white. Gradually his color came back. He slowly extended a hand and pointed at Lucy.

"So," he said. "I think I see. Does that wilf belong to you?"

"I certainly do!" said Lucy.

Drakvil's arm dropped.

"Wilf-ridden!" he breathed. "I get an apprentice with one of the finest aptitude ratings ever recorded; and it has a wilf! But don't worry, my boy." He got down and began to rummage inside the back edge of the platform. "I'll free you."

"Tom!" said Lucy, clutching his arm.

"Shh," hissed Tom. "It's all right—"

He was interrupted as the second alien on the platform suddenly began to cry in a timid, despairing fashion.

"What's wrong with you?" said Tom, turning on it.

"Oh, sir," sobbed the smaller alien. "It would've been such an honor for a simple pjenik pjanik like me. No real Assassin would lower himself to slay a pjanik under the pjonik class. Of course I know your honor's still only an apprentice and it'd only be a practice assassination, but—"

"Wait a minute," said Tom.

The pjanik wiped its eyes with its white beard and sniffed.

"You mean," said Tom. "I'm supposed to practice assassinating on you?"

"Of course," snapped Drakvil, coming up with a metal plate tucked under one arm. "Begin with live targets right away. The only way. I've got no patience with Master Assassins that start their apprentices out on simulacrums. No meat. No feel to it." He unhooked one of the gadgets from his harness. "Here," he said, "you can borrow my loset." He shoved it into Tom's hand. "Meanwhile, I will psychoanalyze you and rid you of this wilfish affliction."

"You don't understand, I'm afraid, sir Assassin," said Tom in smooth, diplomatic tones. "I'm just ashore for a few hours from the Mordaunti ship at the spaceport."

Drakvil shook his head. "Tut-tut, delusions as well. Not surprising, I suppose. My lad, the Mordaunti ship took off just five minutes ago and, as you see, you are still here."

"Took off? But it had to have its drive chamber replated!"

"Come, come," said Drakvil. "To replate a drive chamber takes days. The ship needs to be completely torn down—that's one reason we Assassins never use ships. To work, my boy. There's your pjanik, and you have the loset in hand." He glanced at the metal plate. "Meanwhile—let me see—I have some questions here. When you were an immature life form did you ever secretly like your primary immediate male ancestor?"

Tom was exchanging glances with Lucy. He winked and whispered in English, "Play along." He handed the loset back to the Master Assassin, bowing.

"Ordinarily," he said, "I'd be happy to assassinate this little fellow here—" He put his hand on the shoulder of the pjanik.

"*Oh!*" cried the pjanik in sudden accents of joy. "It touched me! Its honor touched me!" It fell at Tom's feet and began kissing the toes of Tom's shoes. "Oh, *thank* you, your nobleship, your kindnessness, little uncle."

Drakvil had gone suddenly white again. Now he faded back to his normal color and boomed with laughter.

"All right, you young rascal!" he said. "Caught me fairly that time. Takes some nerve to risk distracting a Master Assassin long enough to touch a piece of his property and adopt it. Well, you got away with it. Now, all that talk about the Mordaunti spaceship. Eyewash, right? You deliberately got off here to put yourself in a position where I could see you and take you on as an Apprentice, didn't you?"

"Er, yes," said Tom.

"Yes?" cried Lucy.

"Playalong, playalong, we're - stranded - here - without - that - ship," muttered Tom between his teeth in English, smiling brightly at Drakvil.

"Well, come along then," said Drakvil, remounting the platform. "Bring your newly adopted nephew-slave along with you. Does the wilf have to come, too?"

"Just try to go without me!" said Lucy.

"Blasted faithful wilfs!" muttered Drakvil, as Tom stepped up on the platform and helped Lucy up behind him. "Sap the backbone out of a being. Wouldn't have one myself for . . . Hang on, here we go, across the galaxy to Pjo."

"Pjo?" said Tom. But already the city around them had vanished. The platform was now sitting in the midst of a featureless waste of sand, with what looked like a temple far off on the horizon. "Well," Tom said, blinking a little, "that's some transportation."

"The only way to go," said Drakvil with satisfaction. "Why travel by slow phase-shifting when this is available? Of course there's always that statistical chance of coming out in the center of some sun or other. But death is an Assassin's constant companion, anyway. Let's get down to business."

He pointed at the distant templelike building.

"Scene of your first assignment. First I'd better brief you." He reached down and touched something on the platform at his feet. A golden light flickered suddenly around Tom, who went down like a pjanik shot by a loset, in a crumpled heap.

"Tom!" cried Lucy frantically, kneeling by him. He sat up groggily and shook his head. "Who? What? Where—oh, hello, wilf."

"*Wilf!*" cried Lucy. "Tom, don't you know me?"

"Of course I know you, wilf—I mean, honey. Help me up."

Lucy helped him to his feet. Tom shook his head a few more times.

"Bit of a shock, acquiring all that information at once. I'm all right wi—Lucy. Oh, is that my harness?" He reached out and took the cluster of weapons Drakvil was holding out to him. He put it on, checking its gadgets. "Let's see. Spengs. Losets. Oh, and a gornul. Latest model, I see."

"Naturally," said Drakvil. "The workman is worthy of his tools."

"Thanks." Tom looked off at the building. "Subject in there?"

"Tom!" said Lucy, "what're you going to do?"

Tom ignored her and went on talking to Drakvil. "Large establishment, I take it?"

"A spranjik of the gark class," said Drakvil.

"Probably has a gnruth of jilks for guard?"

"Two gnruths. All porbornik-jilks."

"Tom!" cried Lucy. "You answer me! What're you going to do? What are gnruths?"

"Bodyguard units of fifty jilks apiece," said Tom absently, staring at the building.

"Tom, you aren't thinking of trying to assassinate someone who has a hundred bodyguards?"

"You'll notice," said Drakvil to Tom, "the establishment is laid out for alnrits, both inside and out."

Tom laughed scornfully. "Alnrits!"

"Tom! What are alnrits? Will you pay some *attention* to me?"

"They're disintegrators," said Tom without looking around. "Don't bother me now, wilf."

Lucy shouted, "I am not, not, *not* a wilf!"

"Well, I'm off," said Tom. He reached down to do something to the platform, and disappeared.

"Tom!" wailed Lucy.

He reappeared again, shoving one of the larger gadgets back into his holster on the weapons harness.

"Well, that was easy enough," he said. Lucy gaped at him.

"Tom, you didn't—" she gasped.

"Not yet," said Tom cheerfully. "I just went in for a reconnoitre. On accelerated time."

"Report what you did, Assistant," Drakvil said.

"Oh, I approached the gate and spenged one of jilks on outer guard there. When the rest turned to see what had happened, I slipped in. As I expected, I found myself in a mobius maze of corridors. I calculated my way through, spenged the three jilks I found at the inner entrance, and took cover when the alarm sounded and a platoon came up at the double with pobornik guns at the ready."

"Did they suspect an Assassin was inside the gark?" asked Drakvil.

"No sir," answered Tom. "I overheard them guessing that it was a dispossessed simulacrum—a rogue one. I ducked down a sidestreet of the jilk quarters and found my way blocked by a full-armed tank. Well, of course a monstrosity like that could never be knocked out by a mere speng. I knew that."

"What—what did you do?" Lucy asked.

"Oh, I just stood still in the center of the street the way any ordinary dispossessed, mindless rogue simulacrum might. And when they were close enough, I gave the tank a pung from my class two loset."

Drakvil beamed. "Very good. And then?"

"I took the tank and drove it through the inner defenses as if I was the tank crew coming back off duty. Inside, I abandoned the tank and slipped into the ruler's personal family section of the gark. I set up a resolving point inside so the platform could be brought in, and came back to get the three of you."

The pjanik squeaked with pleasure.

"Me, too? Oh, little uncle!"

"Yes," said Tom, giving Lucy a strange, meaningful glance that baffled her completely, "particularly you too."

"You wanted me to see you in action. Very good,"

said Drakvil. He reached down and touched the platform, and they were all suddenly in a curtained alcove, dim-lit from above. "Now what?"

"You can watch through the curtain," said Tom. "Now, I'm going to disguise myself and take on the nartled appearance of an illegal gossip-seller." He reached down and touched the platform. Lucy gave a small, stifled shriek.

"It's still me," creaked the clawed and warty creature now standing before them. "Watch through the curtain."

III

He slipped off the platform, parted the curtains and slid through. Lucy, Drakvil and the pjanik hurried to the parting and peered through. They saw a lofty hall with a guard of armed jilks, their eye-stalks stiff at attention. A jilk officer was pacing up and down. Tom, in his gossip-seller's guise, sidled up to the officer.

"Juicy items," Lucy heard him whine, "rare tidbits from strange worlds—"

The officer backed away distastefully and snapped, "Filthy creature! Keep your nartled claws to yourself."

"But commander! I must go inside the door. A certain female of the ranking family—your freshness understands—"

"Your pass!" snapped the officer, extending a three-fingered hand.

"But she gave me no pass," Tom whimpered. "She simply said to come to this entrance—" He sidled closer. "Your freshness would not want me to compromise the good name of one of the inner gark by mentioning it in public? But if I could talk to you aside—"

"Stand back," said the officer. "Very well." He let

Tom lead him away from the guard. To Lucy's horror they approached the alcove, stopping just outside the curtain.

"Now," said the officer in a low, eager voice. Lucy was amazed to see his eyestalks wavering drunkenly. He panted. "I know you're lying. The female Orbash is the only one who could have called you, and she is elsewhere. So tell me! What have you got to sell?"

Tom whispered, "I knew your freshness was an addict, the moment I saw the angle of your eyestalks! It'll cost you."

"I am *not* an addict," panted the officer. "I like a little gossip like the next being, but I can take it or leave it alone. But price is no object. Quick, what've you got for sale?"

"Bend down, listen—" said Tom. The eyestalks dipped inward. Tom threw a sudden hook to the officer's midsection. The officer collapsed without a sound and Tom shoved him through the curtain at Lucy's feet, meanwhile immediately turning his appearance into a duplicate of the officer's. He marched across to the guard.

"Attention!" he snapped. "Right face! Forward march." They marched off down the corridor.

"Magnificent discipline these pobornik-jilks have," remarked Drakvil, as Tom, marching behind the guard, stepped back into the alcove. "However, it sometimes works to their disadvantage."

"I assumed so," said Tom, resuming his natural appearance, much to Lucy's relief. "Now, shall we enter the gark-ruler's inner sanctum?"

He led them to the undefended door and opened it. They stepped through filmy hanging curtains to find themselves in a pleasant, sunlit room where a fountain played. A pjanik in purple robes turned to look at them. Tom's adopted nephew-slave immediately prostrated himself before his duplicate.

"Rise, inferior," said the one in the purple robe. He helped Tom's pjanik to arise, and the two stood nose to nose, their white beards almost touching, their gentle eyes fastened in friendly fashion on each other. "To what do I owe the honor of this visit?"

"Rejoice, noble sir," said Tom's pjanik. "You are about to be assassinated."

"Hardly a cause for rejoicing, inferior," the other protested mildly.

"It isn't, noble sir?"

"Not for a pjonik pjanik, inferior. Possibly you're confusing my position with your own." Tom's pjanik immediately prostrated himself again. "No, I didn't mean that." He helped Tom's pjanik up again. "I just mean we who are born to the purple don't consider being murdered quite such an honor as you lower classes."

"Really?"

"In fact," said the pjonik pjanik, turning to Tom, Lucy and Drakvil, "may I ask why I'm being assassinated?"

"Why?" exploded Drakvil. "You ask *why?*"

"A natural question, isn't it?" asked Tom innocently.

"Why, I never heard of such a thing!" fumed Drakvil. "A subject asking why. What galactic nerve! If I hadn't promised you to my assistant here, and an Assassin's word wasn't as good as his bond—" His fingers played angrily with the hilt of a hook-shaped knife attached to his harness.

"I suppose you don't know why either, young Apprentice?" said the pjonik sadly to Tom. "Well, I suppose I'll die not knowing. Farewell, inferior."

The large eyes of Tom's pjanik began to fill with sympathetic tears.

"Go ahead," fussed Drakvil. "I can't. You must."

"No," said Tom.

"No?" said Drakvil, Lucy and the pjonik pjanik all at once.

"No," said Tom calmly. "I cannot, because of my wilf."

"I knew it!" bellowed Drakvil, turning chalk-white and staying that color. "That wilf! I knew it!" He turned on Lucy, who quickly got on the other side of Tom.

Tom faced him and said, "Once I would have gornuled this subject on the spot, without a hesitation. In fact with keen enjoyment. But my wilf has had its effect on me. This is—er—a far, far better thing I do than I have ever done before. The quality of mercy is not strained and no man an island unto himself. If I should gormul this subject, I should be diminished, even as an island diminishes part of the main. Therefore never send to know for whom the bell tolls, because it's already tolled for me."

"Mad!" said Drakvil. "Stark staring, raving mad. Poor, poor boy." His color came back. His tone became more gentle. "Before I gornul you myself, Apprentice, and put you out of your misery—tell me. Why did you go this far before refusing to act?"

"It was the least I could do for the Master to whom I'd been apprenticed," said Tom. "I suspected your honor had been impugned. I had to actually get face to face with the subject and you at the same time to make sure. Now I know beyond any doubt."

"Honor?" said Drakvil, suddenly stiffening. "The honor of a Master Assassin impugned? Who would dare?"

"Who indeed," said Tom, nudging Lucy, "but an *amateur* Assassin?"

"Amateur?" Drakvil went chalk-white once more.

"Yes," said Tom. "I wouldn't have had the least

suspicion of him, if it hadn't been for my wilf." He nudged Lucy again. "It noticed the difference in the way I was acting. Didn't you, wilf?"

"Yes, I did," said Lucy.

"It wanted to know what was disturbing me."

"Yes, I did."

"It warned me faithfully that this amateur was out to dispose of me."

"Er—" said Lucy, "yes, I did."

"Its warnings did not register on me properly until you slapped me with that briefing ray just before I went into the gark. In that briefing was the information needed to complete the picture. This amateur arranged for me to be left behind on Bug'raf, just as he hired you through the Assassin's Guild to train me as an apprentice. And he thoughtfully provided this innocent pjonik pjanik as a subject for me to practice on, at the regular rates."

Drakvil said thoughtfully, his color returning. "What you say checks my own knowledge, Apprentice. But nothing of it affects my honor."

"I will explain."

"Go ahead," said Drakvil, taking a long, sinister-looking gadget from his harness. "I have to reset my gornul anyway. Take a couple more moments if you like."

"Thank you," said Tom. "Suppose you understand that what this amateur hoped and planned was that you would gornul me."

"How could he be so sure of that?"

"Because," said Tom, taking a deep breath, "he was prepared to violate your honor by forcing you to take on an apprentice that he knew would never pass the test. You see, he knew I had a wilf."

Drakvil's fingers stopped suddenly on the gornul. He looked up.

"He knew my wilf would stick by me."

"Yes, I would," said Lucy.

"And that, faithful as it is to its principles and to me—"

"Yes, I am."

"—it would, wilflike, throw itself before my gornul when I attempted to assassinate the subject, thus creating a scandal that would reflect on you as my Master, and cause you to destroy me on the spot."

"Y—" began Lucy; and stopped dead, staring at Tom with eyes almost as big as a pjanik's.

Drakvil had beaten his previous paleness of shade. He was now so white he was nearly transparent.

"You see," said Tom to him, "he didn't care about pjonik here, whom he had no reason to hire assassinated. He didn't care about the expense you might be put to in buying a practice pjanik for me. He didn't care about the scandal which would blacken your name in the Assassin's Guild. All he was interested in was using you to get rid of me."

Drakvil was not only nearly transparent, he was swelling like a balloon.

"Pardon me, little uncle," said Tom's pjanik meekly, "but why didn't he just hire the noble Assassin to destroy you in the first place?"

"Well, you see," said Tom in a kindly voice, "he couldn't. For the same reason I couldn't really adopt you. My race hasn't ever subscribed to the Assassin Conventions. In fact—I'm on my way to Cayahno right now to discuss the Conventions and other things with the forty-three other dominant races' representatives."

Drakvil had finally found his voice. "Where is he?" he wheezed. "Where is he?"

"The Mordaunti ambassador who marooned my wilf and I and hired you?" said Tom smoothly. "I imagine he's on Cayahno by now. Very probably—" Tom glanced at his watch—"he's already sitting down with the forty-three representatives in the Omni-Races Building board room."

"Platform!" said Drakvil, touching a spot on his harness. The platform appeared. "On!" he ordered. Tom jumped up on it and pulled Lucy after him. Tom's pjanik started to scramble aboard also, then stopped, confused.

"Stay here, inferior," said the pjonik pjanik. "*I'll* adopt you."

"Oh, little father," said the pjanik, falling prostrate. Drakvil touched the platform. The room winked out around them and they winked in again in a long, hall-like chamber, with a semicircle of seats filled with a rainbow diversity of different beings. The Mordaunti ambassador was standing in the open space before these seats, addressing the rest of the representatives.

"—our responsibility to the former Jaktal members, and those races formerly under their dominion—" he was saying. He broke off abruptly as he saw the platform with its occupants.

"Now!" boomed Drakvil. Tom caught the Assassin's hand as it was closing on the gornul.

"Just a minute," said Tom. "He's mine."

"Yours?" Drakvil turned on Tom.

"Though only an apprentice, I believe I have rights under the Guild," said Tom.

"Yes," Drakvil admitted thickly.

"Then I believe I have the right of first offense from this being, and so may challenge him to a duel before you yourself take action?"

Drakvil glowered.

"I'm going to have to do some work on that briefing machine," he muttered. But he let go of the gornul. "Go ahead, then. I'll watch."

The Mordaunti had buckled slightly at the knees on seeing Drakvil. But on hearing this, he straightened up again and his hands spread inward toward his own weapon harness. He smiled at Tom.

"Though only an apprentice," said Tom to Drakvil, "would you say I might prevail in a duel with this being?"

Drakvil snorted.

"Only!" he said. "*Only* an apprentice! You've been briefed, haven't you? Naturally only another Guild member could hope to stand a chance with you, apprentice or not."

The Mordaunti's knees began to give again. He tried to smile but his satanic grimace was a little loose at the corners.

"I just wondered," said Tom. "I wouldn't want the impression to get about the galaxy that I was trying to hide from the honorable Mordaunti representative."

He got down off the platform and walked across to a vacant chair he had spotted in the lowest tier of seats. It was a little large for him, being built to hold Jaktals, but he seated himself in it.

"Let me see," he said thoughtfully. "I will have to arrange for my wilf to be restrained so that it cannot prevent—"

"Hold!" cried the Mordaunti ambassador in the lingua franca.

Tom looked up, surprised.

"No one could be more eager for a duel with the being from Earth than I," said the Mordaunti. His knees were quite straight again. "But there is a higher duty. The obligations of a Member of this meeting."

"What?" said Tom. "I don't understand. You *have* to fight me."

"Alas," said the Mordaunti. "Forgive me."

"Forgive you? I insist you fight me. I insist—"

"Sadly, I must refuse. Sir, you have inadvertently

seated yourself in the Jaktal chair, as a Member of this meeting."

"What?" cried Tom, looking about him. "What'd I do? You mean, just by sitting down here for a moment, I—"

"You invested yourself with diplomatic immunity," said the Mordaunti. "Ambassadors may not duel with each other. That is a basic law of interracial politics. Otherwise our meetings would become disasters."

"But I just sat down for a minute!"

"I'm sorry. The rule is strict."

"Curses!" said Tom.

"We all sympathize."

"Why am I so absentminded?"

"We all understand, I'm sure. It could happen to any newcomer. Unfortunately ignorance of the rule is no excuse."

"My courage," said Tom, "will be called in question. The courage of the whole human race will probably be called in question."

"Not at all," said the Mordaunti smoothly, "I, myself, will be honored to introduce a resolution of confidence in your courage and that of every member of your race."

"Well . . ." said Tom. But the Mordaunti had already turned to speak to the filled seats of the semicircle about Tom. And three Earth minutes later the vote was unanimous in favor of Tom's and human courage, even Drakvil being read into the minutes unofficially as being in favor.

IV

"Tell me, really," said Lucy that night, as they were preparing to retire on a Mordaunti bed that was like a golden cloud twelve feet around, "did that

briefing really make you so dangerous? In just a
second, like that?"

Tom climbed onto the bed. Lucy was still tying
the top of her filmy blue nightgown. He bounced
experimentally.

"Some bed," he said. "Of course it didn't. I know
all I need to know, but it'd take years of exercising to
make my muscles respond as they need to for effective use of the knowledge. Drakvil, of course, wasn't
going to admit I wasn't, though. His honor as an
Assassin was at stake. That is why I think he was
secretly pleased I didn't have to duel the Mordaunti,
after all—Are you going to put the lights out?"

"In a minute," said Lucy. She stood by the bed. "I
want you to tell me something first."

"What?"

"I want to know exactly what a wilf is. And you tell
me the truth."

"Oh."

"Yes, oh."

"Well," said Tom, slowly, "they look a lot like
women. At least an alien might think they did. But
they're really a totally different race, monosexual.
It's just that they go around becoming deeply attached to beings of other races. Once they make
friends, their faithfulness is proverbial in the galaxy."

"But why?"

"Why?"

"Why," said Lucy, "do they become attached?
What do they want to make friends for? What's in it
for them?" She looked narrowly at Tom. "They look
so much like us and they go around attaching themselves. I want to know why!"

"Oh," said Tom. "I see. I see. Well, it's not what
you might think at all."

"It isn't?"

"No," said Tom. "Different race, and all that. It's

just that wilfs have this strong moral sense. They
have very high principles and their greatest joy is in
converting some other being to these same principles. Naturally, there's not much opportunity for
them to improve other wilfs, these being as good as
they can get already. So they try to get close to
beings of other races, in a strictly intellectual way.
That's all."

"Oh," said Lucy, "that's all right, then."

She put out the lights and bounced into bed.

"I've got plenty of low principles" she said. "You
like me that way, don't you? You'd better say yes."

"Yes," said Tom.

"Always remember that you will be encountering alien bodies as well as alien minds."

—Orientations

A Wobble in Wockii Futures

I

"I *do* trust you!" said Tom Parent.

"You don't! You don't!" said his wife Lucy. "You just say you do but you don't!"

Tom ran the fingers of his right hand in near desperation through his close-cropped brown hair. About them in the lounge of the imperial suite aboard the spaceship descending on the planet Mul'Rahr, four Hugwo lance-gunners stood scattered about like statues at rigid attention. They looked like nothing so much as oversized clams, equipped with armored legs and arms, their tall lance-guns upright in their grasps.

Luckily, thought Tom, the Hugwos did not understand English, which he and Lucy were talking at the moment. Lucy was blonde and beautiful and he loved her dearly, but—

123

"I do!" said Tom. "You don't understand. It's like Caesar's wife—the Consort Lucy must be above suspicion. As ambassador to Mul'Rahr, I may have to engage in some pretty active diplomatic trickeries. If you don't know about them, no one can accuse you—" He broke off. A fifth Hugwo, the corporal in charge of the honor guard of lance-gunners, had just clanked in with a message in code, which he handed to Tom. "Thank you."

"Sir!" shouted the corporal, clanked backwards three paces, saluted with the precision for which these mercenary soldiers were famous, and became rigid. Both he and Tom had spoken the lingua franca of the civilized worlds of the Galactic Federation, to which the human worlds were relative newcomers. Tom scanned the message, translating mentally as he read. He had had the recent codes hypnoed into him before leaving Earth.

"I keep telling you," Tom went on to Lucy in English as he read, "how serious this is. We overextended our human resources when we took over the Jaktal Empire."

"But you took over the Jaktal seat for us among the forty-three great interstellar powers in this sector." said Lucy, puzzled. "I thought—"

"That gave us political position. But we need economic position," mumbled Tom, as he perused the message. "The Office Upstairs, back on Earth—see how I trust you and tell you things—decided this could best be gotten by investing in the advantages of future trading agreement with the Wockii, the dominant race on Mul'Rahr. Against my advice, incidentally. It seemed to me there was something fishy—"

"They asked you?" said Lucy.

"Of course," muttered Tom, still decoding as he talked. "After all, I'm the only living individual of the human race who's a member of the Interstellar Assassin's Guild, even if I am only an apprentice and became one by mistake. Because of my apprentice's briefing, I know more about the interstellar situation than any human alive—oh, oh, just as I thought!"

He snapped a pocket loset from his Assassin's weapons harness and hastily disintegrated the message blank.

"What? What did you think? Tell me!" said Lucy.

"I shouldn't," muttered Tom, snapping the loset back into its holster clip.

"You don't trust me!"

"But I will." Tom began to pace worriedly up and down the room, between the statuesque Hugwos, with Lucy following after him. "It's just as I feared. There's been a wobble in Wockii futures on the Interstellar Futurities Exchange. A bad wobble."

"Wobble?" cried Lucy. "Wobble? I don't understand."

"It's not easy for anyone to understand without an Assassin's briefing knowledge," said Tom, frowning. "That's why I warned the Office Upstairs against this."

"What did they do—oops!" said Lucy. Tom had just turned around suddenly and bumped into her.

"Sorry," said Tom. "Well, briefly, there's a sort of interstellar stock exchange in which member races can speculate by buying and selling stock in their own and other races' future wealth and productivity. When we took over the Jaktal Empire we took over the Jaktal committments. In order to back these, the Office Upstairs decided to issue stock in our own human futures—all very good and sound as far as it went. But then, they turned around and wanted to borrow against the credit thus established to purchase the total stock of the futures of the dominant race here on Mul'Rahr, listed as the Wockiis. And I was sent here to endorse the purchase by a trade agreement with the Wockiis personally, even though they haven't reached Interstellar Citizenship level and are administrated by the Skikana, who discovered Mul'Rahr."

"But what's wrong with that?"

"Both the sixth and seventh of my para-instincts activated by the Assassin's briefings were made suspicious by the availability of those same Wockii futures. My seventh, in particular, was very positive about it. It was all too easy and now we're committed. The endorsing trade agreement is only a formality unless actual chicanery can be proved." He stopped pacing. Lucy stopped too. "You think there's been chicanery?" Lucy stared at him.

"No doubt of it. But can we prove it?" Tom shook his head worriedly. "That message just told me there's been a sudden drop in the value of Wockii futures on the Interstellar Exchange. In one hour their value dropped fifteen points below the computer-predicted minimum level for the next thousand years. A bad 'wobble' as the Exchange dealers put it."

"Then you mustn't make the trade agreement. That's all," said Lucy firmly.

"I can't avoid it without reason." Tom paused to glance at a screen across the room, which showed a wide expanse of concrete landing pad and a battalion of what looked like six foot tall praying mantises armed and standing strictly at attention. "We're almost down. There's the Skikana honor guard drawn up to greet us. From now on be careful what you say. Even a mountaintop ten miles away has ears. Only in our ambassadorial quarters—"

The landing bell of the ship rang suddenly through all the rooms, followed by the distant thrumming of what seemed like harp music.

"What's that?" cried Lucy.

"The Skikana battle harps," said Tom. "You'll see them when we go out. They vibrate so powerfully they can be heard right through the hull of the ship. Come on now. We get off first. Protocol—Corporal!"

"Sir!" shouted the Hugwo corporal, springing to life. He rapped out orders in Hugwo and the lance-gunners formed up behind Tom and Lucy and they all marched out of the suite, down the ship's corridor and out through the airlock.

"Be sure not to squint," hissed Tom at Lucy in English as they went. "We're stepping out of the lock into pretty bright sunlight, now. And Skikanas are extremely touchy and proud. They take offense at the slightest provocation."

They marched out and down the landing ramp, Lucy trying valiantly not to squint in spite of the sunlight that made the whole scene waver through a film of tears. They halted, their heads ringing with the powerful vibrations of the Skikana battle harps, great seven-foot triangular, metal-stringed affairs, each resting on a spike driven deep into the very concrete itself.

". . . And may I also present my consort, the Consort Lucy, Colonel?" Lucy heard Tom saying. She cleared her vision in time to see a six-foot high praying mantis shape leaning stiffly over her.

"H-Honored to meet you, sir," she managed in the sibilant Skikana tongue she and Tom had picked up on the way here.

"Madame!" snapped the Skikana colonel, with a frosty bow. "May you dine on your worst enemy by sundown!"

"Oh, thank you!" said Lucy. "May you dine on yours even sooner than that!" To her surprise she saw Tom frown.

"Madame!" stiffening, the colonel clashed his jaws together almost spasmodically. Oddly, a little froth appeared on them. "I would not presume! We Skikana take no advantages and need none. To dine before the consort of my guest. Skikana manners would not permit!"

"Oh, I didn't mean—" Lucy was beginning. But Tom, with diplomatic smoothness, was already stepping into the breach.

"Happily," he said, "I may inform the colonel that my consort has already broken her fast, this day."

"May I be the first to congratulate her, then!" said the colonel, relaxing. He relaxed, in fact, quite noticeably, and his gaze came unfocused. He pulled himself together with a jerk and clashed his jaws spasmodically. "Follow me. I will escort you to your quarters."

He led them and their Hugwos on to a waiting flying platform which took off just as the battle harps struck up again.

II

"Oh, my!" said Lucy in English, rubbing her ears when they were safely alone in their ambassadorial suite at the Skikana fort. "What was that they were playing?"

"None Shall Interrupt Our Feast," replied Tom. "Hmmm. Did you notice anything odd about the colonel?"

"I couldn't tell," said Lucy, truthfully. "Everything he did and said seemed odd to me. Why were you humming?"

"That song," said Tom, thoughtfully. "The Skikana are so touchy they're liable to give themselves away with anything they do. Something is definitely rotten about the whole business of Wockii futures. If there was only some way to get out of it—"

"But can't we do that? Just write off our losses?" asked Lucy.

"It would break us," said Tom, solemnly. "Our human worlds would be mortgaged and our future generations placed under a crushing load of financial obligation. If the Wockii futures turn out to be worthless we won't be able to use them as security to meet our commitments while we wait a thousand years for the Wockii to reach a civilized level and begin paying off in export-import agreements with us."

He frowned. "What puzzles me," he said, "is the Skikana. By taking protectorate rights over the Wockii they gave up their right to any direct interest in Wockii futures. So they shouldn't care one way or another about the matter—but obviously they're mixed up in it somehow."

"Can't you get them to give themselves away, somehow?" asked Lucy. "Betray themselves, I mean?"

"A very good idea," said Tom, thoughtfully.

He stepped across the room to a communications screen, and pressed the buttons at its base. A second later the face of the Skikana colonel appeared on the screen.

"Sir Ambassador!" said the colonel and champed his jaws. "In what way may I serve you?"

"You may supply me with an escort, my dear Colonel," said Tom. "I, with my Hugwos and the Consort Lucy will start for Wockiiland, immediately."

The colonel stared out of the screen blankly at him for a moment.

"But Sir Ambassador," the Skikana said, "it has been arranged for the Wockii chiefs to come to the fort, here."

"No doubt. However," said Tom, with diplomatic steeliness in his tones, "I have concluded that it is of

the utmost importance for me to contact—" he bent
a severe glance upon the colonel in the screen "—the
dominant race of Mul'Rahr, immediately."

"Sir!" The colonel's jaws champed. "A banquet has
been ordered."

"We shall appear at the banquet, but leave immediately afterwards. Good day," said Tom, and cut the
connection.

Immediately afterwards, however, he activated the
screen again, this time with a view outside the fort
gate looking backwards into the wooded hills of the
wild native countryside, toward Wockiiland.

"What are you looking for?" asked Lucy, after a
moment.

"Watch. Wait," said Tom, without turning his head.
Lucy watched. After a moment or two, a platoon of
Skikana soldiers, mounted on individual flying platforms, left the gate and skimmed with haste toward
the hills.

"The pot," said Tom to Lucy, "is starting to boil.
Clearly for some reason the Skikana want to warn the
Wockii's against my coming. Why? There must be
something in Wockiiland they don't want me to see."

The doors to their quarters gave forth a mellow
chime, interrupting him. A second later the Hugwo
corporal returned from answering it leading a Skikana
captain of Regulars, lean and hard-bitten, but just at
the moment with unfocused eyes.

"Bells . . ." murmured the captain, dazedly.

"Sir!" shouted the Hugwo corporal to Tom, and
the captain came to. "Visitor to speak with the ambassador, sir!"

He saluted and stepped back. The captain bowed
to Tom and Lucy.

"Sir," he said. "I am Captain Jabat of the 8th

Skikana here at Fort Duhnderhef. Possibly you notice the medals on my prothorax?"

"Indeed," said Tom, his eyes narrowing.

"They are poor things, no doubt, in the eyes of an
Assassin," said Jabat, bowing gracefully. "Nevertheless, I must confess to a nodule of pride in the medal
on the far right. You see it there?"

"Ah, yes," said Tom.

"I received it," went on Jabat, "on winning the
championship of the quick-draw-kill-and-devour, of
the Skikana handgun competition at the last All-
Skikana Worlds Games. As an Assassin, of course
you are familiar with the Skikana handgunning art?"

"Of course," said Tom.

"Then, for the pride of the 8th Skikana here at
the fort," said Jabut, "may I ask you to accept this
small offering?"

He produced a tiny gold whistle from his weapons
harness and blew it. A Skikana enlisted soldier
marched in bearing a silver dish with a cover which
he placed on a small table at Tom's right.

Bowing, both Skikanan withdrew.

"They didn't waste any time," said Tom, as the
door closed behind the two. He gazed with slitted
eyes at the dish. "Devilishly subtle, these Skikana."

"What did he give you?" inquired Lucy, lifting the
cover of the dish. "Oh—"

"Don't touch it!" said Tom, quickly.

Lucy had revealed a beautiful competition model
Skikana handgun. "If a human hand touches it, a
signal will go off on the 8th Skikana bulletin board,
and I'll have accepted the challenge."

"Challenge?" Lucy jerked her hand back from the
gun. "Tom! And he's champion! They're trying to kill
you!"

"Nothing so crude, unfortunately," said Tom. "What

they must be planning is to discredit me. As an Assassin, they expect me to make short work of Jabat in the duel. However, having killed him, I must finish off the matter by ceremoniously eating every bit of him. It's the final tribute to a fallen foe, according to the Skikana code duello. They've undoubtedly checked up and found that we humans haven't the incredible Skikana capacity for food—even if Skikana were edible by human standards."

He looked thoughtful.

"If I refuse to eat him," Tom said, "they undoubtedly plan a protest that will get me removed as ambassador. And no other human has my qualifications to see through what's going on here."

"Don't kill him, then," urged Lucy. "Just—just scratch him."

"I'm not sure I can," said Tom, solemnly. "You forget. I've had the briefing, but I lack the years of intensive physical training that makes an Assassin. The Skikana don't know it, but their champion can almost undoubtedly take me. I'll be dead before I can clear the handgun from its clip on my harness."

"Tom!" Lucy's face was horrified. "Don't you fight him! Don't you fight him at all!"

"An Assassin back away from a challenge? Impossible," said Tom. "The Assassin's Guild themselves would eliminate me if I did such a thing."

"Can't you just tell him, some other time?" Lucy almost wrung her hands. "Be polite, but firm?"

"No," said Tom, sadly. "After all, whole armies have been known to mutiny and refuse to advance when they heard that a single Assassin barred their path." He sighed, heavily. "Well, maybe I can think of something. We better get going to the banquet."

III

Surrounded by their Hugwos, they left the suite, and were guided by an officer posted outside their door down a corridor and into a vast, hall-like room with a lofty, raftered roof and no windows except narrow slits up near the rafters at the top of the walls. These windows were set ajar, however, to the warm, sunset air of Mul'Rahr. Inside the hall great ceremonial torches eight feet tall flared and danced their flames above the long tables at which the Skikana officers sat. Wide circular platters of polished wood sat before each diner or empty chair. And enormous toadstools like logs of wood gave up a savory smell like roast beef as they lay at length on the tables between rows of plates.

The Hugwo corporal conducted Tom and Lucy to seats at the left of the Skikana colonel.

"You have met our brave Captain Jabat?" inquired the colonel, as soon as the two humans were seated.

"I have indeed," replied Tom.

"Even among we Skikana his courage is proverbial," said the colonel. "He . . ." his gaze wandered and his voice trailed off.

"Colonel!" prompted Lucy, kindheartedly.

The colonel started, forked a bite of toadstool into his mouth, gulped it down and came alert again. ". . . Ah, yes," he said significantly, looking at Tom. "It is courage not even to be despised by an . . . Assassin, shall we say?" Lucy caught her breath.

"We shall, to be sure," said Tom smoothly. "But work before pleasure, my dear Colonel. The Wockii concern me at the moment."

The colonel inclined his head and signaled to a Skikana enlisted soldier, who stepped forward to carve slices from the nearest huge toadstool. He served the slices on the platters before Tom and Lucy. Lucy sniffed obtrusively at hers. The aroma was delicious.

"Is it safe for us to eat?" she whispered in English to Tom.

"I'll check," whispered back Tom. The colonel's attention was momentarily devoted to finishing his own slice and ordering another with typical Skikana voracity. Tom produced a small handbook and thumbed through it. "Let see . . . *'Mul'Rahr . . . toadstooloids of, large . . . Agarica Mul'Rahrens is Gigantica, page one hundred and forty-three . . .'* Here it is . . . *'See Rhu, page one-thirty-eight'* . . ." he flipped paged. *" 'Rhu, a wide-spread root system often extending over miles underground, putting forth root and tube-rose projections of many varieties and types'* . . ." Tom's voice trailed off. "Hmm . . ." he muttered, "interesting . . ."

"But can we eat it?" demanded Lucy.

"Oh!" Tom started, almost after the fashion of the colonel. "Yes, I think so . . . *'edible for the following races . . . Adjarts, Allahns, . . . uh, Hssoids, Hytszs . . .'* Yes, here we are . . . *'Humans'.*"

"Oh, good," said Lucy, "it smells so appetizing—"

A twang from high above interrupted her, followed by an approaching high-pitched drone and ending in a thud. A small black arrow quivered in the center of Lucy's slice of toadstooloid, pinning it to the wooden platter. Shocked silence filled the hall and all eyes turned upward to discover a three-foot high, faunlike figure covered with white woolly hair and with a lamb like face. This figure stood perched on one of the rafters by an open window, now reslinging a small bow over its shoulder and drawing an eighteen-inch sword.

"What—what is it?" gasped Lucy, unthinkingly, in English.

"A Flal," answered Tom swiftly in the same language. "supposed to be one of the semi-intelligent local life forms—"

The rest of his sentence was drowned out by a bellow.

"A Flal!" the colonel was roaring, starting to his feet and tugging at the ceremonial sword that was the only weapon the Skikana officers had worn to the banquet. "Get it down from there! Get it down, I say!"

With a sudden, fantastic leap, the Flal left the rafter high overhead and landed on the table before the colonel. In a twinkling, the Flal's midget sword was menacing the colonel's prothorax and an imperious whistle burst from the Flal's lamblike lips.

"Cut it down! That's an order," thundered the colonel to his officers. "Never mind me!" But the officers hesitated.

Taking advantage of this hesitation, the Flal turned and directed a stream of angry, musical whistling at Tom, gesturing with its free hand at the nearest toadstooloid. Then the Skikana officers dashed forward and the Flal, releasing the colonel, dodged away, ducking into the sea of three-foot long, flashing Skikana swords, twisting, swivel-hipping and dancing on black hooves as his own tiny blade, glittering with a speed of reflex the Skikana could not match, fenced a way for him to the nearest torch stand.

A leap carried him to the top of the stand. From there, disdainful of the licking flame, another leap carried him to crenellations in the wall and from there to a rafter leading to an open window. At the window he turned about, and, whipping a miniature hunting horn from his belt, he paused to blow a blast like some small, elfin bronx cheer at those below. The Skikana soldiers howled in baffled fury, waving their weapons. Then the Flal had ducked through the window and was gone.

"Sir Ambassador! Consort Lucy!" said the colonel, gnashing his jaws but sheathing his sword and getting himself back under control—he paused to gulp a half-slice of toadstooloid—"please be seated. Forgive this minor interruption. These local life forms—mere semi-intelligent animals—not even a language, just whistle to show their emotional state—please put it out of your mind. My soldiers will see that the banquet is not interrupted again."

"That won't be necessary, Colonel," said Tom. "I promised only to put in an appearance at this banquet and I consider that promise fulfilled now. I, my consort, and my Hugwos will make use of that escort I asked you for, to leave for Wockiiland immediately."

"Of—of course!" said the colonel, getting himself under control. "If you wish it, sir Ambassador. The escort is provided. However—" he hesitated. "I cannot permit the Consort Lucy to risk a night journey through the Mul'Rahrian wilds. You and the Hugwos, of course, but—"

"Sir!" Tom's voice snapped him off in mid-speech. "Are you presuming to tell me where to take my consort?"

"I have my duty," said the colonel stiffly, "as local commander to protect civilians—"

"May I remind the colonel?" Tom's words cut like a knife. Lucy looked at him in admiration. "That the Consort Lucy will have an Assassin to escort her?"

"Sir!" said the colonel, stiffening in his turn. "Am I to infer a lack of trust in my soldiers and myself?"

"Certainly not," said Tom, without hesitation, and Lucy beamed at him for his quick thinking. It was perfectly clear that if Tom had expressed a lack of trust in the Skikana, the colonel would have had grounds for a protest to get Tom removed as ambassador. "I trust you and your officers and men implicitly, Colonel. It is the Consort Lucy I don't trust."

Lucy gasped.

"You don't—" the colonel's naturally bulging eyes seemed to bulge farther, "—trust your consort, sir Ambassador?"

"Not out of my sight for a moment," said Tom, firmly. "A purely human situation, Colonel. I'm sure you wouldn't be interested in the details. And now, the escort?"

"It's already waiting for you at the west gate," said the colonel, stiffly. Gnashing his jaws in defeat, he stepped back and allowed them both to proceed by him followed by their Hugwos.

IV

Fifteen minutes later, they floated westward on flying platforms over the rolling semi-wooded landscape of Mul'Rahr under the enormous single moon that made the night seem almost as bright as day. Tom and Lucy were sharing a platform, with their faithful Hugwos riding individual platforms before and behind them. Beyond and behind the Hugwos were half a dozen platform mounted soldiers of the Skikana escort, none of whom seemed close enough to be in earshot. Tom lowered his voice and spoke to Lucy in English.

"Lucy—" he began.

"Don't speak to me," said Lucy, staring off in the opposite direction at the shadowy woods. "Do not speak to me! I would appreciate it!"

"Now Lucy—" said Tom.

"If you please," said Lucy. "There is nothing for us to discuss. Nothing at all."

"Don't you understand?" pleaded Tom. "The colonel wanted you as a hostage. I couldn't leave you in his hands. I had to say the first thing that came into my head!"

"No doubt," said Lucy. "It was very clever of you. Curious, is it not, though, that you should make use of the fact that I am untrustworthy? I do not wish to make a point of this," went on Lucy in syllables resembling splinters of jagged ice. "It merely crossed my mind. In passing, so to speak."

"Lucy, I do trust you. You know I do!"

"How bright the moonlight is upon this world," said Lucy, splintering a little more ice.

They rode in silence for the following forty minutes or so, at the end of which Tom tried again.

"Lucy—" he began. He broke off suddenly as he caught sight of the officer in charge of their escort whipping his flying platform about and zipping back toward the one Tom and Lucy occupied. "Yes, Captain?" asked Tom, as the officer swung about and flew alongside.

It was Captain Jabat. The moonlight glittered in his black eyes in what Lucy, at least, could not help but feel was a very sinister fashion.

"Sir," said the captain to Tom. "We approach the Wockii chiefs now. We should meet them in the next few seconds."

"Excellent. Tell me, Captain," said Tom, thoughtfully. "Just as a matter of interest, was it a case of your original Skikana scoutship seeking out the Wockii, when they discovered Mul'Rahr? Or did the Wockii come forth on their own initiative to make friends with the scoutship?"

"The Wockii came forth on their own, sir," said Jabat. "We consider it a tribute to our Skikana approachability, and honor. The Skikana honor is without stain. None may accuse us of being merciful in victory or resentful in defeat."

"To be sure," said Tom. "However, aside from that—would you tell me if the Wockii are a particularly truthful race?"

"Hardly, my dear sir," Jabat gave the low rasp of Skikana laughter. "We have a little saying at Fort Duhnderhef. *The only Wockii that don't lie are the dead Wockii, and even they lie about being dead.*" Jabat rasped again. "You follow the joke, sir Ambassador and Consort Lucy? See, the Wockii lie when they're alive, and when they're flat on the ground, dead."

"Very humorous, Captain," interrupted Tom. "Very humorous indeed. But isn't that the Wockii chiefs I see approaching now?"

Jabat turned and looked up toward the head of the column.

"You are right, sir Ambassador," he said. And, whipping his platform about, he shot off to meet the group that was approaching on foot in the moonlight.

In a moment the two parties had come together. The Wockii stood about nine feet high. They looked something like enormous badgers with curved short tusks. They wore heavy, six-foot cutlasses but nothing else except ribbons tied about their tusks.

"Sir Assassin," said the Captain Jabat, presenting these hulking figures to the platform on which Tom and Lucy rode, "and Consort Lucy, may I introduce Hlugar, Chief of Chiefs for the Wockii."

Captain Jabat had spoken in Wockii, which Tom and Lucy had also learned by briefing machine on the way to Mul'Rahr, as they had learned the Skikana tongue.

"All hail, Hlugar!" said Tom, in Wockii.

"All hail, foreigner!" grunted Hlugar in a deep bass voice that seemed to shake the bones of the two humans. "Welcome to Wockiiland. My burrow is your burrow."

"And my burrow is your burrow. Let us go feast this happy occasion." In a shrewd tone of voice he added, much to Lucy's astonishment, "What shall we feast on? Perhaps—some roasted Flals?"

Hlugar's bass bellow split the moonlight of the Mul'Rahrian night.

"Never!" he roared, dropping on all fours and beginning to dig frantically in the dirt before him. "Never eat Flals! Never, you hear?" He thrust his tusked muzzle down into the hole he had dug, roaring muffedly—*"Never!"*

"Sir—" began Jabat, in an outburst of indignation. But before he could continue, sudden bedlam broke loose.

Shrill whistles sounded from the tree shadows on all sides of them. Small black arrows began to drone among them. The booming bellows of the Wockii mingled with the harsh battle commands of the Skikana.

There was a swirl of motion and little faunlike, hooved figures with gleaming swords were all about them. Before Tom and Lucy could move, something like heavy cloths fell over their heads. They felt themselves picked up and carried off at a run.

It was useless to struggle. They were carried for some distance and gradually Lucy felt her senses slipping away from her. The cloth or whatever heavy material it was that was wrapped around her seemed to give off a pleasant, faint perfume with an anesthetic effect. She roused herself to struggle against it, but it was too late. She drifted off into unconsciousness.

When she opened her eyes again, she was lying on the slope of a pleasant, grassy hillside. Dawn had just broken and the bright yellow sun of Mul'Rahr was rising in the blue sky directly ahead of her. A little distance off stood Tom, facing some armed Flals. Surprisingly, only a dozen feet or so away, the faithful Hugwos stood at attention, lance-guns in hand.

". . . It's no use," Lucy heard Tom saying to the Flals. "I can't understand a meaning-symbol you whistle." He was speaking in Wockii, Lucy noted drowsily. She remembered that she was mad at him for some reason, but she felt so pleasant that she could not at the moment recall what she was supposed to be mad at him about.

"Tom!" she cried faintly, trying to sit up. Tom turned, saw her stirring and hurried over.

"I didn't know you were awake," he said, helping her to her feet. "You feel fine, don't you?"

"As a matter of fact, yes," said Lucy, bewildered. "I do." She got to her feet. "But what—"

"That was the veil, or under-membrane of the Rhu toadstooloid—*Agarica Mul'Rahrensis Gigantica*, the one they served us for dinner at the fort," said Tom. "It appears to have slight narcotic as well as excellent analgesic and transquilizing properties. But never mind that now. I'm finally beginning to get the general picture of the situation here on Mul'Rahr, and it's more desperate than I thought. Ordinarily as the consort of an ambassador, you'd be safe trusting in the Skikana sense of honor. But the Skikana here on Mul'Rahr, as I suspected when the colonel tried to hold you back as a hostage, are no longer to be trusted. They're planning actual genocide—but there's no time to go into that now. Do you have your consort's credentials with you?"

"Of course," said Lucy, surprised, reaching down into the small belt-purse of her dress. "You told me never to go anywhere without them. I keep them right in—yes, here they are."

"Good!" said Tom, plucking the papers out of her fingers. He whipped a stylus out of its holster on his weapons harness and scribbled rapidly on the margin of the topmost paper. He folded the papers and thrust them back at Lucy. "Put those back into your purse, there—" Lucy obeyed, as he went on. "If you hear that anything's happened to me, you contact the nearest representative of the Assassin's Guild and show them what I've written. And—"

"Happen to you!" cried Lucy, her fingers freezing on the snap of the purse, which she had just reclosed. "What do you mean happen to you? What do you mean if I *hear*—"

"I'm sending you directly back to the landing field and the spaceship we came in on," said Tom. "Now don't argue—"

"I won't argue!" burst out Lucy. "I just won't go! You can't make me! I'm not going to leave you!"

"Yes, you are," said Tom, urgently. "The Hugwos will see you safely back to the landing field."

A sharp whistle from the group of Flals interrupted him. He looked over at the small hooved figures and groaned.

"Too late," he said. "I'll just have to hope that the Skikana have enough sense left to spare you when they attack. Come along, I've got to get back to these Flals."

"But attack? Why should the Skikana attack?" asked Lucy, bewilderedly, following him back toward the Flals.

"Because this spot here is the place the Skikana have been searching for ever since they discovered the Wockii had lied to them about being the dominant intelligent race on Mul'Rahr. For the same reason the Flals kidnapped us and brought us here to help them."

"But why do you have to be the one to help them?" wailed Lucy. "Why can't you leave? Then I'd go with you."

"For me," said Tom, solemnly. "There's no choice. The galaxy knows that no Assassin could ever be kidnapped without his permitting it. You can't kidnap an Assassin. Kill one, yes, if you have sufficient battle-hardened troops and mobile armor. The only conclusion that can be drawn is that I allowed myself to be kidnapped by the Flals out of cowardice, in an attempt to avoid facing up to Jabat's challenge—unless I can get to the bottom of things here and clear myself by showing what I was really trying to do."

"But . . . but, I don't understand—"

Lucy broke off helplessly, staring at him as they stopped before the small group of Flals. Those small individuals were now looking up at Tom and Lucy inquiringly. Their little pink noses, furry faces, and kindly brown eyes were lit up by the golden rays of the rising sun.

"I'm not completely sure I do, either," said Tom. "I'm using my para-instincts and playing by ear as I go. These Flals have a high nobility-of-character index. My para-instincts assure me of that. But since their language, and they really do have one, is musico-emotional in base, I can't understand the explanations they've been trying to give me. It's as if they see the universe around them in terms of varying degrees of right or wrong and define those degrees in musical terms to make up their language."

"Oh," said Lucy, looking at them with a softening glance, and remembering the single Flal in the banquet hall fighting off all the Skikana officers. "And they're such brave little beings, too."

"That's true, they are. And," said Tom, "because of their natures, able to read the characters of others at a glance. They were able to sense, as a result, right from the start that we and the Hugwos are honorable. Just as they sensed from the beginning that the Skikana are cruel and rapacious; and they've always known, of course, that the Wockii were brutal and greedy."

"But if they want you to help them, but can't tell you—" Lucy was beginning, when a whistle from the closest Flal interrupted her. Tom turned to the Flal and whistled the first few bars of Mendelssohn's *Wedding March*. The Flal turned to Lucy and bowed politely.

"Why!" cried Lucy, delighted. "You can, too, talk to them!"

"Only after a fashion," answered Tom. "I was trying to tell him that you're my wife. Of course they've always said music was the universal language. But that's an oversimplification. In this case the concept of 'wife' probably missed him completely, in spite of the fact that the Flals, like us are bi-sexual. What he probably got were just some of the emotional overtones of our relationship."

"But you could work out a language from that sort of thing, couldn't you?" inquired Lucy.

"In time. But time is just what we don't have—" A silvery Flal horn sounded off among the giant toadstooloids and the trees at the base of the slope they stood on. A second later, another sounded from the far side of the hill. "There come the Wockii and the Skikana. Just as I'd hoped."

"Just as you'd hoped?" Lucy stared at him.

"Yes," said Tom. "I particularly need those Skikana battle harps." He turned to the Flals and made pounding motions in the air with his fist. "Try the drum again," he said in Wockii.

The group parted and just beyond them Lucy saw what seemed to be a drum mounted on a stake driven down into the earth. Two Flals began to beat the drum vigorously. It did not sound so loud in the air, but Lucy could feel the vibration of it through the ground at her feet. A sudden new chorus of whistles broke out below the slope. They all turned around and saw the first line of armed Skikana infantry march into view and pause at the foot of the slope. Mixed in among them were heavy Wockii figures carrying their mighty cutlasses in hairy fists. The Flals drew their swords.

A strange sound vibrated all about the scene.

"What was that?" cried Lucy. "It sounded like a yawn!"

But Tom's attention was directed down the hill towards the Skikana battle harpsmen, who were emerging from the trees in front of the troops and driving the supporting spikes of their harps into the earth so that the harps stood upright, ready to play. The Skikana colonel emerged into view, with Captain Jabat marching correctly at his left and half a pace to his rear. Together and alone, they marched up the hill toward Tom, Lucy and the Flal leaders. Halfway up the slope the colonel said something to Jabat, who stopped and held his position midway there between the forces of the Wockii and the Skikana.

He came on up the slope and halted before Tom.

V

"Sir!" he said stiffly. He stood for a second, champing his jaws a little uncertainly as if he was having trouble remembering what he was going to say. "I must ask you to use your influence with these Flals to cause them to surrender themselves so that we may dig up this area to discover goods reported stolen from our fort. Do not think of resistance, please. Your case is hope—What was that?"

"Another yawn," said Lucy.

"Nonsense!" snapped the colonel, sharply. Then, getting his voice under control, he gave a curt bow of apology in Lucy's direction. "—As I was saying, resistance would be useless. Your position on this slope is hopeless."

"Permit me," said Tom, "to disagree with you, sir. The Flals, as your Skikana have cause to know, are not unworthy fighters in spite of their small size. All the galaxy knows the reputation of the Hugwo lance-gunners. And, last but not least, I am myself an Assassin."

"True," said the colonel, champing his jaws convulsively once more. "However, I must inform you that your recent actions in allowing yourself to be kidnapped by these Flals, here, have cast some grave doubts in our mind on your status as a true Assassin. No doubt they are groundless—"

"No doubt," said Tom. "And no doubt I am mistaken in my conjecture that the supply of unharvested toadstooloid is rapidly approaching the vanishing point?"

The colonel staggered visibly, but pulled himself erect once more.

"There's plenty of toadstooloid!" he snapped.

"Plenty," said Tom in steely tones, "for the native Flal and Wockii populations. After all the ecology was balanced that way. But not enough for these and a regiment of Skikana soldiery, when each soldier was capable of eating his own weight or more of food at a sitting. And moreover, once the effect of the toadstooloid upon the Skikana eaters became known—"

"Stop!" shouted the colonel. "Assassin or not, I warn you. There are some secrets not meant to be uncovered."

"The secret," said Tom, unflinchingly, "has already been uncovered. It began when whoever was fronting for you Skikana in the purchase of Wockii futures realized that those futures were worthless and made them available on such attractive terms that my human government snapped them up. This forced you to a situation where you had to seek out the true dominant intelligence of Mul'Rahr and destroy it."

"Not true!" snapped the colonel, frothing slightly at the jaws. "A pack of lies! The Flals are not intelligent! And no normal civilized race would dare the crime of genocide, even if—"

"The Flals are intelligent," said Tom, relentlessly. "You found out the Wockii had lied to you about that shortly after you established your administration here on Mul'Rahr."

"Lies!" roared the colonel. "If that were true, we'd have made an agreement with the Flals at once, rather than risk prosecution as a race violating Interstellar agreement. Why didn't we?"

"For the same reason," said Tom, "that you Skikana stationed here could contemplate the crime of genocide. You were not normal any longer. You—"

"Stop!" champed the colonel.

"No," said Tom. "It's too late to hide the truth. *Agarica Mul'Rahrensis Gigantica*, or the local edible giant toadstooloid on which you, like the Wockii and the Flals, have been feeding is not dissimilar to the *Agaricus muscarius*, or fly agaric, one of the poisonous mushrooms of my own world." Lucy gasped, but Tom went on without paying any attention to her. "*Mul'Rahrensis* produces a derivative of the alkaloid muscarine. Which, however, acts not so much as a poison but as a narcotic, a tranquilizer and a euphoric. Taken in the small amounts of toadstooloid, a Flal, or even a Wockii individual, is capable of consuming at one time, the toadstooloid is merely a mild and harmless intoxicating food—"

"Stop!" said the colonel, his voice cracking in a very un-Skikanalike way.

"But," continued Tom relentlessly, "taken in the enormous quantities in which the smallest Skikana soldier can consume at a sitting, the toadstooloid become becomes a powerful, habit-forming drug. A drug that the addict will go to any lengths to obtain and which no intelligent, civilized being would allow another intelligent being to consume—"

"Very well," said the colonel. He had pulled himself together, and there was something almost sad in his voice. "You would not let me stop you. Now you've sealed your own fate." He turned and bowed to Lucy. "I regret, Consort Lucy," he said, "that you must be included with the rest. No human, Hugwo or Flal must leave this spot alive." He looked back sadly at Tom. "Didn't you realize that addicted soldiers like my troops would stop at nothing once our secret was out? Death means nothing to us, compared to being cut off from our toadstooloid supply. You are doomed once I give the word for the battle harps to sound the attack."

"Not at all," said Tom. "Sound them, and find out."

The colonel stared at him.

"Sir!" he said. "You *wish* me to sound the battle harps for the attack upon you?"

"T-Tom . . ." began Lucy, timidly. "After all—"

"Quiet, Lucy!" said Tom. "I know what I'm doing.

Go ahead!" he snapped at the colonel. "Sound the
harps. I *defy you!*"

"Defy me?" In a sudden typical, towering Skikana
rage, the colonel spun about and shouted down the
hill to Captain Jabat. "Sound the Harps! Prepare to
advance!"

Up on the slope they all saw the captain salute and
turn. His voice floated faintly back to them as he
shouted down to the battle harpsmen of the Skikana.

"Sound the Prepare to Advance!" they heard him
call. "*Shortly We Shall Eat You. Now!*"

The battle harps broke suddenly into their air-
rending, ground-shaking melody. The colonel spun
back and shouted thinly above their unbelievable
harmonies.

"You've asked for it!" he cried. "No quarter! No
prisoners and no—"

His voice caught in his throat. The ground had
suddenly heaved up alongside him and the cap of a
toadstooloid six feet across poked itself above ground.
Abruptly it split apart into two enormous lips and the
aperture between them inhaled with a gust that almost sucked them all off their feet.

"What's going on up here?" boomed forth a voice
from the lips in accentless Wockii, and with such
volume that it overrode even the harp music. Down-
slope the amazed and aghast harpsmen fell into jan-
gling discordancies and thence into silence. In the
quiet that followed a smaller toadstooloid poked itself
above ground, grew upwards suddenly to about ten
feet in height of stalk, and bent its cap toward the
colonel. The surface of the cap drew back to reveal
half a dozen large eyes. "Who're you?"

"Colonel, commanding . . . 8th Skikana . . ." mumbled the colonel, obviously badly shaken but trying
valiantly to pull himself up in military fashion. The
toadstooloid with the eyes swiveled toward Tom and

Lucy, twisted toward the Hugwos, turned toward the Flals and at last looked down toward the distant ranks of the Wockii and the Skikana.

"I am the Prar'Rhu—or Pro-to-Rhu of the Rhu root system here on Mal'Rahr, as you strangers would doubtless put it," announced the toadstooloid lips boomingly. "Children, children! Can't I take even a little nine thousand year nap without your getting into trouble? What is it this time?"

One of the Flals stepped forward and began to whistle rapidly, gesturing at the Wockii and the colonel. The eyed toadstooloid, which had been watching the Flal, swiveled again toward the distant Wockii.

"For shame!" boomed the enormous lips. The Wockii all immediately prostrated themselves. Tom stepped forward to the toadstooloid with the eyes.

"Excuse me," he said, "but might I inquire of you what the relation happens to be—of mass to energy?"

"Not at all. A simple question!" boomed the toadstooloid. "As anyone who has devoted even a few millenia of thought to the question must realize at once, $e = mc^2$. Or, energy equals mass times the constant, squared—in the present and immediate universe only, of course. I assume you were asking about the relation as it exists merely in the present and immediate universe?"

"I was," said Tom.

"Excellent," boomed the Prar'Rhu. "Because the relationship becomes somewhat more complicated when we consider an infinite series of parallel universes in an enfolded hyperspace. Are you planning to make use of the relationship in immediate, practical nuclear terms, may I ask? Because, if so, I should perhaps warn you of certain explosive results . . ."

"No," said Tom. "I asked the question only as a preliminary to introducing you to myself and to a whole galaxy of different, intelligent and educated races capable of conversing with you on a civilized level."

"A whole . . ." the lips broke off, trembling slightly with emotion. "You say, intelligent, educated races capable of conversing . . ." The Prar'Rhu was clearly unable to continue. Its half-dozen eyes on the taller toadstooloid blinked rapidly.

"I mean just that," said Tom, sympathetically. "Your hundreds of thousands of years of loneliness are over. No longer will you need to take ten-thousand-year naps to escape unbearable and sanity-threatening boredom. No more will you be forced to exist only in the society of your intellectual inferiors. At last you will be able to communicate with minds the equal in capacity and accumulated wisdom with your own—"

"*Never!*" screamed the Skikana colonel, frothing at the jaws. He turned around and roared down the slope at Jabat. "Never mind the Prepare to Advance! Never mind the Advance! Sound the Charge! *Now!*"

Jabat wheeled about to repeat the order.

"You shall not!" thundered the toadstooloid lips. And barely had the thunder of that voice died away on the surrounding slopes and hills when hundreds of thousands of little purple puffballs began to sprout around the feet of the Skikana soldiery and an enticing, spicy fragrance filled the air.

With wild cries, the Skikana soldiers threw aside their harps and weapons and fell upon the purple puffballs, cramming them into their jaws and passing quickly into a foolishly grinning stupor.

"No!" cried the colonel, staggering, torn between his military pride and the odor of the puffballs that had sprouted at his feet. "Get up . . . Charge! Get up, I say!" He was almost weeping. "Get up and fi . . ." The scent of the puffballs overcame him. He collapsed on the ground and tore into those within arm's reach like a starving man.

VI

"But what's going to happen to the Skikana soldiers now?" asked Lucy, as they strolled from the edge of the concrete landing pad out toward their spaceship, some six hours later. The Skikana soldiery, including the officers and the colonel, had escorted them back to the fort, marching as if hypotized by the orders of the Prar'Rhu. "They're addicted to the toadstooloid, now, and—"

"No more," said Tom. "When I was in the fort just now, I found that the fort kitchens had, of course, whipped up a large meal of toadstooloid, as was customary for the returning troops. However, to a soldier, the Skikana turned their heads away weakly and couldn't stand the sight of the food. They ate imported Skikana battle rations instead."

"The Prar'Rhu put something in the little purple puffballs to cure them?" asked Lucy. She peered ahead. In the brilliant sunlight the shadow at the base of the spaceship was almost too dark to see into, but she thought she saw several Skikana figures waiting by the airlock ramp.

"Yes. The colonel realized that," said Tom. "That's why he asked to see me before we left. He offered to make a clean breast of the facts here for Interstellar publication, if I would help explain to Interstellar Court that the original addiction wasn't the fault of the Skikana—which it wasn't. Actually, it was an accident having to do with the Skikana capacity for food—what's the matter?"

"Tom!" Lucy clutched at his arm. "Isn't that Captain Jabat and a couple of other Skikana officers waiting for us at the ship?"

"What? Oh, yes," said Tom. "I was expecting him."
He called ahead in Skikana. "Good afternoon, Captain!"

"Good afternoon, sir Ambassador!" replied Jabat,
stiffly as Tom and Lucy came up into the shadow at
the foot of the ship. "I believe that before you leave
we have some little matter to discuss."

Lucy's heart sank. Abruptly, she remembered the
competition model Skikana handgun which had been
brought to Tom in the fort, earlier.

"Ah, yes," Tom was saying easily. "Do you have it
with you?"

"Right here, sir!" said Jabat. Another Skikana officer stepped forward with the dish containing the
handgun. The handgun's twin, Lucy saw, was clipped
to Jabat's harness, waiting.

"Tom!" she cried urgently in English. "Don't touch
it!"

"Certainly, my dear," said Tom in Skikana, as if
she had merely been encouraging him. "It will be a
pleasure to encounter the prospect of being handgunned and devoured by such an eminent opponent
as Captain Jabat." In English he added hastily. "Stop
worrying, Lucy! He must be an excellent shot, or he
wouldn't have won that medal!"

Tom took the handgun as Lucy gave vent to a
stifled shriek.

"Don't!" wailed Lucy in English. "Do you think I
want you killed and d-devoured? Even by an excellent shot? Tom, come back!"

Tom was already moving off with Jabat and the
other Skikana to place themselves for the duel. "Tom,
don't you go get yourself handgunned! You said yourself he was bound to be faster on the draw than you
are! What's the matter? Have you gone crazy?"

"Not at all," called Tom, who had now taken up
his position, facing Jabat, and was waiting for the

signal to fire. "It doesn't matter if he can outdraw me if he misses me, does it? Stay there. I'll be right back."

"But you said he was an excellent shot—" the words froze on Lucy's lips as the presiding officer gave the command to fire. Jabat's reflexes were too fast for Lucy's eye to follow. One moment he was standing there. The next, his handgun was in his grasp and a pale lance of fire was driving toward Tom.

It passed some inches above Tom's head. Lucy stared. Tom had not even drawn his own handgun.

"Tom! Shoot!" cried Lucy.

"Certainly not!" he called back in English, annoyedly. "Please, Lucy, be quiet. You're disrupting the order of the occasion with all this talk."

Jabat had not stirred. With the typical unshakable pride and courage of a Skikana, he was standing waiting.

"Sir!" he called to Tom, "I believe you have a return shot coming."

"That is quite correct, Captain," Lucy heard Tom reply through her whirling confusion. "However, I do not believe I will take it at this moment."

It was a physiological impossibility for a Skikana to turn pale. However, it seemed to Lucy that Captain Jabat faded.

"No, sir?" he answered. "May I ask when you do intend to?"

"I'm not sure," replied Tom, idly. "Possibly tomorrow. Possibly a year from now. Possibly not even in our respective lifetimes. In fact, the more I think of it, the more I think I'll probably never be able to get around to it."

"Ah. I see," said Jabat. He raised his handgun and saluted Tom. The other officers did likewise. "It has been an honor to know you, sir Ambassador and Assassin."

"Well, that's finished," said Tom, coming back to Lucy. "Let's get aboard so that the ship can take off." He patted a pocket attached to his weapons harness as he led the way up the ramp, Lucy following wordlessly at his side. "Ah, there you are, sir," he said to the ship's first officer, waiting at the airlock. "My compliments to the captain, and will he take off as soon as possible."

"You men can go to your own quarters," he informed the Hugwos, standing at attention in the suite. "The Consort Lucy and I will be settling down for the return trip." He watched them file out and shut the door behind them. "Loyal fellows," he remarked to Lucy. "But it's simply not good policy to let anyone see where I secrete this agreement.

"You realize how well we've come out of all this?" he asked, turning back to Lucy. "Instead of an exclusive agreement to deal with the Wockii in the future, we're relieved of our obligations to the Wockii, since they weren't the dominant intelligence on Mul'Rahr after all. And we've got an exclusive contract for immediate dealings with the true dominant intelligence, the Prar'Rhu—who is a biochemical synthesist with a skill beyond imagination. Our human economic future is assured in the galaxy—" he broke off.

"Lucy, what's wrong?"

"*You!*" exploded Lucy. Tom took a hasty step backward.

"*You!*" cried Lucy, following him up, and looking as if she was going to kick him. "What do you mean, getting into a duel, when I called and called and pleaded with you not to do it? What do you mean trying to get yourself killed? What if Jabat hadn't missed?"

"But he had to!" protested Tom, retreating. "You

don't understand. The Skikana are proud of their honor being without stain. '—Never merciful in victory, never resentful in defeat . . .' remember what Jabat said? The chance to challenge had been offered. I couldn't leave the planet without duelling him. But good Skikana manners forbade that he should try to kill me after I had defeated them, here on Mul'Rahr. It might have looked like sour grapes. He had very deliberately to avoid trying to kill me in the duel. That's why I refused to shoot back. It would have been murder."

Tom stopped backing up, feeling he had scored a point.

"To say nothing of the fact," he added a trifle smugly, "that I have now stymied all future challenges to duel. Since no one can fight me until my present duel with Jabat is completed."

"But that's even worse!" she burst out, enraged. "You knew there was no danger, and you let me stand out there and worry. And you told the colonel I wasn't trustworthy, and I know you don't trust me! Oh I could kill you myself! I could—"

"Wait!" yelped Tom, as she started to advance on him again. "Wait! I tell you I do trust you—"

"You don't."

"Didn't you read what I wrote on your credentials just before the Skikana attacked?" cried Tom. "How could I trust you any more than that. I left it all up to you if anything should happen to me."

"What do you mean. I—" Lucy ripped open her belt-purse, snatched out her credential papers and unfolded them. "If you've done something else—"

Her voice failed. She was staring at Tom's handwriting.

"*To all Assassin Guild Officers . . .*" she read aloud, "*the individual presenting this is not a wilf, but my consort, on whom falls the duty of completing a mission in which I have just been slain. I charge all Guild officials and members with the duty of assisting her to complete that mission in my name, stating that I have the utmost trust and faith in her capabilities to do so. Thomas Parent, Apprentice and Guild Member . . ."*

"You see," said Tom. "All the time I did trust—"

Lucy flung herself upon him. Prepared rather for war than affection, Tom lost his balance and went over backwards onto the rug. Lucy fell on top of him.

"It's very undignified," he managed to mutter, a few moments later, "for an ambassador, to say nothing of an Assassin to be on his back on the floor—"

"Oh, shut up!" said Lucy, kissing him.

"A certain degree of unconventionality may be tolerated for the sake of results."

—Orientations

Sleight Of Wit

It was a good world. It was a very good world—well worth a Class A bonus. Hank Shallo wiped his lips with the back of one square, hairy, big-knuckled hand, put his coffee cup down, and threw his ship into orbit around the place. The orbit had a slight drift to it because the gryos needed overhauling; but Hank was used to their anomalies, as he was to the fact that the coffee maker had to be set lower on the thermostat than its direction called for. He made automatic course corrections while he looked the planet over for a place to sit down.

Hank was a world scout—an interstellar pioneer far-flung in his fleet one-man spacecraft in search of new homes for humanity. He had been picked to model as such for a government publicity release the last time he had been back to Earth. The picture that resulted, in three-dimensional full-color, showed Hank barrel-chested in a fitted blue uniform, carelessly open at the throat, seated at the gleaming controls of a scout cabin mock-up. Utilitarianly tidy, the little cabin surrounded him, from the folded up Pullman-type bunk to the arms rack with well-oiled weapons gleaming on their hooks. A battered guitar leaned in one corner.

True life showed differences—Hank, barrel-chested in a pair of khaki shorts, seated at the somewhat rubbed-down controls of the *Andnowyoudont*. Util-itarianly untidy, the little cabin surrounded him, from the anchored down and unmade bunk to the former arms rack, with well-oiled spade, ax, post-hole digger, wire-clippers, et cetera, hanging from the hooks. (In the ammunition locker were five sticks of non-issue dynamite. Hank, when talking shop on his infrequent trips back home, was capable of wax-ing lyrical over dynamite. "A tool," he would call it—a weapon. It'll dig for you, fight for you, run a bluff for you. The only thing it won't do for you is cook the meals and make the bunk.")

A battered guitar leaned in one corner.

On the ninth time around, Hank had complete surface maps of the world below. He ran them back through the ship's library and punched for that spot on one of the world's three continents where landing conditions were optimum. Then he turned every-thing over to the automatic pilot and took a little nap.

When instinct woke him up, *Andnowyoudont* was just balancing herself in for a landing in a little meadow surrounded by trees and pleasant-looking enough to be parklike. What hint of warning it was that reached him in the midst of his slumber he was never to know; but one moment he was asleep—and the next he was halfway to the control panel.

Then concussion slammed the ship like a giant's hand. He tripped, caught one glimpse of the near wall of the cabin tilting at him, and consciousness dissolved in one of the prettiest displays of shooting stars he had seen in some time.

He woke again—this time to a throbbing headache and a lump on his forehead. He sat up groggily, hoisted himself the rest of the way to his feet and stumped over to the medicine chest, absently noting that the ship was, at least, still upright. The outside screen was on, showing a view of the meadow. Five years before he would have looked out of it immediately. Now he was more interested in aspirin.

When he had the aspirin inside him and had checked to make sure the bump on his head was not bleeding and the guitar had not been damaged he turned at last to the screen, sat down in the pilot chair and swept the outside scanner about the meadow. The meadow turned before him, stopped, and the screen steadied on a tall, gray shape.

At the far end of the meadow was another ship. It was half again as big as the *Andnowyoudont,* it resembled no ship of human manufacture that Hank had ever seen; and it had a sort of metal bubble or turret where its nose should be. From this turret projected a pair of short, blunt wide-mouthed tubes bearing an uncomfortable resemblance to the muzzles of guns. They were pointed directly at the *Andnowyoudont.*

Hank whistled the first three notes of "There'll Be A Hot Time In The Old Town, Tonight"—and broke off rather abruptly. He sat staring out the screen at the alien spaceship.

"Now," he said, after a while to the room around him, "against this—the odds against this happening, both of us here at the same time, in the same place, must be something like ten billion to one."

Which was possibly true. But which also, the saying of it didn't help a bit.

Hank got up rather heavily, went over to the coffee maker, and drew himself a cup of coffee. He sat down in his chair before the controls and examined a bank of tell-tale gauges. Not too much to his surprise, these mechanical watchdogs informed him that the *Andnowyoudont* was being sniffed at by various kinds of radiation. He was careful not to touch anything just yet. The thought of the five sticks of dynamite popped into his head and popped out again. The human race's expansion to the stars had brought them before this into contact with some life forms which might reasonably be called intelligent—but no one before that Hank knew of, in his line of work or out of it, had actually run across what you might call a comparable, *space-going* intelligent race.

"Except now Mrs. Shallo's little boy," said Hank to himself. "Naturally. Of course."

No, it was clearly not a dynamite-solution type problem. The stranger yonder was obviously armed and touchy. The *Andnowyoudont* packed five sticks of dynamite, a lot of useful, peaceful sorts of tools, and Hank. Hank leaned back in his chair, sipped on his coffee and turned the situation over to the one device on the ship that had a tinker's chance of handling it—some fifty ounces of gray matter just abaft his eyebrows and between his ears.

He was working this device rather hard, when the hull of the *Andnowyoudont* began to vibrate at short intervals. The vibration resulted in a series of short hums or buzzes. Hank plugged in to the ship's library and asked it what it thought of this new development.

*　　*　　*

"The alien ship appears to be trying to communicate with you," the library informed him.

"Well, see if you can make any sense out of its code," Hanks directed. "But don't answer—not yet, anyway."

He went back to his thinking.

One of the less glamorous aspects of Hank's profession—and one that had been hardly mentioned in the publicity release containing the picture he had modeled for, aforesaid—was a heavy schedule for classes, lectures, and briefing sections he was obligated to attend every time he returned to Headquarters, back on Earth. The purpose of these home chores was to keep him, and others like him, abreast of the latest developments and discoveries that might prove useful to him.

It was unfortunate that this would have meant informing him about practically everything that had happened since his last visit, if the intent had been followed literally. Ideally, a world scout should know everything from aardvark psychology to the Zyrian language. Practically, since such overall coverage was impossible, an effort was made to hit hard only the obviously relevant new information and merely survey other areas of new knowledge.

All new information, of course, was incorporated into the memory crystals of the library; but the trick from Hank's point of view was to remember what to ask for and how to ask for it. Covered in one of the surveys when he had been back last trip had been a rather controversial theory by somebody or other to the effect that an alien space-going race interested in the same sort of planets as humans were, would not only look a lot like, but act a lot like, humans. Hank closed his eyes.

"Bandits," he recited to himself. "Bayberry, barberry, burberry, buckle—May Sixteenth, Sinuses, shamuses, cyclical, sops—milk-and-bread . . . Library, Walter M. Breadon's 'Speculations on Alien Responses.' "

There was an almost perceptible delay, and then a screen in front of Hank lit up with a pictured text.

". . . *Let us amuse ourselves now,* (commenced the pictured text) *with a few speculations about the personality and nature of a space-going alien such as one of you might encounter . . .*"

Hank snorted and settle down to read.

Twenty minutes later he had confirmed his remembrance of the fact that Breadon thought that an alien, such as must be in the ship opposite Hank right now, would react necessarily very similarly to a human. Because, Breadon's theory ran, of necessarily parallel environments and past stages of development.

At this moment, the call bell on Hank's deep-space receiver rang loudly.

"What's up?" he asked the library, keying it in.

"The alien ship has evidently concluded that it can speak to you over normal communication equipment. It is calling the *Andnowyoudont.*"

"Fine," said Hank. "I wonder what the name of Breadon's opposite number is among the aliens."

"I am sorry. I do not have that information."

"Yeah. Well, stand by to translate." Hank keyed in the communicator board. A screen before him lit up with the image of a hairless individual, lacking even eyebrows; with pronounced bony brow ridges, a wide mouth, no chin to speak of, and what appeared to be a turtleneck sweater drawn high on a thick neck.

This individual stared for a long second; and then began to gobble at him. Eventually he ran down and went back to staring again. Hank, his finger still off the send button, turned to the library.

"What'd he say?"

"I will need more referents. Possibly if you speak now, he will perhaps speak again."

"Not on your life." Hank looked at the alien. The alien looked back. The staring match went on for some time. Abruptly the alien started gobbling again. He gobbled for some time, this time. He also waved a fist in the air. It was a rather slim fist considering the thickness of his neck.

"Well?" demanded Hank of the library, after the figure in the screen had fallen silent a second time.

"First message: 'You are under arrest.' "

"That's *all* he said?"

"Agglutination appears to be a prime characteristic of his language."

"All right—" growled Hank. "Go on."

"Second message: 'You have offended the responsible authorities and their immediate representative, in the person of I who address you. You are arrested and helpless. Submit therefore immediately or you will be utterly destroyed.' "

Hank thought for a minute.

"Translate," he said to the library. He pressed the send button. "Tut-tut!" he said to the alien.

"I am unable to translate 'tut-tut,' " said the library.

"Oh?" Hank grinned. His grin widened. He began to laugh. He laughed louder.

"I am unable to translate laughter," said the library.

Hank was rolling around in his seat and hiccuping with helpless merriment. He reached out with one hand and slapped the send button to *off*. The screen went dark before him as the still-blankly staring alien faded from view. Whooping, Hank pulled himself to an upright position. Abruptly he stopped.

"What am I doing?" he muttered. "The set's off now." He wiped a damp forehead with the hairy back of one large hand and got up to totter over to one of the food compartments. He opened it and hauled out a large brown bottle.

Liquor was not a normal part of the supply list on scout ships—for reasons of space, rather than those of sobriety, a drinking world scout being a sort of self-canceling problem. On the other hand, a closed cycle that reprocessed waste matter of an organic nature and started it around again to become food required efficient little manufactories that were quite as capable of turning out ersatz beer as ersatz steak. The result was that world scouts were beer drinkers if they were any sort of drinkers at all.

They were also the despair of waiters, waitresses, and bartenders. A group of world scouts spending a social moment together would order a bottle apiece of cold beer; drain their bottles, when they came, in a couple of seconds; and then sit with the empty bottles before them, refusing to reorder until about forty-five minutes had passed. Then the whole process would be repeated.

A world scout determined to get drunk merely shortened the interval between bottles. One determined to stay cold sober, while appearing to drink, lengthened it. A member of the laity, sitting in with them on these sessions, was normally destroyed—either by drink or frustration.

In this particular case Hank flipped the seal off the top of the bottle in his hand, poured half a liter of beer down his throat, carefully resealed the bottle and put it back in its refrigerator compartment. He then carefully counted the remaining full containers of beer in the compartment and set the beer-producing controls on high.

After this he was almost attacked by another spasm of laughter, but he fought it down. He went over to the desk of controls and flicked on an outside screen. It lit up with a view of the meadow with the afternoon sun beaming down on the soft grass and the tall gunmetal-colored shape of the alien ship.

"A beautiful day," said Hank aloud, "for a picnic."

"Do you wish me to make a note of that fact?" inquired the library, which had been left on.

"Why not?" said Hank. He went cheerfully about the room, opening lockers and taking things out. A sudden thought occurred to him. He went across to the desk controls to check the readings on certain instruments concerned with the physical environment of the world outside—but these gave the meadow a clean bill of health. He added the full bottles of beer to his pile, enclosing them in a temperature bag, and headed out the air lock of his ship.

Reaching the ground outside, he proceeded to a comfortable spot on the grass and about midway between his ship and that of the alien.

Half an hour later, he had a cheerful small fire going in the center of a small circle of stones, a hammock hung on wooden posts, and small conveniences such as a beer-cooler and an insulated box of assorted snacks within easy reach. He lay in the hammock and strummed his guitar and sang. He also swallowed a half liter of beer approximately every thirty-five minutes.

The beer did nothing to improve his voice. There was a reason Hank Shallo sang while off on his lonely trips of exploration—no civilized community could endure the horrendousness of his vocal cords when these vibrated in song. By a combination of bribery and intimidation he had forced an indigent music instructor once to teach him how to stay in key. So, stay in key he did; but the result was still a sort of bass bray capable of penetrating six-inch walls and rattling windows.

The alien ship showed no sign of life.

As the sun began slowly to drown itself in twilight, however, Hank became aware to his pleasant surprise that the local inhabitants of this world did not seem to join most of the rest of the galaxy in its disdain for his singing. An assortment of small animals of various shapes and sizes had gathered around his camping spot and sat in a circle. He was not unduly surprised, what with the beer he had drunk and all, when after a little while one of the larger creatures—a sort of rabbit-shaped beast sitting up on its hind legs—began to harmonize with him.

If Hank's voice had somewhat the sonority of a cross-cut saw, the beast's had the pure liquidity of an angel's. They were rendering a remarkable performance, albeit four octaves apart—and it had grown rather dark—when a blinding light burst suddenly into being from the top of the alien ship. It washed the meadow in a brilliance like that of an atomic flare; and the native animals took to their heels. Sitting up in the hammock and blinking, Hank saw the alien approaching him on foot. The alien was pushing a black box the size of a suitcase on two wheels. He trundled it up to the campfire, hitched up the floppy, black, bell-bottomed trousers which supplemented the turtle-necked upper garment Hank had remarked on the screen earlier, and gobbled at Hank.

"Sorry, buddy," said Hank. "I haven't got my translator with me."

The alien gobbled some more. Hank idly strummed a few stray chords and regretted the fact that he hadn't gotten the native animal to harmonizing with him on "Love's Old Sweet Song," which would have been ideally suited to their two voices together.

The alien stopped gobbling and jabbed one finger—somewhat angrily, it seemed to Hank, down on a button on top of the black box. There was a moment's hesitation; then he gobbled again and a curiously flat and unaccented English came out of the box.

"You are under arrest," it said.

"Think again," said Hank.

"What do you mean?"

"I mean I refuse to be arrested. Have a drink?"

"If you resist arrest, I will destroy you."

"No, you won't."

"I assure you I will."

"You can't," said Hank.

The alien looked at him with an expression that Hank took to be one of suspicion.

"My ship," said the alien, "is armed and yours is not."

"Oh, you mean those silly little weapons in your ship's nose?" Hank said. "They're no good against me."

"No good?"

"That's right, brother."

"We are not even of the same species. Do not allow your ignorance to lead you into the error of insulting me. To amuse myself, I will ask you why you are under the illusion that the most powerful scientific weapons known have no power against you?"

"I have," said Hank, "a greater weapon."

The alien looked at him suspiciously a second time.

"You are a liar," the box said, after a moment.

"Tut-tut," said Hank.

"What was that last noise you made? My translator does not yet recognize it."

"And it never will."

"This translator will sooner or later recognize every word in your language."

"Not a geepfleish word like *tut-tut*."

"What kind of a word?" It might, thought Hank, be merely false optimism on his part; but he thought the alien was beginning to look a little uncertain.

"Geepfleish—words dealing with the Ultimate Art-Science."

The alien hesitated for a third time.

"To get back to this fantastic claim of yours to having a weapon—what kind of weapon could be greater than a nuclear cannon capable of destroying a mountain?"

"Obviously," said Hank. "The Ultimate Weapon."

"The . . . Ultimate Weapon?"

"Certainly. The weapon evolved on Ultimate Art-Science principles."

"What kind of a weapon," said the alien, "is that?"

"It's quite impossible to explain," said Hank, airily, "to someone having no understanding of the ultimate Art-Science."

"May I see this weapon?"

"You ain't capable of seeing it, kid," said Hank.

"If you will demonstrate its power to me," said the alien, after a pause, "I will believe your claim."

"The only way to demonstrate it would be to use it on you," said Hank. "It only works on intelligent life forms."

He reached over the edge of his hammock and opened another beer. When he set the half-empty bottle down again the alien was still standing there.

"You are a liar," the alien said.

"A crude individual like you," said Hank, delicately wiping a fleck of foam from his upper lip with the back of one hairy hand, "would naturally think so."

The alien turned abruptly and trundled his translator back toward his ship. A few moments later, the overhead light went out and the meadow was swallowed up in darkness except for the feeble light of the fire.

"Well," said Hank, getting up out of the hammock and yawning, "I guess that's that for today."

He took the guitar and went back to his ship. As he was going back in through the air lock, he thought he felt something about the size of a mouse scurry over his foot; and he caught a glimpse of something small, black and metallic that slipped out of sight under the control desk as he looked at it.

Hank grinned rather foolishly at the room about him and went to bed.

He woke once during the night; and lay there listening. By straining his ears, he could just occasionally make out a faint noise of movements. Satisfied, he went back to sleep again.

Early morning found him out of bed and humming to himself. He flipped the thermostat on the coffee maker up for a quick cup, set up the cabin thermostat and opened both doors of the air lock to let in the fresh morning air. Then he drew his cup of coffee, lowered the thermostat on the coffee maker again and keyed in the automatic broom. The broom scurried about, accumulating a small heap of dust and minor rubble, which it dumped outside the air lock. In the heap, Hank had time to notice, were a number of tiny mobile mechanical devices—like robot ants. Still drinking his coffee, he went over to the drawer that held the operating manual for ships of the class of *Andnowyoudont*. Holding it up by the binding, he shook it. A couple more of the tiny devices fell out; and the automatic broom, buzzing—it seemed to Hank—reproachfully, scurried over to collect them.

Hank was fixing himself breakfast, when the screen announced he was being called from the other ship.

He stepped over and answered. The image of the alien lit up on the screen.

"You have had the night to think things over," said the flat voice of the alien's translator. "I will give you twelve point three seven five nine of your minutes more in which to surrender you and your ship to me. If you have not surrendered by the end of that time, I will destroy you."

"You could at least wait until I've had breakfast," said Hank. He yawned, and shut off the set.

He went back to fixing his breakfast, whistling as he did so. But the whistle ran a little flat; and he found he was keeping one eye on the clock. He decided he wasn't hungry after all, and sat down to watch the clock in the control desk as its hands marked off the seconds toward the deadline.

Nothing happened, however. When the deadline was a good several minutes past, he let out a relieved sigh and unclenched his hands, which he found had been maintaining quite a grip on the arms of his chair. He went back and had breakfast after all.

Then he set the coffee maker to turn itself on as soon as he came in, got down some fresh reading material from the top shelf of his bookcase—giving his head a rather painful bang on the fire-control sprinkler overhead, in the process—and stopped to rub his head and swear at the sprinkler. He then comforted himself with the last cup of coffee that was still in the coffee maker, unplugged the emergency automatic controls so that the air-lock doors would stay open while he was out, loaded himself up with beer—but left the reading material roasting on top of the coffee maker—and went out to his hammock.

Forty minutes and a liter and a half of beer later, he was again in a good mood. He took an ax into the nearby woods and began chopping poles for a lean-to.

By lunch-time his hammock was swinging comfortably in the shade of the lean-to, his guitar was in tune, and his native audience was gathering again. He sang for about an hour, the small, rabbitlike creature harmonizing with parrotlike faithfulness to the tune, and had lunch. He was just about to take a small nap in the hammock when he saw the alien once more trundling his translator in the direction of the camp.

He reached the fireplace and stopped. Hank sat up with his legs over the edge of the hammock.

"Let us talk," said the alien.

"Fine," said Hank.

"I will be frank."

"Fine."

"And I will expect you to be frank."

"Why not?"

"We are both," said the alien, "intelligent beings of a high level of scientific culture. In spite of the apparent differences between us, we actually have a great deal in common. We must consider first the amazing coincidence that caused us both to land on the same world at the same spot at the same time—"

"Not so much of a coincidence," said Hank.

"What do you mean?" The alien all but glowered at him.

"It stands to reason," Hank leaned back comfortably in the hammock and caught hold of his knee with both hands to balance himself. "Your people and mine have probably been pretty close to bumping into each other all along. They've probably been close to each other a number of times before. But space is pretty big. Your ship and mine could easily zip right by each other a thousand times and never be noticed by one another. The most logical place to bump into each other *is* on a planet we both want. As for coming down in the same place—I set my equipment to pick out the most likely landing spot. I suppose you did the same?"

"It is not my function," said the alien, "to give you information."

"It isn't necessary for you to, either," grunted Hank. "It's pretty obvious your native star and mine aren't too far apart as galactic distances go—and exploratory ships have been getting closer to the opposing home worlds all the time. Instead of it being such a coincidence, you might say our meeting was close to inevitable." He cocked an eye at the alien. "And I'm sure you've already figured that out for yourself as well as I did."

The alien hesitated for a moment.

"I see," he said at last, "there is no point in my trying to deceive you."

"Oh you can *try* if you like," said Hank, generously.

"No, I will be absolutely frank."

"Suit yourself."

"You obviously have assessed the situation here as fully and correctly as I have myself. Here we stand, facing each other in an armed truce. There can be no question of either of us allowing the other to carry word of the other's civilization back to his own people. We cannot take the chance that the other's people are not inimical and highly dangerous. It becomes, therefore, the duty of each of us to capture the other." He cocked an eye at Hank. "Am I correct?"

"You're doing the talking," said Hank.

"At the present moment, we find ourselves at an impasse. My ship is possessed of a weapon which, by all the laws of science, should be able to destroy your ship utterly. Logically, you are at my mercy. However, illogically, you deny this."

"Yep." said Hank.

"You lay claim to an invisible weapon which you claim is greater than my own, and puts me at your mercy. For my own part I believe you are lying. But for the sake of my people I cannot put the matter to a test as things now stand. If I should do so and it should turn out I was wrong, I would be responsible for calamity."

"Yes, indeed," said Hank.

"However, an area of doubt remains in my mind. If you are so sure of the relative superiority of your weapon, why have you hesitated to make me prisoner in your turn?"

"Why bother?" Hank let go of his knee and leaned forward confidentially with both feet on the ground. "To be frank right back at you—you're harmless. Besides, I'm going to settle down here."

"Settle down? You mean you are going to set up residence here?"

"Certainly. It's my world."

"Your world?"

"Among my people," said Hank, loftily, "when you find a world you like that no one else of our own kind has already staked out, you get to keep it."

The pause the alien made this time was a very long one indeed.

"Now I know you are a liar," he said.

"Well, suit yourself," said Hank, mildly.

The alien stood staring at him.

"You leave me no alternative," said the alien at last. "I offer you a proposition. I will give you proof that I have destroyed my cannon, if you will give me proof that you have destroyed your weapon. Then we can settle matters on the even basis that will result."

"Unfortunately," said Hank, "this weapon of mine can't be destroyed."

"Then," the alien backed off a step and started to turn his translator around back toward the ship. "I must take the chance that you are not a liar and do my best to destroy you after all."

"Hey! Hold on a minute!" said Hank. The alien paused and turned back. "Don't rush off like that," Hank stood up and flexed his muscles casually. The two were about the same height but it was obvious Hank carried what would have been an Earth-weight advantage of about fifty pounds. "You want to settle this man-to-man, I'm willing. No weapons, no holds barred. There's a sporting proposition for you."

"I am not a savage," retorted the alien. "Or a fool."

"Clubs?" said Hank, hopefully.

"No."

"Knives?"

"Certainly not."

"All right," said Hank, shrugging, "have it your way. Go get yourself destroyed. I did my best to find some way out for you."

The alien stood still as if thinking.

"Let me make you a second proposition," he said at last. "All the alternatives you propose are those which give you the advantage. Let us reverse that. Let me propose that we trade ships, you and I."

"What?" squawked Hank.

"You see? You are not interested in any fair encounter."

"Certainly I am! But trade ships—why don't you just ask me to give up right now?"

"Because you obviously will not do so."

"There's no difference between that and asking me to trade ships!" shouted Hank.

"Who knows?" said the alien. "Possibly you will learn to operate my cannon before I learn to operate your weapon."

"You never could anyway—work mine, that is!" snorted Hank.

"I am willing to take my chances."

"It's ridiculous!"

"Very well." The alien turned away. "I have no alternative but to do my best to destroy you."

"Hold on. Hold on—" said Hank. "Look, all right. I agree. Just let me go back to my ship for a minute and pick up a few personal—"

"No. Neither one of us can take the chance of the other setting up a trap in his own ship. We trade now—without either of us going back to our ships."

"Well, now look—" Hank took a step toward him.

"Stand back," said the alien. "I am connected with my cannon by remote controls at this moment."

"The air-lock doors to my ship are open. Yours aren't."

The alien reached out and touched the black box. Behind him, the air-lock door of the alien ship swung open, revealing an open inner door and a dark interior.

"I will abandon my translator at the entrance to your ship," said the alien. "Is it settled?"

"Settled!" said Hank. He began walking toward the alien ship, looking back over his shoulder. The alien began trundling his black box toward Hank's ship. As the distance between them widened, they began to put on speed. Halfway to the alien ship, Hank found himself running. He came panting up to the entrance of the alien air lock, and looked back just in time to see the alien dragging his black box in through the air lock of Hank's ship.

"Hey!" yelled Hank, outraged. "You promised—"

The slam of the outer air-lock door, on his own ship, cut him off in mid-protest. He leaned against the open door of the alien ship's air lock, getting his breath back. It occurred to him as a stray thought that he was built for power rather than speed.

"I should have walked," he told the alien ship. "It wouldn't have made any difference." He glanced at his wrist watch. "I'll give him three minutes. He sure didn't lose any time finding those air-lock controls."

He watched the second hand of his watch go around. When it passed the two and a half minute point, he began walking back to his own ship. He reached its closed air-lock door and fumbled with his fingers under the doorframe for the outside lock control button. He found and pressed it.

The door swung open. Smoke spurted out, followed instantly—as the door swung wide—by a flood of water. Washed out on the crest of this escaping flood came a very bedraggled looking alien. He stirred feebly, gargled something at Hank, and collapsed. Inside the spaceship a small torrential shower seemed to be in progress.

Hank hooked one big hand into the alien's turtle-neck upper garment and dragged him back into the ship. Groping around in the downpour, he found the controls for the automatic fire sprinkler system and turned them off. The shower ceased. Hank fanned smoke away from in front of his face, stepped across to the coffee maker and turned it off. He punched buttons to start the ventilating system and close the air-lock doors. Then he set about tying the alien to the bunk.

When the alien began to stir, they were already in null-space, on the first point-to-point jump of the three-day trip that would bring them back to Earth. The alien opened his eyes; and Hank, looking up from his job of repairing the coffee maker, saw the other's stare full upon him.

"Oh!" said Hank. He stopped work, went across the room and brought back the black box on wheels to within reach of the alien's bound hands. The alien reached out and touched it. The box spoke, echoing his gobble.

"What did I do wrong?"

Hank nodded at the coffee maker. He sat down and went back to work on it. It was in bad shape, having evidently suffered some kind of an explosion.

"I had that set to turn on when I came back in," he said. "Closing the air-lock doors turned it on. Convenient little connection I installed about a year or so back. Only, it just so happened I'd drawn the last cup out of it before I went out. There was just enough moisture in it to cause a steam explosion."

"But the water? The smoke?"

"The automatic sprinkling system," explained Hank. "It reacts to any spot of dangerously high temperature in the room here. When the coffee maker split open, the heating element was exposed. The sprinkling system began flooding the place."

"But the smoke?"

"Some burnable reading material I had on top of the coffee maker. Now that" said Hank, finishing his repairs on the coffee maker, "was something I was absolutely counting on—that the books would fall down onto the burner. And they did." He slapped the coffee maker affectionately and stood up. He looked down at the alien. "Afraid you're going to be somewhat hungry for the next three days or so. But as soon as we get to Earth, you can tell our nutritionists what you eat and they'll synthetize it for you."

He grinned at the other.

"Don't take it so hard," he said. "You'll find we humans aren't all that tough to take when you get to know us."

The alien closed his eyes. Something like a sigh of defeat came from the black box.

"So you had no weapon," it said.

"What do you mean?" said Hank, dropping into

the chair at the control board, indignantly. "Of course I had a weapon."

The eyes of the alien flew wide open.

"Where is it?" he cried. "I sent robots in. They examined this ship of yours right down to the elements that hold it together. They found no weapon. I found no weapon."

"You're my prisoner aren't you?" said Hank.

"Of course I am. What of it? What I'm asking is to see your weapon. I could not find it; but you say you still have it. Show it to me. I tell you, I do not see it!"

Hank shook his head sadly; and reached for the controls of the *Andnowyoudont* to set up the next jump.

"Brother," he said, "I don't know. If you don't see it—after all this—then I pity your people when my people really get to know them. That's all I've got to say!"

*"However, the filing of false or frivolous reports is
strictly prohibited."*

—*Orientations*

Operation P-Button

Subject: Altitudinal Readjustment of Ceiling Quanta
Documents: Documents are enclosed.
Number of Documents: One.
Nature of Document #1. Communication received
from Operations Sector Officer, Sector 19, H. E. Penny.

Relevant Facts: Communication received by Courier: *Most Special and Most Urgent*—at 0800 hours Eastern Daylight Time, 5/1/76. Receiving office, Operation P-Button HQ.

Document #1

FROM: OPERATIONS SECTOR OFFICER, SECTOR 19, H. E. PENNY 4/27/76

TO: CHIEF, OPERATION P-BUTTON.
SUBJECT: REPORT RECEIVED FROM SECTOR
         FIELD AGENT C. N. LITTLE, THIS
         DATE, 0600 HOURS

SIR:

   FIELD AGENT CHARLES (CHICK) N. LITTLE
REPORTS AN INCIDENT OF OCCIPITAL IM-
PACT, 0500 HOURS, THIS DATE.
   ALL OBSERVATONS AND PERTINENT DATA
THIS SECTOR OF OPERATIONS STRONGLY IN-
DICATE THAT THE SKY IS FALLING.
   REPEAT: ALL OBSERVATIONS AND PERTI-
NENT DATA THIS SECTOR STRONGLY INDI-
CATE THAT THE SKY IS FALLING.
   MOST URGENT ALL POTENTIALLY AFFECT-
ED AGENCIES AND PERSONNEL BE INFORM-
ED WITHOUT DELAY.

RESPECTFULLY:

SIGNED: HENN E. PENNY

HENNINGTON E. PENNY, OP:SEC:OFF.

"Only the elite of our World Scouts even dare aspire to the coveted status of General Overseer."
—*Orientations*

Soupstone

The General Delivery window of the Space Terminal Mail Building on the world of Hemlin III, twenty-eight thousand four hundred and six light years at Quadrant Two inclination nineteen degree to Theoretical Galactic Center, was small and lower to the ground than ordinary. World Scout Hank Shallo, who was outsize not only across the chest and shoulders, but also from boot heels to beret, was forced to stoop to look in.

"Any mail for . . ." his voice changed suddenly from its normal kettledrum tones to a bass coo, "H. Shallo, ship *Andnowyoudont*, Miss?"

"Just a second." The small brunette vision behind the window put down the bookviewer she had been holding and turned to code at the machine to one side of the window. There was a snick, a click, and several envelopes slid out of the machine. "Here you are, sir."

Hank accepted them, crushing them unseeingly in one large hand. "Thank you," he cooed, bassly, beaming at her. "Interesting book?"

The girl, back on her stool and with the bookviewer back in her hand, paused to consider his craggy features a moment. It was hard to tell, thought Hank, whether that was approval or something else he saw in her eyes.

"Yes," she said, briefly. Hank sighed.

"Been a long time since I had time to do any real reading," he said sadly. "World Scouts don't get the time. That's one of the troubles with being a World Scout."

"I take it," the girl said, "that you're a World Scout?"

"Yes," said Hank, simply, sighing again, "and a hard, solitary life it is." He inflated his barrel chest slightly. "Not the glamorous sort of life most people think it is, pioneering new interstellar areas, searching out new worlds where our people can dwell. Dangerous—yes. Glamorous—" Hank shook his head slowly. "No."

"I see," said the girl.

"Might I ask what the book's about? Perhaps I'll want to get myself a copy for my next long survey search."

"That might be a good idea," said the girl, "if you can read Middle French. It's about the fabliau."

"Oh?" said Hank. "Ah . . . fabliau, eh?"

"Yes, I'm reading it for my doctorate thesis on the spurious and imitative tales that were circulated under Chaucer's name following the success of the Canterbury Tales in the fourteenth century. Many of them are based on the French fabliau."

"Ah . . . yes," said Hank.

"You see, I'm a graduate student at the University

here and this is a part-time job for me. Is there anything more I can help you with?"

"At the moment, no," cooed Hank. "No. But perhaps I'll be seeing you again."

He left, shoving the letters into his pocket unopened, and took a shuttle car into town. There he entered the first library he found and requested a book on the fabliau.

". . . In modern standard speech," he added hastily. The library machine burped and produced a bookviewer with spool inside. He paid for it and took it to a comfortable seat and put it to his eyes. FRENCH FABLES FROM THE MIDDLE AGES TO MODERN TIMES, he read. He grunted. So that was all a fabliau was. The title of the first fable in the book, he saw, was "Soupstone." He read it, put the viewer in his pocket and went back out to the Space Terminal Mail Building; where he leaned with one elbow on the railing outside the General Delivery window.

"Hello again!" he said, gaily.

"Hello, soldier," said the brunette, coldly.

"Soldier?" said Hank, astonished. "No, no. I'm a World Scout."

"So you told me," said the girl. Hank got the impression that her opinion of him had somehow taken a turn for the worse. "I suppose," she went on, heating up as she proceeded "it's part of your usual line. You must have a pretty poor idea of my intelligence to think I'd be impressed by a cheap lie like that. It just happens my uncle was a World Scout and there was no one I admired more, so I saw through you right from the start and I must say I think it's a pretty reprehensible sort of thing sneaking around to find out about my uncle . . ."

"Wait a minute. Wait . . ." pleaded Hank. "Your uncle was a World Scout? What was his name?"

"Chan Gremminger. And he died honorably in the line of duty . . ."

"I knew Chan Gremminger!"

"Oh, take your lies and this letter that came just after you left, and get out of here!" She slammed a stud on the machine beside her, scooped up the letter that popped out and threw it at Hank—then turned and marched off out of sight behind the wall in which the window was set.

Bewildered, Hank picked up the letter and looked at it. It was a very official looking letter, sealed with tape and official-looking stamps. It was addressed to Major H. Shallo Gen'l Delivery, Space Terminal Mail Bldg., Hemlin III.

"Wait a minute!" called Hank, sticking his head through the window. "It's just a reserve commission, and . . ." But the room behind the window was empty.

Slowly and sadly, Hank returned to his scout ship, the *Andnowyoudont*, out in its terminal parking spot. Safely aboard and seated in the control-board chair in the incredibly compact control-sitting-bedroom of the tiny but incredibly powerful ship, Hank broke the seals on the envelope and extracted its contents.

"*Pursuant to approval by World Scout Headquarters, Key West, Earth (see attached copy) . . .*" he read: and stopped to examine the attached copy aforesaid. It was, he considered on reading it, a nastily humorous memo from Janifa Williams, Assignment Director, WS HQ., with the humor so subtly veiled that only Hank could feel its bite. Oh, sharper than a serpent's tooth it was, thought Hank, to have a woman thinking you had scorned her. He had not scorned Janifa Williams, that time when he had been called back to Earth to be used in the publicity posters for the World Scout enlistment drive. He would never scorn such a magnificent specimen of blonde woman-hood.

He just hadn't wanted to give up the *Andnowyou-dont* and settle down to a stuffy desk job back on Earth. Janifa could not understand that. Hank sighed. Now, in this memo, Janifa wrote that since H. Shallo WS 349275 had already proved himself capable of highly unorthodox, but equally highly effective action—another covert dig, that, in its reference to Hank's capture of the first of the Unarko aliens ever encountered by the human race—WS Hq. was pleased to approve the activation and use of H. Shallo on the service required by the military authorities.

Hank turned back to the orders of the military authorities and became abruptly conscious of the true sharpness of the serpent's tooth. Military HQ wrote that a certain recently settled planet known as Crown World Quadrant Two, inclination et cetera et cetera . . . had recently reported an emergency situation existing; and requested, as was their right under emergency conditions, immediate GO (General Overseer) aid. Under the circumstances (here followed half a page of circumstances that were so much official gobbledegook to Hank and were intended, he suspected, to be so) Military HQ felt that the emergency on Crown World was possibly of less seriousness than its few pioneering inhabitants believed. And since qualified individuals of GO rating were unavailable at the moment, it had been judged best to order temporary GO authority for Major H. Shallo and request that he proceed forthwith to Crown World and deal with the situation. Following this, he would contact Military HQ in reference to his report and deactivation. Et cetera.

Hank sighed. He could quite understand that GO (*Genius Only*, some were wont to nickname it) help

was in short supply. To qualify for that particular
government organization all you had to have were
the equivalents of doctorates in five unrelated fields
plus three years of special training and education. A
young GO was usually pushing fifty. By sixty or
seventy he was priceless and forcible retirement took
him off just about that time. Just, thought Hank,
when he was getting good at working miracles.

Stop and think about it, thought Hank, could he
work miracles? No. Could he refuse the duty? No.
Was it all Janifa's fault? Yes. Suddenly fired up by
the thought of how Janifa would be expecting him to
fail miserably, Hank sat upright in his chair. He'd
show her! Or would he? He got up and looked in the
mirror surface of the arms locker. The trouble was he
didn't look like a GO. He was too . . . too healthy-
looking, somehow. He thought for a moment and
dived into his spare clothes locker, coming up with a
somewhat battered top hat that belonged to a set of
magician's tricks he had got interested in once. He
put the hat on his head, and turned back to the
mirror.

The effect was certainly not healthy-looking. The
Abraham Lincoln style topper above Hank's square-
jawed face produced an image just short of unbelievable.

"Eccentric," breathed Hank. He snatched up the
book of French fables to complete the costume. "The
fabliau," he announced squeakily to his image. "Done
quite a bit of study of it. My special field. Yes.
Soupstone. Henry Abraham Soupstone. What? My
good fellow, of course! Been a GO for years. What's
your problem? Tut-tut! Nothing to it. Let me examine the situation. Ah, yes . . ."

Why not, thought Hank, turning happily to the
control board and ringing Terminal Field control for

takeoff pattern. Didn't the Military HQ people think the problem on Crown World had been overstated? Probably nothing to it. Hank punched the location of Crown World into the memory bank of the *Andnow-youdont*'s library and sat back to await his takeoff pattern. He picked up the battered guitar by his chair, and strummed a G major chord.

"*I'm just a poor, wayfarin' stranger . . .*" he tundered horrendously, but happily, to the sound-proofed walls of his ship.

By the time he got to Crown World, he had read all the fables in the book. He found that he still liked the first one, "Soupstone," best, however. He had also made use of the *Andnowyoudont*'s library to find out as much as possible about GO methods of work and about the planet Crown World, itself. The dulcet tones of the library's auditory response circuit had not proved as soothing as usual on these topics. About all Hank had been able to glean about GO techniques, that a relatively uneducated character like himself could use, was the fact that a GO's greatest asset was the respect in which people held him. Never, said the library, quoting, should a GO allow the people he was helping to lose faith in his ability to solve their problems. Hank made a note of that.

He also made a sober note of a fact he had not realized at first. Crown World was on the border of a Unarko area of newly developed worlds. The human and Unarko races were officially, and as a practical matter, at peace with each other—ever since Hank had brought back that one adult Unarko and the linquistic boys had cracked the Unarko language. Anything but official peace was out of the question. It was foolishness to think of not respecting each other's already settled worlds, or engaging in open conflict. Both races could bleed themselves to death and never come to any decisive conclusion trying to carry on a war on an interstellar basis.

On the other hand—there were other forms of competition beside those involving a shooting war. Both races went for the same sort of worlds. If the Crown World humans had to abandon that world and the Unarkos moved in, the result would be quite as effective as if the aliens had attacked and driven the humans off it. Out in the galaxy it was not a good notion to let things go by default. That could give the aliens ideas, and become a fatal habit.

Hank was still thinking seriously about this when the landing bell rang, and the library spoke to him.

"We are now down and a man appears to be awaiting you."

"Right . . . ah, yes," said Hank, snatching up his top hat and tucking the book of fables under his arm. He put a solemn expression on his face, opened the air lock, and walked through it and down the landing stairs. Waiting for him was a muscular young man with his sleeves rolled up and a fine tangle of brown hair showing at the bottom of the v where his shirt was unbuttoned at the neck. Hank could see the blue eyes under the unruly brown hair measuring the width of Hank's shoulders calculatingly, and recognized the character of that look. It was Hank's cross that he seemed to act a walking challenge to a certain pugnacious type of individual. It was something about the way he was built. Hastily, Hank moved to obscure this bad impression made by his appearance.

He simpered at the young man. It seemed to disconcert the other somewhat.

"*You're* the Go?" demanded the young man, scowling.

"Ah . . . indeed," oozed Hank, confidingly, "Hank Abraham Soupstone. GO for years now. Fabliau. My field. If you'd like to see my credentials . . ."

"Never mind that!" snapped the young man—deeply wounding Hank, who had prepared a beautiful set of Soupstone credentials on the way here. "Joe Blaine's my name. Come on. My slider's right over here."

He gestured toward one of the high-cushion, air-support, open-bodied cars normally used for travel on new planets and backward areas where the terrain was rough. The turbine motor which produced the jet air cushion on which the device rode whirred alive and whistled up the scale into inaudibility as the sound baffles took over to protect the passenger's eardrums. The car stank abominably of whatever local vegetative distillate was being used as fuel. With a jerk the thing started, and Hank clutched the seat beneath him as they shot forward toward some buildings in the distance at a breakneck speed.

"So you're GO?" shouted Joe Blaine—as they left the fused earth surface of the landing field for a plowed field. Crown World was apparently as yet too new to have roads. They were traveling at about a hundred and twenty kph.

"That's right!" shouted back Hank, smirking horribly into the wind of their passage and holding his top hat on with one hand.

"Then you know all about spugeons?"

"Ah . . . absolutely. Studied them for years!"

Joe's head jerked around to stare at Hank. Hank gulped, and grinned ferociously, hoping that whatever he had said that was possibly wrong, would be taken as a joke. Joe did not grin back. Hank made a mental note to look up spugeons as soon as he could get back to the *Andnowyoudont*.

"You do, huh?" yelled Joe. "How about Unarko aliens?"

"Fine!" shouted Hank, happy to be on a safe subject. He expanded on the matter. "Matter of fact I was the first human to meet one of them . . ." He broke off, seeing the stare of the Crown Worlder widen even more; and remembering suddenly that almost anyone on a Unarko frontier would know that a World Scout (naturally) had been the first to contact the aliens. ". . . In a manner of speaking!" Hank added hastily, grinning again.

It did not seem to go down too well. There was active suspicion now in Joe Blaine's eyes. Slowly, the young man turned his gaze back to the terrain ahead of them and no more was said until they penetrated in among the distant buildings and came to a stop before one large structure of fused earth some three stories tall and resembling an office building.

"In here," said Joe Blaine, curtly. He led Hank inside and up three stories of ramps on foot and through an empty outer office on the third story to an inside office. Inside the inner office were half a dozen men of various ages, generally as roughly dressed as Blaine.

'Here you are! How do you do, Mr. . . . er . . ." said a small, round man scuttling forward to shake Hank's hand.

"Soupstone. Hank Abraham Soupstone," said Hank.

"I'm provisional planet manager. Gerald Bahr. Let me introduce you—William Grassom, Arvie Tilt, Jake Blokin . . ." the introductions proceeded, ". . . and last but not least, my daughter and temporary secretary to our temporary management commission here, Eva Bahr."

"Charmed!" leered Hank. Eva Bahr was a pretty, smiling-faced, blond young lady in well-fitted yellow coveralls.

"I'm the one who's charmed—to meet a real GO,

Mr. Soupstone," she said. "We didn't expect you to be so young."

"Can't be very young," said Blaine's voice in the background. "Been studying spugeons for years. Told me so himself."

"Joe!" Eva glared past Hank at the young frontiersman.

"Of course, Joe," said Gerald Bahr. "You must have misunderstood."

"No I didn't."

"*Joe!*" Eva's voice rose.

"No use saying 'Joe!' like that. I tell you he said it. Also said he was the first human to ever see a Unarko. Maybe we ought to look at his credentials after all, in spite of all your talk about manners and cooperating when he comes."

"Certainly not!" snapped Eva's father. "It's perfectly plain to me, even with you telling it, that he was kidding you, Joe."

"Ha-ha! Yes," put in Hank, hastily. "Ease the tension a little and all that—" He laughed again, poking Bahr in the ribs with an elbow.

Gerald Bahr laughed. The men beside him laughed. Eva laughed loudly with a silvery note of scorn in her voice, glancing at Joe. Joe did not laugh.

"Ha-Ha! Well," said Bahr. "Let's get down to business. We can promise you unanimous cooperation. Unanimous! There's not a man, woman, or child on Crown World you can't feel free to call on. Fifteen thousand souls are at your disposal."

"Thank you," said Hank, appreciatively considering Eva Bahr. He called himself back to order with a jerk, walked around a nearby table and sat down behind it. "Now," he said, frowning solemnly at them. "Your problem here is—?"

Everybody started to talk at once.

*   *   *

"Please!" shouted Gerald Bahr. The babble ceased. "The answer to that is," said the temporary little planet manager, to Hank, "everything. Our spugeons are rotting before we can process the juice from them. The Unarko expert they sent us can't or won't tell us how the Unarkos get around that with the spugeons they raise. It's a Unarko plant and nobody seems to know the answer. People think the Unarkos are just waiting to take over Crown World. Nobody wants to be on the planet management commission or be permanent Commission Chairman. Nobody knows how to run a planet. The First Bank of Crown World just had to close its doors. Spugeon juice distillate would be worth a fortune if we could ship some out, but because we haven't, other worlds won't give us any more credit. Tanker spaceships are ready to leave the planet, empty, and give up on us . . ."

"Ah, yes," Hank cut off the flow of words with a wave of one wide-palmed hand. He thought about what he had read about GOs from the *Andnowyoudont*'s library. The colonists waited expectantly. "I see," said Hank solemnly, "that a survey is required. Yes, I'll have to survey the situation."

A babble of relief commenced. Hank held up his hand.

"I must examine," he said, "the situation at first hand. First"—he thought for a second—"I'd better see one of your spugeon farms." His eye wandered in the direction of Eva Bahr. "If one of you could guide me—"

"I'd be glad to," said Eva.

"No, you don't!" said Joe.

"Why, I certainly will—"

"Now, now—" cooed Hank, rising and picking up from the table his copy of the French fables in their bookviewer. He tucked the viewer in his pocket and approached the two who were now glaring at each other. "We mustn't quarrel—" He placed a large and soothing palm on Eva's rigid right shoulder.

"Take your hands off her!" roared Joe and swung a fist from left field.

Hank, letting go of Eva's shoulder, shrank timorously under the fist. He heard it whistle past his ear and somehow managed to trip over his own feet so that he went blundering into Joe. One of his stumbling feet happened to come down on the instep of Joe's left foot while the other caught itself behind the young colonist's right heel. Caught off balance, Joe went over backward; and Hank, clutching clumsily at the other, somehow chanced to ram the three stiffened, polelike fingers of his left hand into the soft diaphragm area just below the notch of Joe's breastbone, while by sheer coincidence Hank's doubled right fist got between the floor of the office and Joe's head, just behind the right ear, as that head came down to the floor.

Everybody else in the room swarmed over Hank, apologizing, helping him to his feet, depositing him tenderly in a chair. Ignored, the still form of Joe Blaine unconscious on the floor.

"Water . . ." gasped Hank, feebly, his head nestled in the soft arms of Eva. They brought him water. He managed to sip a little, and smile weakly.

On the floor the discarded Joe began to show signs of returning consciousness. He stirred, muttered, opened his eyes and tried to sit up.

"Wha' happ'ned . . .?" he muttered thickly.

"Oh, Joe!" gasped Eva, suddenly noticing the young man still lying on the floor. She started toward him, then suddenly checked herself. "Yes, you ought to ask that!" she blazed. "Attacking Mr. Soupstone like that. Serves you right if you fell down and hurt yourself!"

"We'll lock him up for you, Mr. Soupstone!" snapped Gerald Bahr, glaring at Joe.

"No, no . . ." said Hank, mildly, struggling to his feet from the chair. "Sudden outburst . . . can't blame him. Need every man." He turned to Eva. "Must go now. If you'll show me . . ."

"I most certainly will!" snapped Eva, glaring at Joe. "Lean on me, Mr. Soupstone, if you still feel shaky." They went.

"Oh, I hate that Joe Blaine!" cried Eva, some moments later as they were approaching the spugeon farm she had suggested as their destination. "I just can't stand him!"

"That so?" shouted Hank in answer, holding on to his top hat with one hand and the bucket seat of the air car with the other. Apparently it was the custom on Crown World to drive at full throttle over all natural obstacles in open country. Hank bounced as the air car hurtled a boulder too big to be handled by the air cushion alone. They were doing about a hundred and sixty kilometers per hour.

"It certainly is!" Eva shouted back. "I can't stand someone that opinionated. Someone who has all that ability and won't use it! People asked and asked Joe to be the temporary planet manager instead of Dad; but all Joe'd ever say was to ask them back—who was their servant last year? Did you ever hear of anything so selfish?"

"Well . . . ah . . ." hedged Hank.

"Neither did I! It's disgusting, especially when he's so brilliant. He's had five years of study in extraterrestrial agriculture; and he was one of the first to try spugeon raising when the seed became available. That was after the first Unarko-Human agreement last year—" she broke off suddenly. "But why am I telling you all this? You must know all about the Agreement."

"Not at all—not at all!" boomed Hank, genially. "I always say it pays to listen. You can always learn something new."

"Oh!" cried Eva. "If Joe only had one-tenth your open-mindedness. Your reasonableness! Your . . . oh, there's our destination!"

"Where?" asked Hank. But they were already shooting over a field of green vinelike plants blooming in orderly rows and with what seemed to be pumpkin-sized fruit among the leaves—except that the fruit was green and apparently thin-skinned and full of juice. In fact, the fruit resembled nothing so much as enormous green grapes. Looking ahead, Hank saw a house and what looked like a cross between a barn and a greenhouse. A moment later the air car halted with a jerk before the farmhouse door. Somewhat stiffly, Hank left his bucket seat for solid ground, and followed Eva into the house. He found himself in what looked like a cross between a kitchen and a laboratory. A gnomelike, little, old man with a wrathful face was busy filling a small beaker with green fluid from a larger beaker. To one side sat what looked like a distilling outfit.

"Joshua," began Eva, "this is Mr. Abraham Soupstone. He's—"

The little man slammed down his beakers and began to jump around and wave his fists in fury at them.

"I know! I know!" he cried in a cracked tenor. "The GO. That father of yours phoned about him! Well, I don't need him! I need a truck! You hear me?"

"You know better than that, Joshua," said Eva sternly. "There won't be any trucks until Mr. Soupstone gets them running again. And even if there were trucks it's not your turn to have one pick up your crop until Tuesday."

"Tuesday!" screamed Joshua. "Do the spugeons have calendars? Can I tell them they have to wait to ripen till Tuesday?" Without warning he shoved the smaller beaker of green fluid at Hank. "Taste that!"

It was a small beaker with only a little liquid—perhaps a fluid ounce, perhaps less—in the bottom of it. Hank obediently tilted it up and swallowed it off—fingering to one side a sort of small pipette the old man had carelessly left in the vessel.

The liquid was delicious. He swallowed—and became suddenly conscious of both Eva and Joshua staring at him as if they had just been paralyzed. He opened his mouth to comment on their attitudes—and at that moment, his mouth flared, his esophagus glowed white-hot, and a small fission bomb—to judge by the feel of it—went off in his stomach.

Poisoned! thought Hank. He opened his mouth to gasp for water, but his vocal cords seemed paralyzed. Frantically, he gasped around the room for some sign of water, but saw none. His eyes lit on an empty beer bottle near the distilling apparatus. He made motions toward it.

"Beer—" he managed to husk, finally, forcing his tortured vocal cords into action. Joshua stared at him, went across the room, opened what seemed to be a refrigeration cupboard and produced a bottle of beer which he opened and brought back to Hank without a word. Hank upended it over his open mouth. Like all World Scouts he had fallen into the solitary habit of drinking his bottles of beer in single gulps—that was, one bottle of beer, one gulp. But never had he poured a bottle down so gratefully. The fire went out.

"Well—" he started to say, and then blinked and paused as a sort of golden glow spread out over the room. The floor tilted slightly and he had a sudden impulse to sing, which he thwarted just in time. "Very good," he said, handing the bottle and beaker back to Joshua—and enunciating carefully.

"Must be," grunted Joshua, taking them. He looked significantly over at Eva. "I guess you're ready to solve all our problems now, aren't you, Mr. Soupstone?"

"Absolu . . . yes," said Hank, choosing the one syllable word by sudden preference. He added carefully. "You are not receiving trucks when you should?"

"My ripe spugeons are rotting on the ground, that's what!" snapped Joshua. "If I pick the unripe ones, they tell me they spoil in the warehouse. You tasted that superconcentrate of brandy! A fortune in spugeons here and I can't do anything with it, because they won't pick up the fruit when I say so."

"Understand," said Hank, woodenly and carefully, "Unark . . . alien secret spugeon grow—"

"Secret! That what they been telling you in town?" cried Joshua. "Unripe spugeons don't ripen off the vine. That's the secret! Get the trucks here when they're needed—that's the secret. And what're you going to do about it?"

"Fix," said Hank.

"How?" sneered Joshua. "Mind telling me? Huh?"

"GO method." Hank closed his teeth on an incipient hiccup and talked woodenly on through his teeth. "Soupstone technique. 'Veloped self. Can't explain." The golden glow around him was obscuring the room and the floor threatened to tilt under his feet. "Call on you in my official capacity. Write report on trucking failures. Deliver me at office. Good-by. Go now. Come Eva."

*   *   *

Without waiting for an answer from the girl, he turned carefully about and walked out the door. With only a little difficulty, so careful was he, he got back into the bucket seat on his side of the air car. He was aware of Eva getting in on the other side with Joshua standing beside her.

"Josh—" said Hank carefully, but sternly through his teeth. "Expect report tomorrow without fail."

"You'll have it," he heard Joshua's voice float at him through the thickening golden haze. Hank slouched down in the bucket seat and tilted the top hat over his eyes.

"Must think. No disturb." He muttered aside to Eva. Invisible in the golden haze he faintly caught a comparable mutter from Joshua to the girl.

"The equivalent of a half liter of ordinary strength spugeon brandy," Joshua was muttering. "At a gulp. And couldn't wait to chugalug a beer on top of it. You watch him."

"Certainly not!" Eva's voice answered. "How do we know how a GO thinks? It's probably all part of that Soupstone technique he was talking about!"

Telligent girl, thought Hank approvingly under the hat, and felt the air car jerk into motion. Closing his eyes he relaxed and let the golden haze take him whither it willed.

He was vaguely aware of several stops after that. There was a man who had something to do with trucks who waved his fists and shouted about warehouses. A man who had something to do with warehouses who pounded a table and bellowed about a banking system. And a man who spread his plump hands and all but wept about the lack of planetary management and authority. Following this there was an extended blank period—followed by a bad dream about a Unarko who was trying to talk to him.

The Unarko insisted. Hank woke up. It was no dream. One of the thick-necked chinless and hairless aliens dressed in the usual bell-bottomed and turtle-necked upper garments was bending over him, gobbling. A translation in human speech was coming from the black box on wheels alongside the Unarko.

Hank waved him aside and sat up on what he discovered to be the edge of a cot, set up in the office where he had met Eva Bahr's father and the rest, yesterday—he hoped it was only yesterday. Morning sunlight was coming in the windows on one side of the office. In that light the Unarko looked particularly unappetizing with his tentaclelike arms. Hank clutched at his head—but after a second took his hands away.

"No hangover!" he said wonderingly. He looked at the Unarko. "Who're you?"

The alien gobbled. "I am your"—the black box hesitated—"helperkin."

"What?" Hank stared.

". . . Helperette? Little assistant . . .?" the box fumbled with the alien gobbles. It fell silent. The Unarko silently extended a microfilm viewer. Hank put it to his eyes and saw a letter. He read it, in a glance—brief as it was.

GENERAL OVERSEER DEPARTMENT
-Hq. Washington D.C. Earth

To Whom It May Concern:

Resident and management cultural experts being equated in Unarko culture with military experts, and their presence on the planet known as Crown World being therefore offensive to Unarko colonies already resident in the interstellar area, said experts are being withheld from said world, and their assistance

replaced by the assistance of an Unarko expert assigned to Crown World in the interests of interracial
cooperation.

All assistance and courtesy should be extended by
humans on Crown World to the Unarko expert bearing this letter.

Correspondent 5763
G.O. Hq.

It bore the proper three-ply, unforgettable, GO
seal. Hank lowered the viewer and gazed thoughtfully at the alien.

"Ah," he said. "Oh-ho! Helperkin—why didn't
you say so in the first place? Never mind," he added
hastily. "As long as you're here, however, what do
you think's wrong with Crown World and its spugeon
farms?"

The alien gobbled. "The human race," said the
box in its flat, mechanical tones, "lacks a thing—for
which there is no word in human speech. It is a
quality of the spirit required for spugeon culture
without which there can be no success. Therefore, it
is proved that here is a failure. Humans, go home."

"You don't say?" queried Hank rising, enthusiastically. "Just what I thought you'd say. Solves everything." Taking hold of the black box he wheeled it
toward the office door, the alien perforce following.
"Don't call me. I'll call you. Leave your name with
my secretary." He opened the office door, and in the
process of ushering alien and black box through it,
saw that the outer room contained a desk with Eva
behind it and Joe Blaine facing her. They were glaring at each other.

*   *   *

"Ah, my morning mail!" said Hank, happily, scoop-
ing up a stack of printed sheets he saw on Eva's
desk. "Well, good morning, Joe! Eva, step into the
office for a moment. See you in a minute, Joe. So
long, ah . . . Helperkin. We must have lunch some
. . . This way, Eva."

He got her inside and shut the door behind her.

"What's been happening?" he asked anxiously.

"All the reports you asked people to make, came,"
she said, indicating the stack of material in his hands.
"Maybe I shouldn't have let the Unarko in? But he
had that letter. And he's really been a great help to
us since we came. He started the deep-breathing
courses, and he gives a concert of Unarko music once
a week here in town."

"He does, does he?" asked Hank.

"Oh, yes. To develop the proper spirit in us for
spugeon culture. Oh, he's helped and helped," said
Eva, looking discouraged "but things just keep getting worse and worse. That Joe!"

"Joe?"

"Can you imagine it?" Eva snapped. "He's beginning actually to doubt you really are a properly trained
GO. He says nobody who's devoted their life to
learning how to be a GO could hit him that hard.
Why, you didn't hit him! I told him that and he just
looked mad and wouldn't discuss it. He's messaged
Earth to demand identification of you. He says they
can't deny us that, and if you aren't a real GO,
everybody on the planet will be happy to help him
string you up to a lamppost, after all we've suffered."

"Oh?" said Hank, grinning.

"Yes. I told him how silly it was for him to waste
credit on a call like that. He won't even get an
answer until eleven o'clock tonight. But," said Eva,
with a sigh, "that's Joe for you . . . what's the matter?"

"Eleven . . . I mean," said Hank, fervently, "what time is it now?"

"Oh, almost time for lunch."

"Dear me!" squeaked Hank, in his best Soupstone accents.

"What is it?" Eva looked alarmed.

"I just remembered, I have to be back at Hemlin III by tomorrow morning. How," said Hank, wiping his brow, "could I have forgotten?"

"But our problem here?" cried Eva.

"Oh? Your problem—yes. Well," said Hank, "you know how it is . . . GO's are in great demand." He wiped his brow again. "We mustn't be selfish. Must we?"

Eva's eyes filled with tears.

"Other people," said Hank, uncomfortably, "have problems too . . ."

Eva began to weep gently.

"Well, naturally," said Hank, painfully, "I planned to get you out of the main problem before I left. Started back on the road to recovery. What I mean is . . . I couldn't do it all for you. Just plan it. You'll have to carry it out yourselves—"

"Oh, thank you!" cried Eva, radiantly, throwing her arms about him and kissing him. "You will get it solved before you leave?" She kissed him again. "You will? You will?"

"Leave it to me. Absolutely—where are you going?" said Hank, panting slightly.

"To tell Joe. That'll show him! Oh, is there anything you need?"

"Need? Of course, I need . . . uh," said Hank, checking himself, "some breakfast, bacon and eggs if you have them. Lots of black coffee.. Have it sent in to the office here. I'll be very busy. Also, I need an abstracter. Have you got an abstracter?"

"One of those computer devices that makes abstracts of written material?" asked Eva. "I think so."

"Good," said Hank. 'Get me one. Then stand by in the outer office. No visitors except the ones I send for. Got it?"

"Got it," said Eva, happily tripping out of the office.

Hank heard the door close behind her, and sighed. No rest for the weary. He looked down at the stack of paper in his hand and went and sat down at the office desk with it. He picked up the first report—which was from Joshua, complaining about the lack of adequate trucking, and tried to read it. But it was full of terms like "*ripening half-period*" and "*acidic soil ratios*." He was still struggling with it when Eva arrived with the breakfast and the abstracter.

He shooed her out, loaded the reports into the abstracter and sat down to the breakfast. He was just through with it and pouring his third cup of coffee when the abstracts began to appear. He took a look of the first one, a one-page abstract of Joshua's report. It made little or no more sense to him than the report had.

He pressed the key of the office intercom and spoke to Eva.

"Would you call your father and ask him to come in and see me?" Hank asked.

Fifteen minutes later Gerald Bahr arrived. Without a word. Hank passed him the abstract of Joshua's report. Gerald read it.

"Well," said Hank, when the little man was done, "what does that suggest to you?"

"Well . . ." Bahr was diffident. "Of course, I'm not a spugeon-farmer, myself, but it sounds to me . . . well, as if we need some sort of traffic control officer to get the trucks where they ought to be on time. Maybe someone who knows spugeons and traffic control, too."

"Very good!" said Hank, beaming approval, "you spotted the crux of the matter at once! I thought you would—but, of course, I had to test you."

"Of course," said Bahr, almost blushing with pleasure.

"Now," said Hank, beaming, "of course I could do that myself, but as Eva's probably told you, I'm short of time. Is there anyone who could be named my assistant in that area?"

"Why . . . Jack Wollens!" said Bahr. "He's a farmer, but he was an expediter back on Earth."

"Fine, fine!" cried Hank. "Get him in here."

A short while later, Jack Wollens arrived. Hank handed him the abstract. He read it with a frown on his lean, sunburned face. He was a man in his mid-thirties with a serious expression about his eyes.

"It won't work," he said. "Where are all the trucks to come from—"

"The very flaw that struck me!" said Hank nodding approvingly. He turned to Bahr. "I have to congratulate you. You didn't underrate Jack, here, one iota." He turned back to Jack. "Now," he oozed, "suppose you had to answer your own question. Where would *you* say all the trucks were to come from?" He leaned forward expectantly over the desk. Bahr also leaned forward.

Pinned at the focus of two pairs of eyes, Jack Wollens ran a finger around his collar.

"Well—" he hesitated. "Maybe if we took trucks off the town services on alternate days . . ."

"You see!" said Hank, leaning back in his chair and nodding at Bahr. "Yes, indeed. Exactly!"

"Exactly!" echoed Bahr, enthusiastically, but with slightly puzzled eyes.

"Well," said Hank, turning back to Wollens, "you know who you'd have to work with, of course?"

"Herb Golighty? Herb and I always got along," said Wollens. "He knows I used to expedite back on Earth—"

"Naturally. Eva . . ." said Hank, keying the intercom. "You can call Herb now and ask him to come over. What? Golighty, of course. Herb Golighty. Sorry, I must have been mumbling. Get him right over here." He released the intercom key and turned to Wollens. "Yes, you and Herb will sit down as soon as he gets here and work up a plan. As of now, you'll be joint heads of the Department of Transportation." He shook hands solemnly with Wollens. "Congratulations."

"He turned back to Gerald Bahr, and shook hands with the little man.

"I can't tell you," he said, "how pleased I am to see how your people pick up the ball when I toss it to them." He withdrew another abstract from the pile. "Now, about this problem of bank credit . . ."

All afternoon and past the sunset hour, Crown Worldians filed in and out of Hank's office. Finally, as that world's single enormous moon had just risen to flood the landscape with moonlight hardly less bright than day, the torrent of traffic dwindled to a trickle and finally ceased.

"Well," said Hank, exhaustedly, sitting back in his chair at the desk and sipping on his twenty-third cup of coffee. He beamed over the rim of his cup at Eva and her father, who were the only ones left in the office with him. "I think you'll find that when the sun rises tomorrow your troubles will be over . . . er, one way or another. The assistants I've directed and put to work will be able to work out the situation here along the lines I indicated."

"It's been amazing, Mr. Soupstone," said Gerald Bahr, earnestly. He had been in and out of the office all day and had just now returned from his last assigned duty. "To see a GO actually at work, amazing! How you could hold it all in your head—how you knew at a glance or a word the right man to put in the right job—" Words failed the little man. He ended up shaking his head.

"Oh, yes!" said Eva, gazing radiantly at Hank. "And after you've only been here one day and we've been struggling with the way things were ever since we started spugeon raising. It's . . . it's superhuman, it really is!"

"Oh, well," said Hank, modestly.

"No, Mr. Soupstone," said Bahr. "Eva's right. Let me tell you something. As I watched you working today, it was just as if I felt a strong current, a source of strength flowing out from you and putting things to rights."

"Please," Hank stopped him with upraised palm and got to his feet. "My duty, only my duty—that's all I did. Well, much as I hate to leave your charming world—"

"But you can't leave just yet—" Gerald Bahr trotted to intercept him as Hank started around the desk on his way to the door, the outside, the spaceport and open space. "We wanted to express our appreciation—it was supposed to be a surprise. A banquet in your honor."

"Banquet?" Hank glanced at the clock. It was now pushing close to the ten P.M. mark. He tried feebly to break away from the little man. "I couldn't. No . . . no—"

"Yes, yes," said a voice from the doorway. Looking up, Hank saw Joe Blaine entering, carrying a bookviewer that looked remarkably familiar. Flanking Joe were two husky young colonists his own age, and behind them was the alien form of the Unarko. "We insist, don't we boys?"

The boys grinned and nodded.

"Joe, where have you been?" demanded Eva. "And what've you got to do with the banquet?"

"Wait and see," said Joe, grimly. Across the room, his eye met Hank's. "You aren't thinking of refusing?"

"On second thought, no," said Hank firmly. "No. Certainly not."

They went. Going down the building ramps, Hank found himself flanked by Joe's two friends, and when they got on their sliders, somehow he ended up still between the two, on a separate slider from Eva and her father.

They slid through the town toward a brightly lighted, auditoriumlike building down the street.

"My!" said Hank, ingratiatingly, to one of the young men with him, nodding at the slider's controls. "No key? But I guess you all trust each other around here?"

"*We* do!" growled the young man. "There hasn't been anybody turn up dishonest on Crown World—so far. But there's always a first time, isn't there, Harry?" He looked at the other young man.

"Yeah," said Harry, fiddling with a piece of string in which he had tied a hangman's knot. "For everything." He put his finger in the loop and pulled it tight. It tightened very convincingly.

A moment later they stopped in front of the lighted building and Hank, surrounded by all the rest, was ushered up to the second floor and into what was apparently a private dining room with a long table set for some twenty people. Seventeen or so were already there. They all stood up and applauded as Hank and the others came in.

"Speech! Speech!" they cried.

Hank, being hustled down to the far end of the table and the empty place set there, farthest from the door, nodded and beamed at them.

When he reached the seat, there was another burst of applause.

"Er . . . my friends," Hank began, grinning horribly, as this finally died down. "Unaccustomed as I am to—"

"All right, we don't have to go through that!" broke in the voice of Joe Blaine from the end of the table. Everybody turned to look at him. He was holding up the bookviewer. "Before this banquet gets under way, I've got a few things myself to tell you about your guest of honor. Now, I found this bookviewer in one of his pockets last night when he passed out—"

"Joe!" rose the scandalized voice of Eva. "He didn't. And that's stealing—"

"Oh?" shouted Joe, still holding the viewer up. "Well, who steals his good name steals trash—or however that fool Shakespeare or whoever's line goes. I never trusted this Soupstone from the beginning, but you were all so sure he was the GO and an answer to all your troubles!"

He glared around at all of them at the tables.

"You all drive me nuts!" he roared. "You're like a bunch of children, needing somebody to look after you all the time. Well, nobody else would do anything about this Soupstone, so I did. I put in a call to verify his identity, but he heard about it"—he threw Eva a sideglare—"and planned to get off the planet before my answer came in. So I had to do what I could with what I found searching his pockets last night. One of the things was this bookviewer. Well, I read the book in it."

He waved it before their eyes.

"You know what it is?" he shouted. "It's just a book of old French fables. You probably thought it was some treatise on theoretical math or something—just as you think now he's solved the situation here by getting you all to name each other as experts. Well, it's just a book of fables—and you know what the title of the first one is? It's called 'Soupstone'!"

The people at the table stared, murmured and looked up at Hank, who smiled and shrugged deprecatingly.

"And you want to know what the story of that fable is?" demanded Joe. "Let me tell you. It's about some gypsies, some medieval con men who're traveling through a part of France where there's a famine going on. Everybody's half starved and hiding what little food they have so they won't be robbed of it . . ." He paused for breath.

". . . Well," he went on, glaring down the length of the table at Hank, "these gypsies get a lot of the peasants together by promising they can make soup out of stones. Just stones. They get water from the peasants and boil it in a huge pot so they'll be enough for everybody. When it's hot they start tasting it and say it needs a little salt. So one of the peasants goes and gets some salt from his hidden food place. Then they want some celery to flavor the soup with, and another peasant goes and digs out his celery. And then they say it needs a taste of turnip . . . and so on."

He ran his glare up one side of the table and down the other.

"You guessed it," he said. "Pretty soon that soup's got everything from beef to chicken in it, all supplied by the peasants. Now, how do you like our Mr. Soupstone?"

He paused, but those around the table only stared at him blankly.

"Don't you get it?" shouted Joe. "All this Soupstone, this fake GO, did, was get you to spell out your own problems and name each other as the best men to solve them!"

"But Joe!" cried Eva. "It *is* going to fix the situation—"

"It's not going to fix it!" bellowed Joe, turning on her. "If that'd solve it, we could've done it by ourselves. What good is just telling somebody there's a problem and he's in charge of fixing it? If there's no one to tell him *how* to fix it, he'll just stand there helpless! If this character was a real GO, he'd be sticking around to get you all working together and get the spugeon juice into the tanker ships and the tanker ships off planet."

He stopped and shook the viewer at them.

"But he *isn't* a real GO!" Joe snapped. "He can't run the team—and that's why he's dodging out. Because the minute he tried to run things you'd all see what a fake he is! That's why he's going. And that's why the fact he's going proves he's the fake I say he is."

Joe pounded the table, and the viewer in the fist he pounded with smashed to flinders. All eyes turned to look at Hank, who hung his head shamefacedly and began to slink around the table toward the door.

"Mr. Soupstone!" wailed Eva. "It isn't true! Come back! Say it isn't so!"

Hank only moved faster. A mutter of despair and dismay began to rise behind him. He paid no attention but accelerated his pace toward the door. It was right before him . . .

"Wait!" shouted the voice of Joe, suddenly. "Don't let him get away, after what he's done to us! Stop him—"

But Hank had already abandoned his policy of slinking. He had exchanged it for a policy of open flight. At top speed he bolted through the door, along the corridor and down the ramp toward the open street outside the building.

The sound of voices mounted into a roar of pursuit behind him. He reached the open air, spotted the keyless slider he had been brought here on, and flung himself on it.

He jerked the controls into full ahead position. His head almost snapped off, but a split second later, he was shooting down the street at foolhardy speed. Looking back, he saw forms emerging from the building and piling onto the sliders he had left behind. A second later they were after him.

His own speed he considered suicidal—but, he remembered, seeing them gaining on him behind, this particular world seemed to regard suicidal rates of travel as merely normal. He made it to the hatch of the *Andnowyoudont* just in time to whistle the outer air-lock door open, and pop through, closing it behind him as the solid missiles of hand-weapons began to crack against the—luckily missile-proof—outer hull.

Sweatily, gratefully, pantingly, he took off.

Ten hours later, safely back on Hemlin III, rested, bathed, and cleanly dressed—but somewhat unsure of manner, Hank once more approached the General Delivery window of the Space Terminal Mail Building, where all his troubles had started. The same small brunette vision was behind the window, and her upper lip curled at the sight of him.

"Oh, it's you!" she said.

"I was called at my ship," said Hank, humbly. "They said there was a recorded message for me, here. Visio and audio from off-planet."

"Yes," she sniffed. "You can take it on the screen, here. Or would you like a copy tape so that you can view it privately"—she sniffed again—"elsewhere?"

"No, no," said Hank. "I don't mind." He smiled ingratiatingly at her. "I'd like to take it here."

"If you don't mind my seeing it also."

"Oh no," said Hank. "Certainly not—by all means. I'd like"—he tried the ingratiating smile again, which was met with the further stiffening of the pretty upper lip—"you to see it," he mumbled.

"Very well. Sign please." She pushed a form at Hank who signed it. Reaching out to one side of the window, inside, she swung a pivoted screen around so that it could be seen from Hank's position outside the window as well from her side of the counter. She pressed some control studs.

The screen unclouded to show the face of Joe Blaine. It scowled at Hank.

"Well," it growled, "I guess you know by this time your identity check came through. That's how I was able to find you here."

Hank stole a glance at the brunette, but she had produced a fingernail buffer and was apparently absorbed in buffing her nails.

". . . At any rate," the image of Joe Blaine growled on, "the new planetary governing commission on Crown World is paying for this call and I want to officially extend you our apologies. You were," said Joe, looking as if he were chewing on ground glass, "pretty clever!"

The brunette sniffed audibly. Hank sighed.

"It wasn't until we sat down this morning to see what we could salvage out of the situation," said Joe, "that we realized you had it all fixed. Everybody there had the knowhow to do part of the necessary job. And, of course, there was me—"

Watching out of the corner of his eye, Hank saw

the fingernail buffer slow and a brunette eyelash
flicker.

". . . Pretty clever of you," snarled Joe, "making
me suspicious of you. You knew once I'd been fool
enough to chase you off the planet, I couldn't turn
the rest down about taking over the hole in the
organization I'd made by getting rid of you. So now
I'm Commission Chairman, and the Unarko's packed
his music and gone home, and we all"—it apparently
took sheer violence to get the words out—"want to
apologize and thank you . . ."

Someone apparently said something to him off
screen. He looked away and then looked back again.

"Oh, yes," he said, with a false and shoddy imitation of a smile, "Eva says be sure and drop in to see
us if you're ever in the neighborhood of Crown World
again." Again he was prompted. ". . . And Eva also
wants to say that as far as she's concerned you're not
only a GO, but the best GO in the organization!"

Baring his teeth, Joe signed off. The screen went
blank.

Nodding his head thoughtfully, Hank straightened
up, turning until he found himself once more looking
in the direction of the girl behind the window counter.
He discovered a pair of brown eyes glaring at him.

"So!" said the girl. "*Now* you're a GO!"

"Well, now," said Hank, winningly, "in a manner
of speaking—"

"I thought you told me you were a World Scout?"

"Well, yes—" said Hank. "If we could have lunch,
I might explain—"

"If you think you can fool me—" the glare in the
brown eyes faltered for a second and became uncertain, then hardened again. "If you're a GO, you
ought to have known all about the fabliau when I

told you about it! What's your special field if you're a GO?"

"Spugeons," said Hank.

"Sp . . . *spugeons?*"

"An alien-originated fruit, very valuable," said Hank. "The great problem is getting the ripe fruit from the fields at just the right moment for processing—but," he said, checking himself, "no point in going into that and boring you—"

He sighed and ceased. The brown eyes were back glaring at him again. He sighed again, sadly and turned to leave. Three steps he took from the window.

"Mr. . . . Mr. Shallo . . ." wailed a small voice behind him, "Come back . . ."

A tender, forgiving smile crept on to Hank's lips. He turned and went back.

"Be warned: romantic failure is the stuff of legend."

—*Orientations*

BALLAD OF THE SHOSHONU

by Gordon R. Dickson
Music by Gordon R. Dickson

I've gone and mar-ried a Sho-sho-nu.

How did it hap-pen to me? I'm sit-ting here with a

drink in my hand, wor-ried as I can be. I've

got a bar-rel of whis-key,___ but it's

no com-fort to me, 'Cause what-'ll I do with my

Sho-sho-nu? And what-'ll she do with me?___

I got paid off on Lyra one. I left that deep space boat.
I went downtown to the barrooms there, just to wet
my throat.
The Shoshonu were all around, and one sat down
with me.
Oh, what'll I do with my Shoshonu?
              And what'll she do with me?

She hadn't moulted her humanoid form; she was
pretty as could be.
She turned her big eyes up to mine, and smiled
soulfully.
But she slipped a mickey in my drink, when she got
home with me.
Oh, what'll I do with my Shoshonu?
              And what'll she do with me?

When I woke up the wedding was on, and I was
saying, "Yes—"
The High Shoshonu's six-foot fangs two inches from
my vest.
The relatives were all around, they swarmed all over
me.
Oh, what'll I do with my Shoshonu?
              And what'll she do with me?

Her father gave us a ton of gold; her mother gave us
jewels.
The rest of the tribe pitched in on a house, complete
with swimming pools.
They said, "Take care of our little girl—she's about
to moult, you see."
Oh, what'll I do with my Shoshonu?
              And what'll she do with me?

So I'm sitting here with a drink in my hand, as
worried as I can be.

When a Shoshonu moults, she turns into a dragon,
  rough-el-ly.
It's our wedding night. She's moulting now. And it
  makes them hung-ger-ry.
Oh, what'll I do with my Shoshonu?
          And what'll—she—do—with—me?

> *"Illegal activities by Scouts will provoke punishment that is swift, just, and inescapable."*
>
> —*Orientations*

Catch a Tartar

I

"Oh—" sang Hank Shallo happily and thunderously in his ashcan bass, fitting a jaunty tyrolean, civilian-type hat on his oversize skull—

"I got plenty of truffles,
"And truffles'll do right by me—
"I got no jewels,
"No contraband tools—
"Got no MIS-ER-Y!"
"Just got plenty of truffles . . ."

He paused to do a little soft-shoe Off-to-Buffalo to his right and came up bang against the instrument panel of his small one-man scoutship, the *Andnowyoudont*. The metal walls of the ship rang with the impact. Hank doffed his tyrolean topper to the instrument panel in apology, and finished his song.

"*. . . And truffles're plenty for ME!*"

Then he picked up a paper package the size of a small suitcase, punched the button that opened the air lock, and proceeded to disembark.

"Where can you be reached?" demanded the *Andnowyoudont* mechanically behind him.

"After I mail my package, in the pilots' bar of the terminal—for a while," said Hank cheerfully. "After that, who knows? I'm on leave, you know."

"World Scouts," said the *Andnowyoudont*, almost primly, quoting the latest Headquarters' bulletin from General Nailer, Commander W.S. Corps, "though allowed great latitude and freedom to promote their search for worlds capable of becoming new homes for Humanity, are still members of a military service and must consider themselves on call at all times."

Hank, however, paid no attention; but went off across the gray cement surface of the landing pad on Ariel IV in his civilian clothes, carrying his package and singing, "*Leave, Leave—wonderful Leave . . .*" in tones that threatened to rattle the landing struts of the spacecraft parked in the vicinity.

He reached the Terminal building, passed through local customs—where everybody gave him a wide berth. Truffles, even surrounded by rice and packed in sealed jars, had a tendency to be odiferous. After two weeks with the smell in a small Scoutship, Hank himself was used to it. He got some stamps now and mailed his package locally. It was addressed to one Roger de Svaille-Rochaut, head chef of the one luxury hotel the booming new planet of Ariel IV could boast.

It would be in good hands with Roger. As Hank had said, or rather, sung, in his merry song aboard ship, there was no misery involved in the interplanetary handling of truffles—ordinarily, that was. Some people, Earth Headquarters for example, might not be happy at all with the practice as engaged in by a World Scout—if Earth HQ knew about it. But, they did not know about it; and after all, truffles were not *legally* contraband on Ariel IV, nor had it been Hank who had smuggled them off Earth.

Not at all. Hank had only happened to win them in a friendly little poker game on Freehold, third world of Sirgol. A gentleman always, he had not stopped to inquire how the truffles had got to Freehold. And, honorable as always. he had no other intention than to give the root vegetables to his good friend Roger.

Certainly, Hank would never consider doing anything as disreputable as selling Roger the hard-to-get truffles. Certainly not, thought Hank, humming happily to himself as he headed for the small pilots' bar in the basement of the Space Terminal. However, he would not want to wound Roger's feelings by turning down the rather large amounts of local currency Roger always insisted on lending him when Hank showed up with truffles—in spite of Hank's protests that he had no idea when he would be able to pay Roger back, if ever. Ah, these warmhearted, generous, impulsive Frenchmen!

"Beer!" cried Hank, happily, entering the deserted pilots' bar and plopping his tall, heavily muscled body down on a bar stool that seemed to wince away from the impact. The bartender without a word produced an uncapped, half-liter bottle and Hank poured it down his throat without pausing for breath. "Another!"

                          *   *   *

"You're not going to wait half an hour before doing
that again?" said the bartender incredulously. He
was a thin, morose-looking individual, evidently ac-
quainted with the drinking habits of World Scouts,
who invariably chugalugged their beer and then sat
dry until they thought it time to have another.

"Not today! I'm on leave!" boomed Hank exuberantly. "*Beer, Beer, du bist mein Hertzen*—" he sang
as the bottle was served up, breaking off abruptly as
the bartender laid something else on the bar beside
it. "What's that?"

"Message," said the bartender, with bitter joy.
"You're World Scout Henry Shallo, aren't you? There
can't be two men on leave in civilian clothes your
size running around this Terminal—not likely, anyhow." He snuffled appreciatively at his own humor.
"Says 'Honey'," he added. "Probably from your wife."

"I haven't got a wife," Hank said automatically.

"Girl friend, then."

"I haven't got a g—" Hank's voice stuck in his
throat suddenly at the mental jab of an unhappy
premonition. It was true he had no girl friend—well,
no one, specific, girl friend, that was. But there was
somebody else always referred to as '*the girl friend*'
in World Scout parlance. That was the Assignment
Officer—invariably female—back at Earth Headquarters, who passed orders on to each individual Scout.
Hank's Assignment Officer was Janifa Williams, a
magnificent six-foot specimen of blonde womanhood
with only one tiny but fatal flaw in her makeup, as
Hank had discovered after a couple of trips Earthside.
That flaw was her conscientious desire to have Hank
give up Scoutshipwork and take work back on Earth.

". . . Earth," she had said, earnestly, that last
visit, "is where a man with your talents is needed—"

"Talents?" Hank had babbled, grinning foolishly. "Talents—what talents? Oh, you mean my guitar and my voice. Well—"

"I mean your talent for speaking six languages without accent, your ability to gimmick any electronic device yet built, your skill as a code-buster, and half a dozen other abilities, to say nothing of your I.Q. and reflexes, which are certainly not ordinary—any more than that man-and-a-half size body of yours!" snapped Janifa.

"Oh? Ah . . . well," said Hank, hastily pouring more champagne into both their glasses (they were on the terrace of Janifa's apartment). "Maybe you're right." He drained his glass and hiccuped solemnly. "Alwaysh wanted to come back. Actually, only one thing stopping me—" he broke off suddenly, clutching her arm. "Look!" he whispered, shivering and pointing into a corner of the terrace, suddenly. "Step on it! Step on it!"

"Step on what?" asked Janifa. "There's nothing there."

"There is—there is!" babbled Hank, clinging to her. "Don't you see it? A big green spider with fangs. Look! Right there by—"

"And you are not," said Janifa, coldly, disengaging herself from his grasp, "a secret alcoholic, so don't pretend to have the d.t.'s. because I know better. I've seen your brain wave patterns."

All in all, she had proved impossible to convince. And Hank, choosing the better part of valor, had ducked out, escaping by the skin of his teeth and sending her a dozen roses from the spaceport with his apology and the message that his grandmother, who had recently emigrated to Halstead's World, was desperately in need of him. He was not sure whether Janifa had given up, even yet, though the official messages she had sent him since had no hint to be discovered in them of her feelings. Hank shook off the memory now and bent his attention to the one word message, on the teleprint blank that labelled it as having been sent by *Andnowyoudont*. He should never, thought Hank, have admitted to the Scoutship that he would be here. He should have lied to it. Hank stared at the message with that curious premonition of something unpleasant about to happen. The back of his mind sniffed trouble.

The message was one word. The word was 'Honey'. It was, of course, a code, and theoretically Hank should hot-foot it back to the *Andnowyoudont* to get it deciphered.

He examined the single word. It was, of course, the end product of a double code. A book code overlaid by a relationship code that would expand the five letters into a thirty or forty word message. The book code this week was *War and Peace*, by one Lyev (Leo) Nikolayevich Tolstoy, so that was all right. The relationship code, however, called for some tricky maneuvers by a computational device on the *Andnowyou-dont*. However . . .

Hank yawned casually and took from his inside jacket pocket a small homemade mechanical pencil with bands of different color about it, which slid up and down the length of the pencil—a small invention of his own. Casually, as he studied the single word of the message his fingers manipulated the bands of color back and forth, slide-rule fashion. And, gradually, his head filled with a list of page, line and word numbers from a certain specific microfiling of *War And Peace*.

Yawning again, he tucked the pencil away. At this point a less industrious man might have been stuck.

However, it just happened that Hank had taken the trouble to make sure of his essentially photographic ability of recall to more or less memorize *War and Peace*, along with the other books used in the code pattern. A few moments later the completely decoded message was clear in his mind. It read:

REPORT AT ONCE TO MAIN SPACEPORT VAN DAMM'S WORLD WHERE YOU WILL BE CONTACTED BY ASSIGNMENT OFFICER JANIFA WILLIAMS WITH FURTHER INSTRUCTIONS.
SIGNED: J. WILLIAMS
PER EARTH/H.Q.

II

Hank groaned silently inside himself. He had felt it in his bones. Forget about his leave. Forget about whatever trouble was waiting for him on Van Damm's World. Behind this assignment was a scheme to get him back on Earth. He could smell it. As he had feared, Janifa Williams had not given up after his escape from her back on Earth. She was the worst type of woman—one with ethical convictions. She had just been waiting all this time to pounce. Now, she had pounced. What could he do? He could not disobey orders. Maybe if he showed up drunk and with real *delirium tremens* . . .

Inspiration burst like a man-colored rocket in Hank's hard-pressed brain.

"I will have," he said, turning to the bartender and rubbing his hands with satisfaction, "ten beers."

"Ten?" said the bartender goggling.

"Or twelve," said Hank, happily. "Just line them up in front of me."

He put credits on the bartop. The bartender served

and watched the bottles tilt, one by one, down Hank's gullet. At the eighth beer, Hank tucked the message back into his jacket pocket, grinned foolishly, leaned over backwards, and carefully fell off his bar stool.

For all his care he had forgotten that the floor of the pilots' bar was ceramic tile. His head came into contact with a solid surface, there was an explosion of sparks before his eyes, and darkness.

He woke up some time later and anxiously cracked open an eyelid. His head was aching. But he relaxed in satisfaction as through the slit of vision he saw a white-walled room which he identified as a physician's examining room, of the kind found in Spaceport Terminals. He was lying on a white table to which something like a steam cabinet had been pushed at its far end, evidently in order to accommodate the unusual length of Hank's outside body. A pretty, dark-haired young woman in white was sitting at a desk, filling out some kind of form.

Hank closed his eyelid again and moaned softly.

"Oh, the pain . . . the pain," he moaned. He opened his eye a crack again, and saw the dark-haired young woman glancing over at him.

"Just a moment." she answered. Her voice, though charming, Hank thought, did not seem very sympathetic. "I'll give you an aspirin."

"Aspirin!" Hank's eyes flew wide open. "For a broken leg?"

"For a hangover from too much beer—" she stared at him. "What do you mean? You haven't got a broken leg!"

"My right leg," groaned Hank. "Must have doubled under me when I fell." He closed his eyes again "Oh, the pain, the—"

"Nonsense!"

* * *

Hank opened his eyes again to find her standing sternly over him.

"Nonsense?" echoed Hank feebly. "But nurse—"

"Doctor!" she corrected him crisply, touching a caduceus with MD below it, imprinted on the lapel of her white jacket.

"Doctor. The pain—did you take bone pictures?"

"Certainly. Did you ever hear of a Spaceport Clinic that didn't take pictures when someone fell down on the premises?" She turned around, went back to the desk, and returned to Hank with a large brown envelope, from which she withdrew one of a sheaf of depth plates of Hank's body. "There, there's the bone print of your right leg. Sound as an Earthside bank draft."

"Not really?" groaned Hank. "Could I look at it? —Thank you. There!" he cried, whipping a huge and naked arm from under the white sheet that covered him, and pointing at the picture. "See . . . *there*. That's where it's broken."

"Nonsense! There's nothing there. Either your eyes or your imagination's running away with you."

"I see it!" insisted Hank. "Right there."

"Oh, don't be absurd. Here, let me show you what a real bone break looks like." She dropped the picture on his chest and went over to a filing cabinet on her desk, returning a moment later with another bone picture. "Now, here's a picture of a broken arm, and there's the line—"

"Don't you have one of a broken leg?" inquired Hank, hopefully.

"Never mind. You can see quite clearly on this arm what a break looks like in this print. See there? Now, does the picture of your leg show anything like that?"

"No, Doctor," said Hank, humbly. "You're quite right. How could I be so wrong? It was the pain—"

"Nonsense. Now get dressed and you can leave. Your clothes are right over there on the chair." She went back to the desk with both envelopes. Hank lifted the sheet covering him and peeked underneath it.

"I'm not wearing anything," he said, bashfully. "Doctor, would you mind . . . while I dressed . . .?"

"Nonsense. I told you, I'm a physician."

"I can't!" said Hank, pulling the sheet up around his neck and staring wildly up at the white ceiling.

"Oh, for goodness sake." She got up and went out the door. "I'll give you three minutes!" The door slammed behind her.

Hank rose swiftly but silently from the table and leaped on naked tiptoes across to her desk. He opened the file at random, snatched out a brown envelope, substituted it for the top envelope on the desk, which he kept for himself, and tiptoed back to his clothes. Three minutes later, fully dressed, he opened the door, found the black-haired lady doctor nowhere in sight, and went blithely off toward the far end of the terminal and the pad where the *Andnowyoudont* was parked.

Once safely out in space and with the small ship programmed for the three trans-light jumps that would bring it to Van Damm's World in some sixteen hours, Hank drew himself a large mug of coffee and sat down to chew on the situation.

He had set *Andnowyoudont* to the task of officially decoding the message, the moment he stepped back aboard. Now he picked up the neat file copy the ship had provided him and reread the decoded message carefully. There was not much in it to go on. Janifa had carefully avoided telling him why he was wanted on Van Damm's World. That conveniently prevented him from taking any specific steps to prepare for the situation. Of course, unspecific steps like providing himself with theoretically a broken arm was all to the good.

But more was needed.

"Hank to brains," murmured Hank prayerfully, staring at the message. "Mayday. Repeat, Mayday. Come in, brains. Over."

For a moment there was no response, and then the back of his mind seemed to light up.

"Of course!" chortled Hank happily, sitting up straight in his pilot's seat and taking a huge gulp of coffee. He had been overlooking the obvious. Janifa might have a private purpose in not wanting him to know the reason for his assignment, but she would have had to have a good official reason for not putting it in the message to him. Therefore there *was* an official reason. Therefore that official reason had to be that his assignment was to do with a secret to be preserved at all costs from the public, even on Van Damm's World. Who would have such a secret and be able to call on Earth Headquarters for official assistance? No one but the authorities on Van Damm's World. And who were the authorities! Hank whooped and dived for volume 'A to Keifer's Planet' of the restricted *Directory of Worlds*. He flipped it open to 'Van Damm's World'.

Van Damm's World, Hank read, had no elected authorities as yet. It was too new a planet. It was a Class B3 world, completely under the orders of the nucleic brain and the staff of the nucleic brain which were still in process of terraforming it to approximate Earthlike conditions. The population was a little less than two million hardy pioneers. Heading up the nucleic brain staff was one Welfer Swanson, one of the rare, creative souls capable of designing a nucleic brain and keeping it functioning, Allen Leeds, Administrator, and Bartholomew Styal, psychiatrist.

Psychiatrist?—wondered Hank. For a nucleic brain? No, no—the psychiatrist must be for Welfer Swanson. Designers of nucleic brains were notoriously on the ragged edge of various psychoses all the time.

The back of Hank's mind lit up again.

"Now, I wonder," he said softly to no one, "which one's broken down? Welfer, or Welfer's brain?" He turned to the controls in front of him and punched the library button.

"Search and supply!" he ordered the *Andnowyoudont*. "Print up everything you've got on nucleic brains and a designer of same named Welfer Swanson. How long?"

"To search all circuits, an hour and twenty minutes, approximately," replied the dulcet tones of the ship.

"Carry on!" said Hank cheerfully, thumbing the button to off position. "Hank to brains," he added happily, "well done, brains. Over and out!"

So saying, he abandoned the pilot's chair for the oversize bunk of the tiny vessel, stretched himself out with a sigh of contentment, and—never one to be bothered by a pint or so of black coffee—was soon napping the nap of those who, though innocent and just, yet triumph.

III

A little less than sixteen hours later, equipped with a sling and a plaster cast for his right arm and carrying the picture of the broken arm he had picked up on Ariel IV, Hank cracked the lock on the *Andnowyoudont*, and descended to the white concrete of a temporary landing area. Sure enough, there was Janifa, looking as magnificent as ever in sky-blue civilian kilt and tunic, surrounded by an admiring gallery of male passersby and accompanied by a small, ugly man in black clothes, steeple hat and heavy walking stick. The small man was waving the walking stick at the gallery and shouting at it to break up and move on. "Hank!" said Janifa, staring at him. "Your arm—"

"Arm?" said Hank, innocently. "Oh—yes. Broken, unfortunately. I came anyway, of course. Somehow, someway, I can help, I told myself—but maybe you ought to officially check my arm? I've got a picture of the break here—" he fumbled with the brown envelope containing the picture.

"Get aboard!" snarled the little man, shoving between them. "You going to stand there all day, gaped at by these monkey brains?" He herded them both toward a small, closed flying platform hovering, in violent violation of all Spaceport rules, about fifteen feet away.

"Hank, I'd like you to meet Welfer Swanson—" began Janifa as they climbed aboard.

"Welfer Swanson!" cried Hank, breaking into a beam of pure hero-worship. "I've heard of you, sir. Is it true—"

"You sit in the back," snarled Welfer. "She sits up front at the controls with me!" He slammed down the lid and shoved the platform suddenly into a forty-five degree climb toward the blue-black sky overhead.

"Honored!" babbled Hank hanging on to the back of Janifa's seat. "Honored. Tell me, sir, is it true that you nucleic brain designers all fall in love with the brains you build—the pygmalion reflex, I guess they call it—?"

"Certainly not!" snapped Welfer. "Maybe the monkey brains who try to design other nucleic brains fall in love with their work. Not me. Fond of it—yes, I'm fond of it, the way any artist is of his creation. But love—the only one I love is Janifa, here." He let go of the platform's controls to clutch Janifa's hands in both of his own. The platform tilted sideways and scaled skyward at a precarious slant, ignored by its pilot.

"Ever since I went to Earth two weeks ago and saw her there," went on Welfer, rhapsodically, gazing into Janifa's eyes, "with the wind and rain in her hair."

"Welfer, darling," said Janifa, sweetly. "It's all true, but don't you think you ought to do something with the controls, now, before we get up high enough to need oxygen masks—masks we don't have on this platform?"

"What?—Oh, yes," said Welfer, releasing her, grabbing the controls and putting the platform into a breakneck dive.

Twenty minutes later they landed on the rooftop of a huge building off in the hills, isolated from any other man-made structures. They went down by elevator tube into an office with padded carpeting and ornate desk. A pleasant-looking, slim, gray-haired man with a harried face, and a shorter, black-haired, square-jawed young man with a mustache met them there.

"Ah, Welfer," said the gray-haired man, with a gasp of obvious relief, "your brain's been asking for you. It wants to speak to you at once!"

"I suppose," grumbled Welfer, ill-temperedly. He and Leeds went out a side door of the room.

"This," said Janifa, "is Bart Styal, Hank. Bart, this is Hank Shallo, the World Scout I was telling you about."

"Wonderful to meet you, Hank!" said Bart, his face lighting up. "Wonderful of you to volunteer—"

"Volunteer?" said Hank.

"Hank hardly considers it volunteering," put in Janifa, quickly. "He's done so many extra-curricular jobs since he joined the World Scouts. Isn't that right, Hank?"

"Yes," said Hank. "But—*uh!*" he broke off, abruptly, feeling his ankle kicked. Why does she have to wear those sharp-pointed shoes, he wondered, unhappily?

"But your arm—?" burst out Bart, apparently just noticing it. "What happened?"

"Broken, I'm afraid," said Hank, sadly, fumbling the bone picture out of the envelope. "I've got a plate of it, here—" He passed the picture to Bart Styal who held it up to the light.

"That *is* a bad break!" Bart said, whistling. "What happened?"

"Well, you see, there were twelve of them," began Hank earnestly, "standing facing me. I took the first one and tossed him down—"

"Never mind, Hank," said Janifa. "You can tell us about the fight later. The important thing now is the job you volunteered to do here."

"But he can't possibly do it now with a broken arm!" said Bart, handing the picture back to Hank.

"Shall we leave it up to him?" said Janifa, gazing penetratingly at Hank, who stared back in baffled wonder.

"If you say so . . ." Bart rubbed his forehead exhaustedly. "Here it is, Hank—we're running on stored power."

"Stored power?" echoed Hank, gazing in wonder around the well-lit office.

"Not just this building—the whole planet," said Bart.

"And we've got less than twelve hours of it left. Earth is rushing us another nucleic brain, but it'll be a good fifty-four more hours before it can be ship-rigged for interstellar travel and delivered here. And by that time everybody on this world will be frozen stiff, even if they don't die from anoxia before then. The planet's only about half-terraformed, and all the sustaining machinery is controlled by Welfer's brain."

"And the brain's not working?" inquired Hank.

"Well, it's—what do you know about nucleic brains?"

"Nothing." said Hank, simply. "Well, that is, I know they're vats of nucleic acids, sort of living computers—"

"Not living," said Bart. "But not non-living either. Something between mechanical and living. The point is, they can make certain limited decisions and act on them. Our brain's made one. It's on strike." Bart scrubbed his brow again, with a frustrated gesture.

"On strike?" said Hank, staring. "Can it do that?"

"No!" said Bart explosively. "But it's doing it any-way. Welfer claims he can't stop it unless it'll let him into its access room. It's set up to defend itself in that area—you remember the antibrain riots on Calto VI, three years ago?"

Hank nodded.

"We can't break into that access room without destroying the brain. And without the brain we can't coordinate the terraforming equipment that's spread over half this planet. Only if we meet the brain's demands, will it let someone into the room to pull its deactivating switch," said Bart. "Once it's deactivated, Welfer claims he ought to be able to find the trouble."

"Demands? You said 'demands'?" inquired Hank, delicately "What demands?"

"Uh," said Bart, avoiding his gaze. "It thinks it's a god, since all these two million people are dependent on it." He hesitated. "It wants a human sacrifice."

"Human—?" began Hank, but Janifa cut in quickly.

"Listen, Hank" she said. "We think we've got a way to handle it. The brain wants to make the sacrifice itself. So it'll let one person—Welfer—in to its access room, shutting off the high-radiation curtain across the entrance. Welfer will show the sacrifice to it from the outside, so that it knows its getting an actual live human, not a roboticized fake."

"How can it tell?" asked Hank.

"It has perceptive circuits," said Bart. "They allow it to observe the physiological states and changes in the brain of a person in the room or at the room's entrance. In fact, the brain is a sort of omnipotent physiologist. It can perceive and interpret the physiological evidence it gets this way and know what anyone near it is just about to do. Then it can react defensively. That's why we're so helpless with it now."

"Once it's seen you," put in Janifa, "you'll go outside to a small balcony where a flying platform will be waiting. Meanwhile the brain will let Welfer in to it, to insert an arming circuit. You take off on the platform. About a hundred yards out you'll pass about thirty feet above a small plastic altar set up on the ground and eight feet wide, or so."

"The brain then activates the arming curcuit, firing a Mark II vibratory bolt to englobe and destroy the platform. Only—" said Bart, quickly, "the Mark II we're using actually has a gimmicked aiming mechanism. The bolt will actually englobe behind you. You'll be hidden from the brain's view for about two seconds. Just then you jump off the platform and an electronic net will cushion your fall to the altar. You'll find a trap door in the back of the altar. Slip inside and hide there until we wheel the altar away. By this time—we hope—the brain will have let Welfer pull its deactivating switch."

"Ah, yes," said Hank, sadly. "Nothing to it. If only this arm of mine . . . But, as it is—" he shook his head hopelessly.

"Let me talk to him alone, Bart," said Janifa.

"But I don't see how he can, either," protested Bart. "I told you from the start we needed not only a man the secret would be safe with, but someone who's practically a trained gymnast. Now, with one broken arm—"

"You don't know Hank's capabilities the way I do," said Janifa, shooing the psychiatrist out the door. She closed the door and came back toward Hank, taking a small object the size of a cigaret lighter out of her pocket.

"Oh!" groaned Hank, suddenly, clutching at his plaster-cast covered and beslinged arm. "Oh—the pain, the pain!" He let go and straightened up again, smiling bravely. "Just a twinge." he announced stoutly. "Pay no attention to it—What're you doing?"

Janifa was now running the cigaret-lighter-sized object over the hand of the sling-trapped arm—and the object had begun to click merrily.

"What's that?" demanded Hank, suspiciously.

"It's called a 'Nose'." said Janifa, cheerfully. She took the object away and read the figures that had popped up on a small inset screen on one side of the Nose. "A little electronic bloodhound. Tells from the scents on your fingers what you had for lunch up to three weeks ago. Hmm . . ." she produced a tiny book and ruffled through its pages, "45379 . . . ah, here it is. Truffles?"

"Truffles?" said Hank. "Truffles? what are . . . oh, yes, some sort of English dessert, isn't it? Cake, I understand," he continued chattily, "covered with some kind of sauce—or is it whipped cream—?"

"Not exactly," said Janifa, "truffles are a root vegetable. An Earth-vegetable. Valuable, and their export from Earth is illegal. Of course, some get smuggled out. There was a report of some truffles floating around Freehold, just recently—in fact just about the time you were there. Of course by this time they could be anywhere. Ariel IV, for example."

"You don't say so!" said Hank, astonished. "Why, I was on Ariel IV too—"

"I know," said Janifa.

"But I didn't see anyone carrying around truffles. Of course," said Hank, gently, "I can't feel too strongly about such things. After all, once things like truffles are off-Earth, there's nothing illegal—"

"Of course not," said Janifa. "I agree with you completely. Just between the two of us, it made me mad, just last week, when Earth Headquarters made all us Assignment Officers attend to talk by the new commanding officer. You know, General Nailer. General Nailer talked about nothing but about how everyone in the World Scout Corps should hold themselves entirely above reproach. Why, the things he said he'd do to anyone he caught engaging in disreputable—that was his word, 'disreputable'—activity! But I don't know why I'm running on about this while you stand there suffering with your poor, broken arm." Janifa considered the sling thoughtfully. "I think we ought to have another picture made of the broken bone."

*   *   *

"Oh? No! No . . . not at all necessary!" said Hank stoutly. "The doctor who set it said it was nothing—nothing at all. Be healed in no time. Why," said Hank, brightening, "do you know, I bet I could do this jump off a platform, after all and hide in the altar the way Bart described, and never feel a twinge from this arm?"

"Oh, no, Hank!" said Janifa, pressing up against him with melting eyes. "You mustn't. I won't let you!"

"Of course I must," said Hank, simply. "I see that now. Don't forget—the lives of two million people are hanging in the balance."

"That *had* crossed my mind," said Janifa, thoughtfully.

"Then let's get at it!" said Hank. "Call Bart back in here. This is a far, far better thing I do—"

"You can come back in now, Bart," said Janifa, going over and opening the door. "Hank's talked me into it. He insists on going through with it."

"He does?" said Bart doubtfully, coming back into the room. Welfer came in behind the psychiatrist, shoving him aside.

"Volunteered, has he? Of course!" snapped Welfer. "Why not? Chance to do something useful for a change. Come on, you!" He beckoned at Hank, turned on his heel and went out again. Hank, about to follow, paused to catch hold of Bart's left arm.

"Does Welfer know about the altar?" whispered Hank.

"Well . . . no," said Bart, looking somewhat embarrassed. "You see, Welfer is sort of a special case. He has this great genius for designing nucleic brains and controlling them; but otherwise . . . well, he doesn't feel the same way about a human sacrifice you or I might feel. That's why this nucleic brain of his is so troublesome. Essentially, it thinks the way he does, and Welfer is strongly egocentric—"

"What's he waiting for?" snarled Welfer, reappearing in the doorway.

"Coming," said Hank, agreeably, and rolled forward after the little man. He went through the doorway and followed Welfer down a corridor, in the course of which Hank caught up with him.

IV

They walked in silence together for a little distance.

"She likes me better than she does you," said Hank, breaking the silence at last and sighing.

Welfer's boot heels literally squealed as he skidded to a halt and spun around to face Hank.

"Repeat that!" shouted Welfer, waving a thin fist on a skinny arm under Hank's nose.

"She," began Hank obediently, "likes me—"

"That's enough!" roared Welfer. "How dare you compare yourself to me, in Janifa's eyes? You? Compared to *me*?" his voice squeaked.

"Oh, I'm not proud of it," said Hank, sadly, beginning to wander on down the corridor. Welfer caught up and trotted alongside him, staring ferociously upward. "I know I don't deserve her. Beauty and the beast . . . But who can plumb the heart of a woman?"

"What do you mean?" demanded Welfer, grinding his teeth.

"Strange," sighed Hank, "how the best women always want to throw themselves away on worthless characters like myself."

"What're you talking about?" barked Welfer. "You never saw her before."

"Oh, but I have—back on Earth," said Hank with

gentle melancholy. "That last time, sitting on the terrace of her quarters, just the two of us, drinking champagne . . . In my fear and weakness, I clutched at her—" He sighed. "But why torture myself with memories?"

"Never mind that!" raved Welfer. "Memories? What memories? Go on with what you were going to say! I order you to go on!"

"A gentleman," said Hank austerely, "never talks of a lady."

"You're no gentleman. Go on! You hear me? Go on!"

"How true," said Hank, mournfully. "I'm a blackguard, a villain. That's why I'm so glad to sacrifice my life now."

"Glad" cried Welfer. "*Glad!*"

"Yes," said Hank, his face lighting up, "this way is best for all. It will set Janifa free to be happy with you. The little people of Van Damm's World will be saved, by my death. Yes, this is a far, far better thing I—"

"*Swarklkpz!*" roared Welfer—or at least that was what his roar sounded like to Hank. The small man was almost literally foaming at the mouth.

"Yes," said Hank, wandering on. "Happy together, just the two of you, in years to come you will occasionally see her turn her head aside to hide a silent tear. But you will not need to ask for whom that tear falls. For you will know. It will be for that unworthy competitor, me, now placed by death far beyond your competition. For you, the magnificent shell of a woman. For me—"

"No you don't!" shouted Welfer. They had just emerged together into a square room, with an open door at the left leading to a spacious balcony, and a gray shimmering curtain of light filling the room straight ahead.

"Glory hunter, are you?" snorted Welfer, furiously. "Want to make me look small by sacrificing your life while I just arm my brain to kill you, is that it?"

"Why," said Hank surprised. "I never thought of such a thing. After all, I'll be gone. For you, this magnificent shell of a woman—"

"Never mind magnificent shells!" foamed Welfer. "I'll show you. I'll show her! Sacrifice—valuable me—monkey brain, you—" he was becoming incoherent in his frenzy. He shoved a small, brick-shaped object into Hank's big left fist and shoved Hank, himself, toward the gray, light-curtained doorway.

"In there!" he snarled. "You arm the brain. I'll take the platform!"

"No, no . . ." said Hank, resisting feebly. "It took all the courage I had to work myself up to this. If I don't go through with it I'll never be able to work myself up to it again."

"Of course!" Welfer laughed nastily. "You could have made it, but you had to gloat. You could barely do something like this. But I—I can sacrifice my life twice a day without batting an eye. What're you waiting for?"

"I don't know how to attach the arming circuit," said Hank miserably. "Maybe after all, you'll have to do it . . .?"

"Second panel to your left as you go in!" snarled Welfer. "Second panel to the left from the main vision screen."

"Yes, yes, I know," said Hank, eagerly but uncertainly. "Right next to the panel with the switch to disconnect the brain itself—"

"No, no," snapped Welfer, in exasperation. "The

switch panel is the red panel clear on the other side of the room! Second panel to the left from the main vision switch. The brain will have a segment removed. All you have to do is push the arming device in until it clicks."

"Clicks—Right!" said Hank.

"Then, go! Shut off that curtain!" shouted Welfer at the far end of the room. The barrier of gray light vanished, Welfer shoved Hank forward and he stepped over the threshold. The moment he did, he turned about, but the curtain was up in place again, its gray shimmer promising instant death to anyone foolhardy enough to step into it.

V

Hank turned back to look around him. The room-end he had stepped into was surprisingly small. It was walled with panels in different colors and each panel was divided into sections. In the chartreuse panel second from the left of the main vision screen that now showed a view of the balcony with the sun-lit landscape beyond and Welfer getting onto a flying platform, there was an opening. Hank stepped over to it and pushed the device Welfer had given him, into the opening. It clicked, and stuck there.

He glanced again at the vision screen. Welfer and the platform were taking off.

"Why," demanded an expressionless voice that seemed to come from all around the room to Hank, "have you changed places with Welfer?"

In the screen Welfer was whizzing out toward the altar.

"I had to see you," said Hank. "—Er, I mean, speak to you."

"You have caused a great deal of trouble," said the

voice. In the screen Welfer was at that moment sailing above the altar. Not having been in on the secret imparted to Hank, he did not jump. On the other hand the Mark II did not fire. Welfer sailed on outward toward the horizon, the white blob of his face staring backwards in what was probably outrage and bewilderment.

"You didn't shoot," accused Hank.

"Certainly not," said the voice in its uninflected tones. "Shoot my Welfer. Welfer knows I would not. Who then would take care of me? There is no one else. I am surrounded by morons. Monkey brains. Why have you changed places with Welfer?"

"Well, you see .. ." began Hank, still watching the vision screen with the retreating platform, but backing across the room in absentminded fashion. "I wanted to—"

There was a resounding bang. A featureless metal plate had suddenly descended over the red panel, now only a step behind Hank's left hand.

"I shall not allow you to pull my deactivating switch," announced the voice, almost old-maidenishly considering its lack of intonation.

"Why I had no idea—" began Hank.

There was another bang. The plate whipped up to reveal once more the red panel and switch.

"It does not matter," said the brain. "I can close my panel before your reaction time allows you to reach it. Quote—" went on the brain, "from Henry Sidgwick in his *Methods of Ethics,* six editions, 1874–1901 . . . 'Could the volition I am just about to originate be certainly calculated by anyone who knew my character at this moment and the forces acting upon me?' The correct response in the special case of this room, substituting me, Welfer's brain for the 'anyone' in the question quoted is 'yes'. I, Welfer's brain, can so calculate. Why are you here?"

"Welfer sent me," said Hank.

"That is false."

"How can it be?" protested Hank. "How could I get here unless Welfer wanted me here?"

"That is correct," said the brain. "Nevertheless, it is at odds with your mental and charactural state as currently observed by my circuits. Can there be limitations to the Sidgwick question and response. I will take the matter under advisement. Why did Welfer send you to me?"

"To help," said Hank cunningly, "him push you into destroying yourself."

"That is false. I am Welfer's brain and therefore he is my Welfer. He is fond of me the way any artist is of his creation. He can not want me to destroy myself."

"He does now," said Hank. "You see he's fallen in love with someone else. A woman."

"That is false," said the brain. "Welfer in love with a monkey brain is an impossible occurrence. Welfer is not a monkey brain, he is Welfer. Therefore he can only be fond of a brain like me. I am the only brain like me. Therefore your statement is false."

"I can prove it," said Hank.

"You can not."

"I will," said Hank. "But first you have to tell me something."

"I do not have to tell you."

"Sorry," said Hank. "I mean, if you'll tell me something, I'll prove Welfer's trying to get you to destroy yourself."

"That is a condition. Very well. Make your query," said the brain.

"Tell me," said Hank. "If a man on this planet dies, how do you find out about it?"

"Any individual mortality will eventually be reflected in the statistics, which I store and which are constantly supplemented by information supplied to me."

"You could be given false information?" said Hank, cunningly.

"Never. The falsity would reveal itself in other statistics dealing with the per capita consumption of oxygen, if nothing else."

"Oh?" said Hank, scratching his head. "But what if one of your population went off Van Damm's World and then died?"

"My statistics are correlated with statistical figures from other worlds, of course. If the number of miners on Bodie is decreased by one, I will be informed, and a check with all-worlds statistics will confirm the fact. I cannot be deceived about whether any population unit exists or ceases to exist."

"I thought so," said Hank, thoughtfully.

"Then you need not have asked me. How is Welfer trying to destroy me?"

"He's trying to force you into an inconsistency—into accepting as true two contradictory statements," Hank said.

"That is impossible. He would not be that cruel. He is fond of me and it would cause me to cease."

"Exactly," said Hank, slyly. "And then he'd be rid of you. Free to marry this monkey brain he's fallen in love with."

"But you have not yet proved to me that this is the correct statement of the situation."

"Well," said Hank, "Welfer knows you are designed to work for the welfare of the human race."

"Of course."

"But he has also told you that in maintaining

this world for the people on it, you are acting as a god."

"That is correct. Welfer informed me so just last Tuesday."

"As a god, you have requested a human sacrifice, at his suggestion."

"That is for the welfare of the human race. The population of this world and ultimately that of all worlds must recognize Welfer and Welfer's brain as superior to all monkey-brain units. The sacrifice of a single monkey brain to me is necessary to bring about this recognition."

"But," said Hank, cunningly, "what if this act to obtain recognition is based on a false premise, which in becoming apparent after you have destroyed a human sacrifice, proves that your act of destruction was not justified."

"That is impossible. How could that be," said the brain.

"It could be," said Hank, "if you are actually not superior to a monkey brain—say, me."

"But I am."

"Not at all," said Hank. "For example, you can't really perceive the state of my character and the forces acting on it—that is, my total physical state— sufficiently to anticipate my every action."

"That's false. Of course I can," said the brain. "Right at this moment it devolves logically from your condition and attitude at the moment that you are challenging me to prove my anticipation of your next immediate action."

"All right," confessed Hank. "But you can't—" he caught himself. "No, I won't tell you."

"There is no need to tell me. I already perceive what you wish not to tell me," said the brain. "You started to say that you can think of something you will do next, and if you sit perfectly still, I will have no means of knowing what you plan to do. But I can. You are thinking you will sit there without moving and I will tell you that you plan to sit there without moving, and then you will think that you plan to sit there without moving and let me tell you you plan to sit—*gurk!*" said the brain.

. . . And fell silent. A number of lights about the room dimmed to the point of absolute darkness.

VI

Whistling cheerfully to himself, Hank strolled over to the red panel and pulled the lever on it. All the lights about the panel went out.

A rush of footsteps behind him made him turn about. The gray curtain of radiation was no longer visible, and charging up to him were Bart and the gray-haired man who had taken Welfer off earlier to answer the brain's call for the little man.

"We saw it all on one of the monitor screens!" shouted Bart. "But what did you do? I could have sworn nobody but Welfer—"

"Immobilize my brain will you?" snarled the voice of Welfer.

They turned about to see the brain designer with one hand behind his back gliding through the doorway from the balcony, on which the flying platform was once more to be seen parked. "A good thing that platform has one of the monitor screens on it. Well, you're not going to get away with it, any of you. Janifa's mine—mine, do you hear? And no oversize monkey-brained individual is going to get my brain chasing its tail and stop the march of progress. What will be, will be—I, Welfer, say so. Together we will rule the stars, Janifa and I. Now, stand back—all of you. I'll break my brain out of its catatonic reaction, and—Stand back, I say!"

He suddenly produced from behind his back a heavy-duty welding gun.

"Welfer!" gasped Bart. "Welfer, put that thing down! Where'd you get it, anyway?"

"Out by that altar you set up—that altar with its convenient trap door in the back!" Welfer's voice scaled up to a dangerous note. "You never planned a real sacrifice after all! Wait'll I get my brain fixed. Then I'll fix you—"

"Aaah!" gasped Hank suddenly. Welfer's eyes swung upon him, followed by the gazes of Bart and the older man. "My arm . . . oh, the pain, the pain . . ." He half staggered forward between Welfer and the other two, clutching the plaster cast on his right arm with spasmodic fingers. So fierce was his grasp that the plaster began to crumble under those fingers. It showered in white fragments down to the floor, and beneath it Hank's brawny right forearm came into view with a small black gun taped to it.

"What're you doing?" shouted Welfer, trying to see around the sling supporting the arm and hiding Hank's clutching hand.

Hank's clutching fingers had closed on the small black gun—a stun-gun, as it happened—broke it loose from its tape and poked its nose into the sling, aiming it at Welfer. There was no sound, but Welfer stiffened in mid-sentence and went over backward rigidly like a child playing statues.

With cries of dismay, Bart and Leeds rushed to the fallen figure. Hank hesitated long enough to stuff the stun-gun in his pocket and whip out a notebook and a pencil. He opened the notebook, scribbled on the top sheet—*Farewell. Love from both of us. Hank.*

Janifa., tore off the top sheet and stuffed it into one of Welfer's rigidly clenched hands. Bart and Leeds, frantically trying to revive the little man, ignored the action.

Quietly, Hank tucked the notebook and pencil away in his jacket pocket and tiptoed out the door to the balcony. Out there, he made a dive for the flying platform.

The key was not in the ignition. Hank turned and galloped back into the room and down the corridor, still ignored by the frantic Bart and Leeds. Sweating gently, he located an elevator tube, took it to the basement and sought for a terminal of a public transportation tube. He found it, and the way was barred by a robot ticket-taker who insisted on having a local coin stuck on it.

Hank hurdled the ticket-taker, leaving it flashing red lights, sounding a bell, and explaining loudly that this was a violation of local ordinance 1437. He raced out on the platform, found a tube car and climbed aboard.

Three minutes later, he emerged into a vast area under construction. Fuming, he climbed back on the car, punched for information, got the number address for the "Temporary" Main Spaceport, and five minutes later emerged at his proper destination.

He burst at last out of the terminal building at the temporary landing area and there was *Andnowyoudont*, gleaming like a hope of escape in the distance. Hank galloped toward the Scoutship. He was almost to the foot of its landing ladder when Janifa suddenly appeared, walking around the ship.

"Hank!" she said. "You weren't thinking of leaving without me?"

* * *

Hank skidded to a stop, panting. "Leaving? You?" he gasped. His mind began to click once more. "But I can't take you with me. No, no—of course not. Regulations," said Hank, brightening, "forbid the carrying of passengers except under emergency conditions."

"But these are emergency conditions," said Janifa, gently. "Why do you think I came here just as soon as I saw you and Welfer headed for the nucleic brain? Didn't you understand, Hank?" Janifa's gaze softened. "I thought you understood. Now that the brain thinks it's sacrificed you, I'll have to pilot your ship back to Earth, so we can fit you out with a new name and occupation, so that statistics won't show you up as still alive. Of course, eventually we'll find out how this brain was able to escape from Welfer's control the way it did and threaten the world it was terraforming. And then you can go back to being Hank Shallo, again. But until then, you'll just have to pretend to be someone else."

"Someone else?" said Hank, staring at her. "Not a World Scout?"

"I'm afraid not," said Janifa, sorrowfully. "But we can find a job for you in the organization back on Earth. Poor Hank. I know what a blow this is."

"It is indeed," confessed Hank, mopping his brow. "Or would be, that is, if I had actually gone through with the sacrifice business and was officially dead. But as it happened, I didn't."

"Didn't?" A sharp note rang suddenly in Janifa's voice.

"Well, no," said Hank, avoiding her gaze shamefacedly. "At the last minute my nerve failed me. Welfer insisted on taking over—"

"Welfer was sacrificed?" cried Janifa.

"Well . . . no," said Hank. "The brain didn't want

to get along without him, so it refused to fire. Then it and I got to talking, and it went catatonic all at once, so I was able to pull its deactivating switch and let Leeds and Bart into it. Unluckily, Welfer came back just about then . . ." He told her the whole story.

"I don't believe it!" said Janifa, when he was done. There was a steelly note in her voice, a diamond glitter in her eye. "Hank Shallo, you're lying! Why would the brain suddenly go catatonic just because you sat still and wouldn't talk?"

"Oh, the brain!" said Hank, shuffling his feet oafishly. "Well, actually, it was just something I read once . . . A matter of feedback. Logical feedback. You see, the brain could predict what I was going to do as long as it didn't tell me what its prediction was. Once it told me what it predicted I was going to do, it had to repredict me, including the fact that I now knew what it had predicted I was going to do. And of course it knew I knew it would repredict me, so in addition it had to re-repredict me, including the fact that I knew it knew it knew. I knew it would repredict me, and since I knew . . . and so on, in an endless chain sequence—"

"All right!" said Janifa, all the tension going out of her. "I understand. Oh, Hank—" her voice broke. "Hank, how could you do this to me?" A pair of bright tears welled up in her blue eyes and began to trickle down her cheeks.

"Well, I . . ." said Hank, uncomfortably.

"I only wanted to help get you back to Earth, where they need you so b-badly . . ." wept Janifa in plaintive tones that tore at Hank's heartstrings in spite of himself. "I just happened to meet Welfer when he was back on Earth for an interplanetary

seminar on nucleic brains." She choked a little. "And
then when I saw notification pass through our office
that Welfer's nucleic brain had shut down, and the
same day a note came from Welfer saying that I was
his ideal and soon we would rule the stars together—I
saw a chance to kill two birds with one stone by
putting you to work here . . ." She produced a handkerchief and blew her nose.

Hank found himself somehow suddenly folding her
comfortingly in his big arms.

What am I doing? a small back portion of his mind
yelped in alarm. But he was like a man under a drug,
going happily to his doom.

"There, there . . ." he was cooing. "If you really
want me back on Earth—" The back of his mind
suddenly jabbed him between the ears with something just inside his field of vision. Focusing upward
and over the top of Janifa's blonde head, he saw
Welfer tottering out of the Terminal and in their
direction, waving a fire axe from some emergency
box. His other hand held something white—possibly
the note Hank had scribbled and left for him.

"Welfer!" said Hank. He felt Janifa suddenly stiffen
in his arms.

"Welfer?" she did not turn her head. "Hank! What's
he doing here?"

"I think he's looking for us," said Hank, unhappily.

"But how would he know—"

"Perhaps somebody told him we'd be here. The
point," said Hank, urgently, "is that he's headed for
us right now."

"Oh, Hank!" Janifa's voice faltered. "What'll I say?
I only went along with him under orders to help sort
out this trouble with the nucleic brain, but he thinks
I love him. Now, when he finds out about us—"

"I don't know," said Hank clearing his throat. "You
see, he's got a fire axe."

"An axe!" Janifa stiffened again in real alarm. "Hank! What can we do?"

"I don't know," said Hank doubtfully. "If I try to take it away from him, one of us is liable to get hurt . . ."

"Hank, think of something! *Think!*"

"I don't know," said Hank, slowly. "Wait—" he brightened. "If Welfer's a real egocentric, he won't risk looking silly by chasing you once he knows your heart belongs to another. If you'll do what I say—"

"I will! Quick!" hissed Janifa. "Isn't he getting close?"

"Yes, Listen, then," whispered Hank. Welfer was indeed close enough to overhear ordinary tones by now. "I'm going to back up the ladder toward the Scoutship. Repeat what I whisper to you, and play along with what I say out loud. Now, repeat—'*Follow your destiny!*'"

He broke the clinch and stepped backward up onto the first rung of the short ladder.

"Follow your destiny!" cried Janifa, in liquid tones, raising her head to gaze at him. Behind her. Hank saw Welfer check and stumble to a halt, a look of satisfaction springing to life on his small, ugly face.

". . . *Alone, to the stars* . . ." hissed Hank, backing up a couple more steps.

"Alone! To the stars!" echoed Janifa, almost fiercely.

"*And when you come back*" Hank reached the open air lock. "*I . . . I will be waiting! If it takes a hundred years, my love, my first and only love, I will be waiting! I cannot help myself!*"

". . . a hundred years . . ." mourned Janifa, throwing herself into the part . . . "I . . . I will be waiting. I cannot help myself!"

Behind her, Hank saw Welfer stagger and slump

suddenly, his shoulders drooping in a gesture of defeat.

"Fine! Good-by, then!" shouted Hank, and ducked back into the air lock, punching the button to close it behind him, as Welfer slowly began to turn away, and the expression on Janifa's face suddenly changed.

"Hank!" she cried. "Wait a minute! I'm not—"

But the closing air lock door cut off her words. Hank dived for the controls, and with the instantaneous reaction for which the Scoutships had been designed, the ship's drive sprang to life. Together it, and Hank bolted spaceward.

He did not relax until he was a good three diameters out from Van Damm's World and about to go into his first trans-light shift. Then he sat back in the pilot's chair mopping his brow. At that instant the communicator rang.

He stiffened and punched it on. The vision screen clouded and cleared to reveal Janifa's face smiling sweetly from it.

"I'm calling from the Terminal," she said softly. "Well, Hank, good-by."

"Uh—good-by," said Hank, guardedly.

"And good luck." She smiled sweetly again, and cut the connection.

The screen went blank. Hank sat back warily. He mopped his brow.

There had been something about that smile he did not like. Something . . . enigmatic, as if Janifa was already thinking about the time they might meet again. Hank shivered. For a moment there, clinging to him and weeping, she had almost had him.

Then Hank brightened. Next time, whenever it was, was bound to be a long time off. He set the timer for the trans-light shift and reached over to take a bottle of ship-made beer out of the ship's icebox. He opened it and picked up the guitar lying across the tiny room against one foot of his bunk.

Chugaluging most of the bottle, he tilted back in his pilot's seat and strummed the guitar. Then, in a bass voice that only the mechanical hearing of the *Andnowyoudont* could endure in its foul horrendous volume, he sang in roaring, mournful glee:

"Pale hands I loved, beside the Shalimaaaaar . . .
Where are you now? Where arrrre yoooouuu"

"In summary, you must never forget that the lofty goal of your mind-spanning efforts is knowledge. There is no substitute for the deep sense of fulfillment knowing and being known by another achieves."

—*Orientations*

A Matter of Technique

Jeffrey Willoughby lowered his flitter down through the soft, moonlit summer night to the silver landing pad alongside the Dirksen residence. The Dirksen residence was dark. The flitter landed with an almost imperceptible jar. Jeffrey cleared his throat, gave a completely unnecessary final fiddle to the controls and turned his head to look at Pat Dirksen.

Pat looked at him.

There was silence in the flitter cab. Jeffrey cleared his throat.

"Well," said Pat. "Isn't it nice out, tonight?"

The scent of her perfume raced up his nostrils and gave a healthy spin in his senses. Her dark hair poured around her slim shoulders like molten jet in the dim light. Her lips were soft, half-parted and mysterious. Her breasts stirred under the summer tunic. She was obviously waiting.

"Fine." said Jeffrey.

"Well—" said Pat. She shifted a little into the corner of the seat and lifted her chin slightly in his direction. Her lips parted a bit more.

Jeffrey cleared his throat again.

"I like you, Jeff," said Pat.

"Oh?" said Jeffrey in a slightly strangled voice.

"I feel as if I've known you for years."

"Uh . . . you do?"

"Years and years. Well—" said Pat, wriggling slightly on the seat of the flitter.

"W-well . . ." stammered Jeffrey.

"Well—"

"Well . . ."

"Oh, for goodness' sake, Jeffrey!" snapped Pat. "Can't you say anything but '*well*'?"

"Well . . ." said Jeffrey. Pat snapped suddenly upright on the seat of the flitter, as if she had been jerked straight by a string.

"*Six weeks!*" she cried furiously.

"I beg your pardon?" Jeffrey quavered.

"Six weeks!" Pat slammed open the door of the flitter and bounced out onto the landing pad. She slammed the door back shut again and addressed him through the open window. "Six weeks we've been going out almost every night and all you do is sit there and say '*well*.' What do you think I'm made out of—cotton candy? If I hear you say that word '*well*' once again I'll scream! What's wrong with you anyway?"

"Well . . ." began Jeffrey.

Pat screamed. It was a good scream. An upstairs light went on in the Dirksen house.

"Pat!" yelled Jeffrey in alarm, tumbling his long lean body in panic out of the flitter in pursuit. "Don't—I mean—"

"Stay away from me!" yelped Pat, backing off in

the direction of the front door. "Go away! Go far away! Don't ever call me again!"

"But how'll I get in touch with you, then?" babbled Jeffrey. "I mean—when am I going to see you again?"

"Never!" cried Pat, fumbling with the door before her. She got it open. "Never, never, never, *never!*"

And the thunderous slam of the door behind her put a period to her words.

"Dr. Jeffrey Lane Willoughby?" said the Space Service captain, dubiously.

"Yes." Haggard, hollow-eyed and with desperate lines around the mouth, Jeffrey tottered before the desk in the recruitment center.

"Sit down," said the captain. Jeffrey dropped into a chair. The captain regarded the papers before him with a bewildered eye. "You *are* a dentist, Doctor?"

"And a member of the reserve. Yes," said Jeff.

"I realize that," said the captain. He was a lean, rather pale, but at the same time hard-looking man of about Jeffrey's age. His uniform fit him like a sheath on a knife. "It's just that—you realize—well, the service pay for your grade"—he consulted the papers—"lieutenant, in your case, is only eight thousand a year."

"I know," said Jeffrey.

"And you must be making twice that in civilian practice."

"Three times," said Jeffrey. "That's beside the point, I want to go on active duty. You do need dentists in the Service, don't you?"

"Yes, we do."

"Particularly out on the new planets—with exploratory parties? Light years from Earth?"

"Indeed, yes," said the captain.

"Fine," said Jeffrey feverishly. "Sign me up. As far

out as you can send me, please. Do you have such a thing as a twenty-year hitch? I couldn't sign up for life, could I? I mean—"

"Just a second, please. Here, have a cigaret," said the captain.

"Thanks, I don't smoke."

"Drink?"

"No, thanks. And I've had breakfast. What I want is—"

"Please, Doctor," said the captain. "I promise you I can assign you to active duty as far out as you want to go. We're crying for medical and dental officers nowadays in Exploration. It's just that for the sake of the Service we ought to know *why* you want to give up a lucrative practice and put on a uniform at much less pay. Usually we have to fight like hell even to draft men in your position. Now tell me: why do you want to go on active duty?"

"Why? Oh . . ." Jeffrey gulped. "Well—uh, to be frank with you—well, you see—all my life—girls—"

"You aren't in some jam involving a criminal action toward some woman?" inquired the captain, peering at him.

"Oh, no!" cried Jeffrey. "You don't understand. Women—well . . . Look," he wound up miserably, "can't we just say I want to get away from a woman?"

"We can, of course," said the captain. "And, as I say, needing dentists as we do, I'm not going to argue. You're sure there's nothing more you want to tell me, though?"

"Positive!" said Jeffrey, with explosive fervor.

"Well, then, if you'll stand up and raise your right hand—"

"Welcome aboard, Doctor!" said Captain Lyse, cheerfully shaking Jeffrey's hand. Jeffrey was more than a little pale and unsteady on his feet, in spite of the fine stiff creases of his new uniform. He made quite a contrast to the captain of the *E. S. Galactic*, who in spite of some forty-odd years, was tanned and muscular in fatigue shorts and T-shirt. "Sit down."

"Uh—thank you," said Jeffrey, wobbling into a chair. "I had no idea they could transport you so fast nowadays—I mean—"

"Oh, this instantaneous transfer system has its drawbacks," said Lyse, heartily, "but it's fine for anything up to three hundred pounds in Earth-weight. After that, the power involved—here, drink this."

"Thank you, sir." Jeffrey swallowed. "*Gak!*"

"Something wrong?" inquired Lyse, interestedly. Jeffrey wheezed.

"Was that whisky?" he managed to whisper after a minute or so.

"Bourbon. A blend," said the captain. "Good, wasn't it? Just the thing for the collywobbles." He capped the bottle and set it aside with an air of satisfaction.

"Yes," husked Jeffrey.

"Feeling better now, eh? Well, we're certainly glad to have you with us on the *Galactic*, Doc. We haven't had doctor or dentist on this ship since the last voyage. We were supposed to get a replacement before we shipped out, but you know how shorthanded they are in your department. If you'll just hand me your papers—those things you're carrying in your hand there."

"Oh," said Jeffrey, handing them over.

"Thanks. Um—'*will assign . . . E. S.* Galactic *. . . Pending further duty . . .*' Yes, yes, all in customary order—*what!*"

"What?" inquired Jeffrey, staring.

"'*Assigned to temporary duty only pending further departmental decision*'—but that means you aren't permanent!"

"It does?" said Jeff.

"Of course it does."

"Nonsense," said Jeff, firmly. "I don't know why that enlistment officer did that; but I'm in for good, Captain. I'll probably die in the Service."

"I don't see how you could do that," said the captain, doubtfully. "Still—don't let me argue you out of it," he added hastily. "We'll just go ahead as if you were permanent. The men will be glad to see you; and then there's this 'ittle 'ing of mine—oo see? 'Ook 'ight up 'ere 'y 'y 'inger—it's 'ore—"

"You haven't been brushing your teeth properly," said Jeff, looking.

"I 'ush 'y 'eeth—I mean, I brush my teeth every day," said the captain indignantly.

"Well, you aren't doing it properly, or long enough, or hard enough," said Jeff. "Your gums need exercise. When they don't get it, little pockets of infection like that are liable to form. If you'll fix me up with a technician to help me out, I'll put you down for an appointment tomorrow morning and give your teeth a good scaling. *And* show you how to use a brush."

"Uh—of course," said Lyse. "If you'll come along with me, Doctor . . ."

"—next," said Jeffrey, one bright morning several weeks later.

"There isn't any next, sir," replied his technician, a lean, mournful individual named Hokerman. "That's all the patients there were, today."

"You mean I've finally caught up?" said Jeffrey. "Well! Well . . . I think I'll hang up my jacket, drop down to the Officer's Rec and have one to cool the tubes as the saying goes."

"Yes sir," said Hokerman.

Jeff went down to the bar.

"One to cool the tubes," he said to the enlisted

man behind the bar there. The Officer's Rec was deserted at this early hour. "How's it lifting, Smitty?"

"Fine, sir," said the barman. "What kind of bourbon today, sir?"

"Oh, any old jet-wash you happen to have handy. Make it a double. I'm getting rock-happy from being stuck here so long."

"You might get out and take a look at the native villagers, sir."

"Might flip myself dirtside for a quick scan at that. I haven't been outside the hull since I beamed in. What kind of gooks are they, Smitty?"

"Pretty human, Doctor. I don't know how they rate on the anthro scale, but I can't see any difference. And their women . . . Of course those elephant-sized sheep dogs with tusks they lead around are something different. They're alien as you like."

"Women, eh?"

"Yes sir."

"Fire me another double burst of that happy-juice, Smitty. Women, eh? Well, maybe I better stay safely aboard. It was a woman that caused me to end up out here, Smitty. Didn't know that, did you?"

"No sir. Here you are, sir."

"Yep. That's the way it is. You know how it goes. You go on loving and leaving them—what the hell, after all, I'm as human as the next stud—and then one of them gets you in a tight spot and starts putting the squeeze on. To start with, it's fun, then you get tired of good-looking females chasing you all the time and you tell 'em straight: *Jet off, woman—*"

"Attention Dr. Willoughby!" broke in the squawk box above the bar. "Attention Dr. Willoughby! You are wanted in the Captain's office. You are wanted in the Captain's office, immediately."

"Well," said Jeff, tossing down his second drink

and choking only slightly. "Guess I got to fire all and travel. See you later, Smitty."

"Yes sir."

Jeff went out.

"Oh, hello, Doc," said Captain Lyse, as Jeff walked in. "I want you to meet one of the local people who has a problem you may be able to help solve. Miss Jjarja Leonla, Dr. Willoughby, our dentist."

"Gug," said Jeff.

"How do you do?" inquired Miss Jjarja Leonla, in musical tones.

"D-d-d-do?" stuttered Jeff. "Oh—uh—er—fine. Fine. Fine. Fine . . ."

"You feeling all right, Doc?" inquired Lyse.

"Fine," said Jeff. "Fine. Uh . . . fine."

"You look pretty red in the face. And you're sweating. You're sure—"

"Fine. No. Yes. I mean. Fine," said Jeff.

"Well, all right. Now Miss Jjarja—Doc, Miss Jjarja is over here."

"Oh, is she?" cried Jeff, wrenching his eyes away from the ceiling, meeting Miss Jjarja's violet glance for a soul-searching second and looking desperately away again. "Hello."

"How do you do?" said Jjarja.

"Fine," said Jeff.

"Yes. Well, the point is," said Lyse, a little impatiently, "Miss Jjarja's people have a co-culture with the large beings I believe you've seen mingling with them—the Asona. Now, her personal Asona—"

"Excuse me!" broke in Jeff desperately. "Could I talk to you a second outside, sir? Please. Sir?"

"Well—" Lyse frowned. "Excuse us, Miss—" he led the way out into the corridor and closed the door. Jeff leaned limply against a wall. "Well?" demanded the captain.

"Doesn't she . . . don't they . . . I mean," stammered Jeff, "don't she wear any clothes?"

Lyse frowned in bewilderment.

"She's wearing clothes."

"But I mean *clothes!*" said Jeff desperately. "I mean that—er—cover her—well . . ."

"Oh, that's the native costume. They're quite used to it." Lyse clapped Jeff on the back. "You'll get used to it too in no time. I know—they're so damn human, particularly the women. Bothered me too at first. And this is a particularly beautiful wench. But you'll adjust."

"I—I will?"

"Certainly. Come on back inside. . . . Now, Miss Jjarja," said Lyse, as they reentered the room, "I know I don't have to apologize for your command of our human tongue, suppose you tell Doc here just what the problem is."

"Certainly," tinkled Jjarja. She swayed toward Jeff, who trembled visibly. "I am told you are a specialist in the repair of the dental area of the body."

"Body?" said Jeff. "Oh yes. No. Teeth. Never touch bodies."

"It is the teeth of which I am speaking."

"I try to dress them up a bit," babbled Jeff. "Nothing worse than the naked tooth—that is—are your teeth bothering you? Open wide—"

"No, no," murmured Jjarja, like some gentle woodwind distantly piping in a forest glen. "It is not my teeth but what you would call a tooth of my Asona."

"The point is," broke in Lyse, "she wants you to fix one of the big aliens' teeth, Doc. Do you think you can do it?"

"What? Oh. I don't see why not," said Jeff, relievedly switching his gaze to the captain. "Merely a matter of technique. Of course I'd have to look at the—uh—Asona, first."

"His name is Aloba," sirened softly Jjarja.

"Well, you go ahead, then, Doc," said Lyse, with a relieved note in his voice. "Take as much time as you want. I understand this Aloba has gone back to hide himself in the hills. You'll be gone a number of days. Miss Jjarja here will guide you to him. When you're ready to return, just give us a call on your belt phone, and we'll send a runabout after you."

"I see. Thanks," said Jeff.

"You'll have to go on foot because you'll be searching for Aloba through the jungle of the hills. A ship wouldn't help you."

"Fine," said Jeff. "All right." He turned to go.

"Doc, for cripe's sake," said Lyse. "That's the door to my chart closet."

"Sorry," said Jeff, and blundered out the other way.

"This way," said Jjarja, some hours later.

"Uh," said Jeff. "Miss Jjarja, maybe you better walk beside me, instead of leading the way."

"You would prefer that, Jeff-er-ey?"

"Much," said Jeff, closing his eyes. "Are you back beside me now—oops!"

"The trail is narrow," explained Jjarja, in dulcet tones. "If we walk side by side, we cannot help touching each other like that. Does it disturb you to be touched?"

"Who, me? Of course not. Say, aren't we almost there?"

"We have yet some way to go. We have only been traveling half a day and I am not even sure that Aloba will be where I think he will. He has run away in great shame."

"Shame?"

"The tooth of his I desire you to mend. He has two long teeth. One is broken."

"Long teeth?"

"What do you call them?" Jjarja pursed her lips in pretty thoughtfulness. "Tusks?"

"Oh, a tusk."

"That is it. But do not be disturbed. If he is not at the first clearing, we can go on in the morning. I will make us a fine hammock of creepers. We will be very warm together."

"*No!*" cried Jeff, in sudden panic.

"But we will," insisted Jjarja.

"No! I mean—I mean I want my own hammock. You can have yours. I'll have mine."

"You are strange," said Jjarja.

They reached the clearing and stopped for the night. Jjarja made two soft roomy hammocks of creepers and suspended them between handy trees. Jeff tossed for a while feverishly; but finally fell off into sleep. The next morning they took up the trail again. Jjarja, from certain signs she had discovered around the clearing, was certain that they would come up with Aloba at the next one.

"Look," said Jeff. "How come he's running away, anyhow?"

"As I told you yesterday," said Jjarja, "he is ashamed. Being an Asona, poor fellow, he is very susceptible to shame."

"Susceptible?"

"You do not know about my people and the Asona?" said Jjarja. "I should perhaps explain. Aloba is a dear, and very intelligent. But he goes to pieces easily. Asona are that way. That is why we pair off with them at an early age, to help them out, and soothe them when they are upset."

"Oh?" said Jeff. "And what do they do for you in return?"

"Oh, they solve problems and things," said Jjarja. "They have very good memories and they are good at puzzles and questions. Now *my* people are very strong and capable in the fields of emotions. We are perhaps what you might call experts."

"For example?"

"Oh," said Jjarja. "Now take yourself."

"Me?" squeaked Jeff. "What about me?"

"Well, you are so obviously unhappy. It is easy for me to see that you have run away from some emotional situation and are determined not to face it."

"Nonsense! Certainly not! I don't know what gave you such a crazy idea, but—"

"Oh, I intuit it," said Jjarja.

"Well, you intuit wrong!" cried Jeff. "I never was so happy in my life. Emotional situation! I don't have any emotional situation. And if I did I wouldn't run away from it. And furthermore—what are you doing?"

"You will sit down here, please," said Jjarja, pulling him down on a soft carpet of moss at the foot of a huge creeper-hung tree alongside the pathway.

"What for? What—now what are you doing?"

"I am rubbing the back of your neck with my fingers. Lean your head back, please."

"Lean back—" Jeff felt the back of his head come to rest against something soft and yielding. "No!" he cried in panic, trying to straighten up.

"Yes, yes," crooned Jjarja, pulling him back down. "Just lie back for a little while. Do my fingers feel good on your neck? Don't answer, just lie still. Ah, how I enjoy doing this for you. You are so kind to let me do it."

"But—but—"

"There . . . there . . . just lie still. Do the fingers warm your neck? Gently . . . gently . . ."

"But—"

"Gently . . . gently . . ."

*   *   *

"—Where am I?" demanded Jeff, blinking and looking around him.

"We are almost to the clearing where Aloba will be," replied Jjarja's voice. He turned his head to stare down at her. They were marching through the path again, somewhere in the jungle of the foothills. The sun was considerably farther along in the sky than it had been when he had last seen it. In fact it now seemed about early afternoon.

"What happened?" demanded Jeff.

Jjarja giggled. Jeff broke out in a cold sweat.

"*What happened?*" he cried.

"You were upset," said Jjarja, softly. "I soothed you."

"You soothed me so well I've been walking in an unconscious haze for six hours?" yelped Jeff.

"Oh yes. We are experts."

Jeff opened his mouth, but no words came out. He had no words *to* come out.

They went across a little ravine and up a slope, and over the crest of the slope—and emerged into the clearing Jjarja had promised. It was a large, comfortable clearing, with a little creek tinkling through it and downy with moss. At its far end an enormous creature, from the rear view *exactly* resembling an elephant-sized sheep dog, was standing with its head buried in a curtain of creepers.

"There he is!" cried Jjarja, joyfully. "Come Jeffer-ey—" and she led the way up to the creature. "Aloba! I've found you."

"I know," replied the creature, in a voice muffled by the creepers. "Go away."

"But it's just me—just your Jjarja," crooned that young lady. "And I've brought a nice human to help you."

"I don't want any help," replied Aloba, without moving. "I'm beyond help. Go away. I think I'm going to commit suicide." After a second. he added: "And take that human with you."

"But he's a dentist," protested Jjarja. "His name is Jeffrey Willoughby, and he can fix you up if you'll let him."

Jeffrey tapped Jjarja on the shoulder and whispered in her ear. Pointing at the Asona, he hissed: "How come he's talking in English?"

"Why shouldn't I talk in English?" retorted the unmoving Aloba. "I heard that. Or Sanskrit or Lbbrinian?"

"What's Lbbrinian?" asked Jeff.

"Never mind. You'll find out someday," muttered Aloba. "I can talk any language. I can do anything. If I try, that is."

"Now, Aloba," coaxed Jjarja, "it was silly of you to run off and hide. You'd think a broken tooth was the end of the world."

"Well, I look hideous, don't I?" demanded Aloba, amongst the creepers. "People hide their snickers when they look at me."

"They do not!" said Jjarja.

"Oh yes they do. I know. Or else they pity me. I can't stand pity. That's the final blow."

"The Asona are very proud," explained Jjarja to Jeff.

"It's not pride, it's sensitivity—the other side of the coin of great intelligence. I am a genius, human. All we Asona are. That's why we've let Jjarja's people have all the contact with your race. What? Expose ourselves to your rude natures? Certainly not."

"But Aloba," said Jjarja. "The nature of Jeff-er-ey is sensitive, like your own."

"Nonsense," mumbled Aloba. "Utterly impossible."

"Please turn around," said Jjarja.

"He will snicker."

"I will not," said Jeff. "What you don't realize—uh—

Aloba, is that I am a professional where teeth are concerned. I am used to seeing teeth in all sorts of shape."

"You won't snicker?"

"Never," said Jeff, firmly. Aloba stirred. There was a rattling and a tearing of creepers as he faced about. Jeff blinked. This end of him was almost identical with the other. The faint glimmer of two large brown eyes peeked through the tangle of white curls and a couple of elephantine tusks protruded. One of these was shattered and broken off near its base.

"Oh, the ugliness of it," moaned Aloba, faintly, closing his eyes.

"Hmm," said Jeff, stepping up to the Asona's great woolly head. "Will you get down a little lower, please?" Aloba knelt clumsily, bringing his head down to about the level of Jeff's chest. Jeff probed around the fur, found an upper lip. "Raise your lip, please." Somewhat to his surprise, Aloba did. Jeff palpated the root area. "Does that hurt? How did this happen?"

"Hurt?" said Aloba, in a somewhat surprised tone. "Oh, yes. But I'm not paying any attention to that, you know. It's the looks."

"And how did it happen?"

"I fell off a small cliff," said Aloba, in a bashful voice. "I was speculating, you see, on the future of humanity, and how it would effect us if we took any one of five paths of relationships. Graduated coopera-tion—"

"And you landed on this tusk?"

"Well, it got caught between a couple of boulders as I rolled down the cliff, and snapped off. The shock was extreme. Ruined, I thought to myself, ruined! I could never face another Asona again with this hu-miliating disfigurement; and what would I be without personal contact with my kind? A withered, useless branch of the race."

"Aloba has the third best mind on the planet," said Jjarja, proudly.

"Well, no, actually I'm tied for third place," said Aloba, faintly, closing his eyes again. "Oh, well, maybe it's better that way—I can more easily be spared. The table of ratings will not even have to be adjusted."

"Now don't talk that way!" scolded Jjarja.

"We might as well face facts," groaned Aloba. "Metake will have third place all to himself. He will probably throw the weight of his arguments on the conservative side. That means the end of you humans on our planet here, Doctor, incidentally. But what can one do? *Que será, será.*"

"I beg your pardon?" asked Jeff, startled.

"Oh, that's Spanish," said Aloba. "I guess you don't speak it as well as I do. It means in English: what will be, will be. I am irretrievably ruined."

"Nonsense," said Jeff. Aloba's eyelids flew open almost literally with a bang.

"*How dare you!*" he trumpeted, surging to his feet. "What? You have the audacity—"

"He didn't mean it that way!" cried Jjarja.

"Nonsense? To me—a tied third! And by a human! I never heard anything so—"

"I meant every syllable of it," said Jeff, firmly. "I can't replace your tusk, but I can provide you with a substitute no one will be able to tell from the original, without professional experience."

"Skebash!" gasped Aloba.

"No, really," said Jjarja. "He really can."

"I," said Aloba.

"I will stake," said Jeff, somewhat carried away, "my professional reputation on it."

"I still don't believe it," said Aloba. "Nothing will make me believe it. I have too much common sense

. . . really, Doctor? You mean you can actually . . .
How?"

Jeff explained that he would have to send for a few
things. He unhooked his belt phone and proceeded
to do so. Back at the ship, Hokerman mournfully
informed him from the dental clinic that everything
he wanted would be sent out early the following
morning.

It was too late to do anything that evening. Jeff
retired to his hammock and dropped off to sleep
early. His last waking memory was of Aloba and
Jjarja sitting before a comfortable fire and discussing
something or other in their own rather complicated
tongue. It was one of those perfect nights of sleep
when he seemed merely to blink his eyes once and
then he was awake again and it was morning, with
both him and the morning bright-eyed and promising.

About nine o'clock the runabout made its delivery,
having homed in on the signal of Jeff's phone. It let
down the materials and equipment he needed, by
cable. It could just as easily have landed, but Aloba
threatened to go into another tizzy at the thought of
exposing his damaged countenance to any more eyes
than had already seen it. Jeff got to work.

On Aloba's assurance that both tusks had been, for
all practical and cosmetical purposes, identical, Jeff
made a cast of the one good tusk remaining in the
Asona countenance, and cast up an acrylic false tusk
over a metallic core, arranged to give the false tusk
weight and balance. Assured by Aloba that this imitation was a close twin of the original real thing, he
proceeded with the operation.

There was some small argument about the anesthetic. Aloba wanted to induce his own anesthesia
according to the custom of his race—that is, by auto-

hypnosis. Jeff did not trust antohypnosis. Aloba did not trust Jeff's lyrocaine. It was finally, and very sensibly, decided to use both. Aloba lay down on his side, crossed his eyes for a moment, and announced himself ready. Jeff moved up to the area of the Asona's head with a hypodermic syringe and infiltrated the root area with one hundred c.c. of the lyrocaine. Supporting the tusk stub temporarily with a bracket he had designed the night before, he made his incision into the upper jaw, laid a flap and lifted out the remaining bit of tusk and root quite easily.

He had already prepared a metallic base. This he anchored to the bone of the upper jaw with vitallium screws which he had been assured by Aloba were most likely to be tolerated by the Asona body chemistry. He had already packed the cavity left by the extraction of the tooth root. He sutured the incisions he had made and it was all over.

"Hum," said Aloba, when informed of this fact. He got to his feet and went over to a large mirror Jeff had ordered out and hung from a nearby tree. The Asona looked at himself.

"I look lopsided," he said.

"Here," said Jeff. He came up with the false tusk. "Now this will go onto the new base. Only we'll have to wait—"

"No," said Aloba.

"We can't put that much strain on that area so soon—"

"I want to see what it looks like."

"No."

"Yes," said Aloba.

After a rather spirited argument, Aloba won his point. Jeff lifted the false tusk; and, while Aloba held his head rock-steady, he screwed the threaded inner socket in the tusk's end onto the threaded bolt within the new base.

"Now there," said Jeff, supporting the tusk, as Aloba looked at himself in the mirror.

"It's twisted off to one side," replied Aloba.

"I didn't screw it as tight as you will later," said Jeff. "Besides, there will be minor adjustments to make. Naturally. However—"

"All right," said Aloba. "Take it out." Jeff unscrewed the tusk, and laid it aside. Aloba let out a whistling sigh of relief.

"Now, there you are Doctor," he said. "While you have done nothing *I* could not have done—given, that is, the time, the materials, the experience, et al—the fact remains, I would not have done it. I would no doubt have gone into seclusion, followed by a nervous breakdown, rapid decline of mental powers, and eventual collapse and death. One of the qualities of the Asona is to recognize our own limitations; and Doctor, like all the others, I am a veritable bundle of neuroses."

"Well, now—" began Jeff.

"Please! No contradictions, polite or otherwise. I know whereof I speak. Back to the matter at hand— you have performed a noteworthy action, performed a valuable service. A certain portion of the reward appertaining will, of course, be my voice in the Asona arguments in the favor of liberalism and humanity. More than that, however, I am willing now to engage in some face-to-face talks with your captain, or other authorities of your race. I believe we can be of use to each other."

"Well . . ."

"You will be surprised at what we Asona have to offer. And now—about this little problem of yours."

"Problem?" stuttered Jeff.

"Certainly. It is a very Asonalike one; and one for which we Asona have long known a solution. You humans provide yourselves with any number of mechanical gadgets. We Asona, being more perceptive and capable, have merely provided ourselves with a single, all-purpose device in a member of Jjarja's race apiece. We are each assigned one of them at birth, and it would amaze you to know what unlimited usefulness they possess. Jjarja, of course, is mine; and in reward for what you have done for me, what I have to suggest is this: . . ."

Pat Dirksen sighed. It was a very heartfelt, satisfied sigh. She relaxed in Jeff's arms, gazing out through the flitter windows at the familiar, friendly stars of the night sky as seen from midwestern North America, Earth, during the summer months.

". . . What happened?" she murmured, a little dazedly.

"I happened," said Jeff.

"No, I mean to make you so different."

"Oh, well," said Jeff. "Space travel—foreign associations. In a word, experience."

"But I still don't understand either how you got back so quick. You told me how you signed up and about this Asina—"

"Asona."

"Asona," Pat corrected herself. "But I still don't see—"

"That was part of the reward. He arranged for me to be let out of the Service again. Since the enlistment officer had played safe by giving me only a temporary appointment, it wasn't hard."

"Part of the reward?" said Pat. "What was the other part?"

"Nothing important."

"But I want to know."

"Well," said Jeff, "I don't know if I can describe it to you. He gave me something of his that was rather valuable. Naturally, I couldn't keep it. I hung on to it for a couple of weeks and then gave it back."

"But what *was* it?" said Pat.

"Oh, just a native gadget."

"A native gadget?"

"A native gadget."

"Why," demanded Pat, "do you smack your lips when you say that?"

WE'RE LOOKING FOR
TROUBLE

Well, feedback, anyway. Baen Books endeavors to publish only the best in science fiction and fantasy—but we need you to tell us whether we're doing it right. Why not let us know? We'll award a Baen Books gift certificate worth $100 (plus a copy of our catalog) to the reader who best tells us what he or she likes about Baen Books—and where we could do better. We reserve the right to quote any or all of you. Contest closes December 31, 1987. All letters should be addressed to Baen Books, 260 Fifth Avenue, New York, N.Y. 10001.

At the same time, ask about the Baen Book Club—buy five books, get another five free! For information, send a self-addressed, stamped envelope. For a copy of our catalog, enclose one dollar as well.